Harvest

of

Dreams

ALISON HENDERSON

Harvest of Dreams

Cover Art by Creative Author Services

Publishing History
Originally published by The Wild Rose Press, Adams Basin, NY, 2010
Second Edition, published by Alison Henderson 2018

Published in the United States of America
ISBN-13: 978-1-0906-3097-1

DEDICATION

To my wonderful husband, Michael,
for his inspiration and support on
this long and winding road.
And to Gram, who taught me the power of
perseverance.

Chapter One

December 24, 1865
Weston, Missouri

Lisa Culpepper McAllister squeezed her eyes shut and focused her energy on the simple act of breathing. Waves of overwhelming sensation rolled over her body from head to toe. She couldn't even call it pain anymore.

The conscious portion of her mind drifted outside her body for a moment to wonder why huge unseen hands squeezed her distended abdomen like a rolling pin squeezes dough. Surely the task would be finished soon.

But it wasn't. Drawing strength from some unknown source, Lisa's muscles toiled on. She no longer had the power to deny, control, or even assist the forceful contractions racking her body. Her long hair, damp with perspiration, twisted beneath her head. She could only lie on the bed with her eyes closed, struggling to catch an occasional breath against the forces pressing upwards on her lungs and downwards on her belly. The rock-hard mound seemed to have a life of its own, requiring no assistance from her as it labored to push forth the child it had nurtured and sheltered for so long.

Lisa's splintered thoughts came together and centered on the baby. Could it survive such an arduous entry into the world? And if it did, what would it be like? Would it be a boy or a girl? Would it have her dark coloring or Dan's fair hair and blue eyes?

Dan. Her pain-hazed mind refused to call up his features. Try as she might, his face remained shrouded in a soft fog.

"Mrs. McAllister?" A deep male voice called from somewhere outside the room.

A frenzied jolt shot through Lisa. She struggled to sit up. "Dan?"

But it couldn't be Dan. He would never call her *Mrs. McAllister*. Besides, Dan was gone.

It must be Dr. Hutchins. Her mother must have brought him from town. Now she wouldn't be alone through the rest of this ordeal. Dr. Hutchins would know what to do. Grateful to put herself in the doctor's experienced hands, Lisa collapsed back against the pillows waiting for the next wave to hit.

****

Jared Tanner shook the snow from his hat and bounded up the stairs of the two-story brick farmhouse to the second-floor bedroom where he'd heard the woman's faint call. He glanced around the spacious, high-ceilinged room and spotted her, clad in a white nightdress, lying still and taut in the middle of a large carved walnut bed. She groaned and twisted, her fingers clutching the rumpled sheet beneath her. His heart thudded in his chest.

What in the name of heaven was he doing here? He must have taken leave of his senses. Any fool could see this woman needed a doctor, and he was no doctor. Why had he ever agreed to this? An hour ago, he'd been warm and dry in the little parlor of his old friend, Ben Wainwright, getting ready for a game of checkers on a snowy afternoon. Then Martha Culpepper had burst through the door in frantic distress, and now here he was, alone with a woman in labor.

He hoped Martha, the young woman's mother, would be along soon in the wagon with Ben, and he wouldn't have to do much more than boil water. But what if they didn't make it in time? What if the raging blizzard outside held them up? Could he deliver the baby alone? He hoped to God he wouldn't have to find out.

He had just begun to pull off his heavy leather riding gloves when another moan from the bed drew his attention. He tossed his hat, coat, and gloves onto a chair and walked over to get a closer look at his patient.

She was young, perhaps ten years younger than his own age of thirty-one, and had a tangled mass of sweat-soaked hair flowing away from her temples in dark waves. Her brows and lashes were equally lush and dark. The rest of her features contorted in an agonized grimace as a tremendous spasm gripped her. Jared's gut twisted at the sight of the woman's suffering. She was helpless without him. His feelings had no place here. He reached forward and brushed her hair away from her brow.

"Hang on, ma'am. It's going to be all right."

The contraction passed its peak, and the woman's face relaxed. It was an arresting face with high

3

cheekbones, strong planes, and a small black mole high on her right cheek near her eye like a natural beauty mark. Her mouth, gasping for breath, was full and wide. Without seeing her eyes, he could only guess she was a real beauty, not delicate and fair in the current fashion but stronger and more dramatic.

The woman's brow furrowed, and she tossed her head from side to side. Her forehead glistened in the dim afternoon light seeping through the storm.

"Aaaah!"

Her groan jerked Jared back to his current predicament. He pondered his next step. How far along was she? How much longer was her labor likely to last?

He checked the room to see what preparations Martha had made before leaving for town to bring back the doctor. A basin of water, a towel, and a stack of folded white flannel cloths sat on the round marble-topped table, and a pair of leather straps with a loop at each end dangled from the posts at the head of the bed.

Jared didn't know much about the intricacies of childbirth, but he had once watched a friend deliver a foal and hoped a human baby wouldn't be too different. If memory served, he would need his knife, a ball of twine, and hot water. He would have to go back downstairs to the kitchen for more water. Maybe he could find some twine there, too. But first he had to try to make the woman more comfortable.

The fire in the fireplace had nearly gone out, so he added a couple of logs. Despite the chill in the room, sweat beaded on the young woman's forehead and upper lip. He sat on the side of the bed, wrung out the wet towel, and blotted the droplets. She stirred and mumbled something that might have been "thank you." He rinsed the towel again and moistened her parched lips. They sought the cool liquid, sucking greedily. Again he soaked the towel, and again she drank.

Then her eyes opened. Beautiful, pain-filled, confused brown eyes. She blinked twice, as though trying to focus.

"Wh-who are you? Where are my mother and Dr. Hutchins?" Her voice held a note of rising panic.

"They're coming. I'm here to help you. My name is Jared Tanner. Don't worry."

She still looked confused. Then another contraction hit, and her eyes pinched shut.

When her expression eased, he asked, "Would you like more to drink?"

"Yes, please." Her words were soft but clear. She sucked on the rag again.

The contractions developed their own rhythm like a steam locomotive picking up speed. After a while, time ceased to register. He sat on the edge of the bed, bathing her brow with the wet cloth and offering the comfort of his presence. He talked to her of unimportant things in a deep, quiet voice, hoping the sound would reassure her she was not alone in her travail. When her pains grew stronger, he held her hands and marveled at their slender strength as she nearly crushed his bones at the peak of her spasms.

Soon there was no respite between contractions. Jared didn't know how close the actual birth might be, but the woman beside him couldn't go on much longer. Her grasp had weakened and her breath came in rapid, shallow pants.

He carefully extricated his hands and stood. "Mrs. McAllister."

"Ahhh!" She acknowledged her name with a cross between a groan and a cry.

"I have to go downstairs for a few minutes, but I'll be right back."

"Hurry...please!"

From the high-pitched urgency in her voice, he sensed her time was near. He strode out the door, down the stairs, and through the hall to the kitchen. Thank God, the coals in the large open fireplace still glowed, and a copper kettle hung over them on a cast iron hook. He spotted a ball of twine on a cupboard against one wall. He grabbed what he needed and was back upstairs in a flash.

The woman lay still, keening softly, as if all hope and strength had deserted her. Her knees were bent, and both hands gripped the sides of her distended abdomen. Icy fear stabbed his chest. What if something was wrong? He had no idea what to do if the baby was out of position. He might harm one or both of them in his ignorance.

But he had to do something. He couldn't let her suffer if there was any chance he could help.

He reached over to slide the creamy flannel nightdress up to her hips, and the full impact of his action hit him. Even though she was beyond modesty, his natural sense of decency rebelled. He shouldn't be seeing her like this. He didn't know this woman. She should have a doctor or her own husband, not some untrained stranger. But he was all she had, and he would do what he could to bring her baby safely into the world.

"Ma'am, I'm going to touch you for a minute. I'll try not to hurt you."

She moaned and tossed her head but didn't resist

when he slowly separated her knees.

The gathering gloom of the late afternoon cloaked the depths of her body in mysterious shadow, so he lit the kerosene lamp on the bedside table and held it closer. Relief mixed with fear flooded through him. A tiny patch of dark, wet hair showed at the peak of each contraction. The baby was about to come.

"It's time, Mrs. McAllister. It'll all be over soon."

Her eyes focused on his face and held. Jared stared hard into their rich, coffee-brown depths, willing her to scrape together enough strength to withstand the culmination of her labor. The baby wouldn't wait much longer.

"Please try to sit up."

She opened her mouth to speak, but no words came. A mighty contraction struck, and the physical imperatives of her body demanded her full attention. Jared slid his arm beneath her shoulders and helped her. Without hesitation, she accepted the leather straps when he placed the loops around her hands.

"Hold onto these and push as hard as you can."

Calm settled over her. She closed her eyes, but not in agony this time. She seemed to be gathering her strength to concentrate on the task at hand, no longer a passive victim of the forces of nature.

A victorious scream accompanied the tremendous push that delivered the head. Her body did the rest of the work on its own, and two more contractions slid the body of the child into the waiting blanket in his hands.

It was alive. Slippery and a little purplish maybe, but a wonderful, wriggling miracle.

He wiped the little face, and a thin wail of protest arose from the rosy mouth. He stared, transfixed, at the toothless gums, plump cheeks, and waving fists of the infant. Everything was so small, yet so perfect, down to the delicate eyebrows and minute fingernails. His shaking hands dwarfed the tiny creature they held. As soon as he was able, he tied off and cut the cord.

Another soft moan reminded him the woman's labor was not yet complete. He wrapped the baby in the blanket and set it on the bed before returning his attention to the mother.

The afterbirth came easily, but the flow of blood that followed shocked him. She couldn't die now. He wouldn't let her. He grabbed a cloth from the pile on the table and pressed it between her legs to staunch the flow, discarding it when it became soaked. He took another cloth. Then another. And another.

The sharp, metallic smell of blood filled the room. Fear gripped him—he might lose her yet. A clock on the mantel ticked off the minutes in a loud, insistent rhythm. Finally, the bleeding slowed.

After wiping off most of the remaining birth residue and wrapping the baby in a clean blanket, he laid it in the carved wooden cradle on the floor beside the bed. The woman's legs began to quake, and soon she was quivering all over. He needed to get her warm but couldn't just throw a quilt over her and leave her lying in all that blood.

Martha had left a pile of fresh bedding on top of a small walnut chest across the room. If he was careful, he could probably get the soiled sheets off the bed and clean ones on without having to move the young woman too much. He was afraid if she stood, she might start bleeding heavily again.

"Ma'am, if you could roll this way a bit."

It wasn't easy and it wasn't perfect, but he

managed to strip away the bloody sheets and replace them with clean ones just as violent shivers overcame her exhausted body. She must be freezing, half-naked and damp from sweat and blood. He reached for the kettle and poured warm water onto one of the clean cloths.

"Ma'am, if you can help me, we'll get you cleaned up and into a fresh nightdress."

She opened her eyes as soon as the warmth touched her chilled skin, and their gazes met. Neither spoke. Jared's breath caught in his chest and held. He felt as if he were drowning. Free from pain, her dark eyes mesmerized him.

He dropped the cloth into the basin. What had gotten into him? He didn't know this woman from Eve. For all he knew she had a husband and six other children somewhere. Besides, he'd spent the last nineteen years avoiding connections of any kind. The last thing he needed was the tug he felt when he looked at this woman and her baby.

He finished washing her as quickly as possible, assuring himself the gentleness in his touch was only out of deference to her condition.

"Where do you keep your clean clothes? In the wardrobe?"

She nodded.

He crossed the room, opened the double doors, and rifled through two drawers of delicate, feminine garments before finding what he was looking for. When he returned, he handed her the folded nightdress and turned his back.

"I...I'm sorry, but I can't seem to..." Her voice quavered with weakness.

He bit back a reply and whirled around, jerking

the gown from her hands. His response annoyed him. A man who had just delivered a baby ought to be able to change a woman's nightdress without blinking an eye, particularly one in obvious need of help. But it was her need that made him so uncomfortable.

"Can you raise your arms? There, let me lift your hair. All right, all done now."

"Thank you." She turned her head, searching the room. "Where is my baby?"

He reached down and lifted the flannel-wrapped bundle, laying it in its mother's arms. The baby's eyes were closed, but its cheeks flexed as it sucked its tongue.

The woman's face glowed with wonder at the miracle of new life she held. Jared's earlier discomfort was nudged aside by a sense of kinship with these two people who should have been strangers to him but were so much more. Unfamiliar feelings of pride and responsibility stirred inside him.

"Is it a boy or a girl?"

Her question broke into his thoughts and drew him up short. "I know you won't believe this," he admitted, "but I forgot to look."

She glanced up with a hint of a smile twitching around the corners of her soft, full mouth. "Then I think we should check." She returned her attention to the baby and unwrapped the soft folds of the blanket.

"A boy," she murmured. "Hello, Andrew." She stroked the baby's round cheek with her forefinger, and he turned his head.

"After your husband?"

"What?" The woman dragged her gaze away from the child.

"Andrew. Did you name him after your

husband?"

"Oh...no." She turned back to the baby.

She wore a gold wedding band. She must have a husband somewhere. Unreasonable anger surged through him. Jared frowned. What right did he have to be angry? He didn't know this woman's husband.

"Excuse me, ma'am, but where is your husband? I ought to try to get word to him as soon as possible."

Her face lifted. "I'm afraid that would be difficult."

"Why is that?"

"Dan...He can't...He's not..." She struggled to get the words out.

Suddenly it was very important to find her husband. Jared felt like a poacher in the absent man's territory and didn't like it one bit. "Can't what?" he prompted. "Where is he?"

She leaned down and kissed the baby on his forehead. "He's gone."

She eased the baby onto her lap and stared past Jared toward the window. "He's gone, and he'll never come back."

Never come back. She must mean—

She looked back at him with a steady gaze. "He's dead, Mr. Tanner."

"I'm sorry, ma'am." He didn't know what else to say. She had suffered a grievous loss but seemed to have accepted it. He was sorry, but loss was a part of life. He had suffered loss, too—he just refused to think about it.

He glanced back at her face and found her staring at him as if she'd never seen him before.

"Mr. Tanner, you seem to know who I am, but I don't know you. I'm grateful for your help, but why are you here? Where are my mother and Dr. Hutchins?"

Jared was about to speak when footsteps clattered up the stairs, and Martha Culpepper burst into the room with Ben Wainwright following behind her.

"Lisa, honey, are you all right?" Martha shook out her scarf and brushed the snow from her coat as she hurried to her daughter's side.

"Mama!" Lisa's face lit, and she tightened her grip on the baby, who squalled in protest.

Martha slid one arm around her daughter's shoulders and gently loosened Lisa's grasp on Andrew with the other hand. She soothed the baby before laying him back in the cradle then looked at Jared with glittering eyes. "Mr. Tanner, I can never thank you enough."

"Glad to be of assistance, ma'am." He wasn't quite sure he meant it. He had an uneasy feeling his life would have been a lot simpler if he'd never met this woman and her daughter.

"Ben, why don't you take Mr. Tanner down to the kitchen and fix him a cup of coffee? I'm sure he's had quite an afternoon. I'll take care of everything here."

Jared followed the older man down the stairs and into the attached kitchen. Ben moved around the room with practiced ease, procuring a small burlap sack of coffee beans from the pantry and the grinder and blue and white enameled pot from a cupboard. Jared held his questions until the coffee came to a boil over the fire and they were both seated at the scarred wooden table. He glanced at his hands, which looked big and clumsy in comparison to the delicate porcelain cup they held. The sharp, rich aroma rose on the steam. He took a long, careful sip of the revitalizing brew and set the cup down.

"You seem right at home here, Ben."

Ben snorted. "I should. I've been courting Martha Culpepper for seven years."

Seven years? Jared couldn't understand that kind of patience. He liked to look over a situation, decide on a course of action, and then do whatever was necessary to achieve the desired result. He couldn't imagine waiting patiently for seven years for a woman he wanted. But then, he'd never wanted anyone that much.

****

Upstairs, Lisa was content to watch her mother fuss around, gathering the bloody linens and tidying the room.

"How are you feeling, dear?" Martha asked. "I do so wish I'd been with you. Are you in pain?"

"Not really, not any more. It's funny how you forget, isn't it?"

Her mother smiled. "Yes, it's funny." She brushed the damp hair back from Lisa's forehead. "Sometimes forgetfulness is one of the greatest blessings of motherhood. You'll come to appreciate it even more over the next twenty years or so."

Lisa struggled to bring order to her jumbled thoughts and feelings. She couldn't remember much about the actual birth. She remembered strong hands and a gentle, commanding voice steering her through a sea of pain. Afterwards, she remembered the tall, dark man helping her, caring for her.

Jared Tanner.

"Who is Jared Tanner, Mama? Why did he come here?" She struggled to sit upright in the bed.

"Be careful now, dear." Martha patted her and

guided her back against the pillows. "You must know I would never have left you if I'd had any idea it was going to snow like this."

Lisa nodded in unquestioning acknowledgement. "I know."

"The snow didn't start until I was halfway to town. By the time I got there, the blizzard had come on hard. I could barely reach Dr. Hutchins's house. When I did, I found he was away on a call. I was able to get as far as Ben's, where I found Ben and Mr. Tanner.

"When he heard of our predicament, Mr. Tanner offered to ride out here through the storm to help. Ben and I followed in the wagon as quickly as we could, but you know how slow Old Pete is in the snow. We got stuck in a rut, and one of the wheels came off." She shook her head and clucked her tongue. "I'm afraid I got pretty worked up. I'm so sorry we didn't make it in time."

"So am I. But I still need to know, who is Jared Tanner?"

"He works with Ben for the stage company. Apparently, they've known each other for several years, but Mr. Tanner has just arrived from Denver to take on some special assignment. I didn't pay much attention to the details. I was only concerned about you."

"But, Mama, he isn't a doctor, is he? He might have done more harm than good." Lisa's cheeks flamed at the memory of everything he'd done.

"He didn't hurt you, did he?" A frown puckered Martha's brow. "He seemed like such a competent young man, and I was so grateful when he offered to help."

"No, he didn't hurt me. He seemed to know what

he was doing, but—"

"Fine," interrupted her mother, "then we won't worry any more about it. I'd much rather concentrate on what's really important—you and my new grandchild."

Mention of the baby distracted Lisa from her thoughts of Jared Tanner. "Have you seen him yet?"

Martha lifted one brow. "Not very well, dear. When I arrived, you were holding him as if a ravenous bear were about to snatch him away." She bent and lifted the infant from the cradle, snuggling him against her breast and beaming with grandmotherly pride.

Lisa smiled. "He's perfect, isn't he?"

Martha stroked a tiny fist. "Absolutely."

"And he has so much hair."

"He looks just like you did."

Lisa's throat swelled. "Mama, I'm so happy."

Martha glanced up, her eyes glistening. "I felt the same way when you and Seth were born."

Lisa's heart contracted at the mention of her brother's name. How did her mother live, day after day, with the loss of her firstborn? She never could. "I couldn't bear to lose him."

Tears trickled down Martha's cheeks as she reached out to pat Lisa's arm. "And I hope you never have to. The good Lord willing, he'll be a comfort to you all your days. Have you thought of a name for him?"

"Andrew Culpepper McAllister."

"Dan would have been very proud."

"Yes." Dan. Lisa tried again to picture him. The image faded back and forth between the carefree teenage boy she'd thought she loved and the battered, broken man she'd hardly known.

Life could be so hard to understand. She'd lost so much—her father, her brother, her husband—but in return she had been given this marvelous gift, a whole new beginning.

"Have you tried feeding him?" Martha asked, breaking into her thoughts.

"No, not yet."

"It would do you both good, even though he doesn't seem to be hungry right now." She handed Andrew to Lisa.

She settled the baby into the crook of her left arm and regarded him with uncertainty. "What do I do?"

Martha laughed. "Just unbutton your bodice and let him do the rest."

Lisa guided her nipple to the baby's mouth and watched in wonder as he instinctively began to suck. The sensation was like nothing she had ever felt, intense yet soothing. The pace of his suckling suggested a lack of true hunger and lulled her with its slow, regular rhythm.

She yawned.

Martha gently replaced Andrew in his cradle. "Why don't you try to get some rest now, dear? It's been a very eventful day."

Lisa nodded, barely able to hold her eyes open. The last thing she heard was the click of the latch.

****

From the kitchen table where he sat with Ben, Jared heard footsteps coming down the back hall and glanced up just as Martha entered. Ben was quick to stand and offer her a chair.

"Martha, honey, you sit down now, and I'll pour you a cup of coffee. You must be done in."

Martha collapsed onto the chair. "Thank you, Ben.

I am. I think we all are."

The trio drank their coffee in silence until Martha had finished hers. She set her pink-rosed cup down on its delicate saucer and looked across at Jared.

"How are Mrs. McAllister and the baby doing?" he asked.

"Very well, thanks to you. They're both asleep." Shadows of fatigue circled her eyes, but she faced the men with a gracious smile. "You've both been such a help to us today. Since it's still snowing and tomorrow is Christmas Day, I hope I can persuade you to spend the night here as our guests and join us tomorrow for our modest celebration."

Jared glanced at Ben, then back at Martha. "I wouldn't want to put you out, ma'am. You have enough to do without worrying about guests."

"Nonsense, Mr. Tanner. It's no trouble at all. Besides, you'd just have to drive back out here in the morning with Ben for dinner. Unless, of course, you'd rather spend Christmas alone."

Jared thought back over the years of Christmases spent alone or in the accidental company of strangers. The thought of spending the holiday in the Culpepper home held surprising appeal. Besides, with no man around the place, there were bound to be chores he could do to repay their hospitality.

He nodded. "I'd be honored to spend Christmas with you."

"Fine. After supper, I'll show you both to the hired hand's room."

Supper was a simple affair, and after they finished eating, Jared and Ben made sure the animals in the barn were fed and bedded down for the night. Then they followed Martha up the flight of outside stairs leading from the back veranda to the hired hand's room on the second floor above the kitchen. Although the room was attached to the house, it had no connecting doors. The only way in or out was by way of the outside staircase, allowing privacy for both the occupant of the room and the family in the main house.

Jared glanced around. Martha kept the room made up and well stocked with linens and towels. A set of bone-handled shaving utensils lay on the washstand next to the bowl and pitcher. He assumed this was her hint to the hired help that she expected a certain level of basic grooming from anyone in her employ.

He ran a hand over the thick bristles along his jaw and realized he was grateful not to have to appear before Lisa tomorrow looking like a renegade bushwhacker.

He lay down on the crackling cornhusk mattress, shrugged the quilts up over his shoulders, and wondered why he should care. He couldn't figure out why his last conscious image should be of a beautiful, dark-haired Madonna with eyes like sparkling black pools.

Chapter Two

The next morning, Christmas morning, Lisa awoke late. Pale winter light peered through the front windows of her room. Her first thoughts were of Andrew, and she sat up quickly, but sank back against her pillow almost as fast when a wave of weakness and lightheadedness washed over her. It wasn't pain so much as leaden exhaustion.

Determined to see her baby, she tried again, more slowly this time, and managed to scoot to the edge of the high bed. She leaned over and saw Andrew, still fast asleep in the simple wooden cradle her father had carved for her brother Seth twenty-five years earlier.

"What do you think you're doing?"

She jerked up to see her mother bustling through the door with a laden breakfast tray in her hands and a look of consternation on her face. Martha hurried to the bed and set the tray on the table next to it.

Lisa leaned back, trying to avoid putting weight on the more tender parts of her anatomy. If she kept still, she was reasonably comfortable, but any sudden movement sent a throbbing ache straight up through her.

"I just wanted to see Andrew. Shouldn't he be awake by now?"

Martha laughed and tucked a large napkin into the neck of Lisa's worn nightdress. "Be grateful for the peace. In a day or two, he'll wake up for good, and you'll be asking me why he never sleeps."

"Won't he be hungry?"

"I'm sure he'll make his wishes known before much longer. In the meantime, you need to eat and rest so you can get your strength back."

Lisa glanced at the plate of eggs, toast, milk, and preserved apple slices and realized she was famished. She hadn't eaten since her labor had begun almost thirty-six hours earlier. When she finished, Martha smiled and removed the tray.

"You keep eating like that, and we'll have you up and around before you know it. I'll take these to the kitchen. Then I'll be back to help you wash and brush your hair."

Lisa touched her tangled curls, which were stiff with sweat in places. She grimaced at the picture she must make. "That would feel wonderful."

After her mother left, she lay back and closed her eyes. Her tired mind drifted from Andrew to thoughts of Dan. Why couldn't she remember him clearly? She'd known him all her life. Maybe she didn't want to remember. To remember would bring back the distant, dying man as well as the laughing, teasing boy.

When he first came home from the war, she had been shocked beyond words. He could barely walk. His skin was gray, old-man eyes stared out of the once familiar face, and he'd lost a frightening amount of weight. He seemed to improve a little as the wedding drew closer.

On their wedding night, she'd urged him to conserve his strength, but he had seemed driven to consummate their vows, and she hadn't had the heart to deny him. The encounter was awkward, painful, and brief. And it had marked a turning point for Dan. It was as if he'd passed to her all the life force he had left. By the time she discovered she was pregnant, he was gone.

She should have listened to her mother when Martha had tried to talk her out of marrying, but she'd given Dan her word when he left for war, and a promise was a promise. At the time, she'd still been struggling to accept the reality of Seth's death. Then Dan left her, too.

At least now she had Andrew. He couldn't leave. He wouldn't leave. Or would he? Accident and illness made childhood a perilous time. Her heart contracted painfully, and she whispered a fervent prayer for her son's health and safety.

A few minutes later, Martha walked into the room carrying a basin of steaming water and an armful of clean towels. "Let's get you freshened up so Andrew can see what a beautiful mother he has, if he ever opens his eyes." They both smiled, and Martha set to work.

Lisa thrust aside the hazy, but mortifying, memories of other hands, a stranger's hands, bathing her the night before. She forced herself to relax and accept the luxury of having her mother wash her from head to toe without having to get out of bed. Martha worked quickly and efficiently so Lisa didn't become too chilled. Although the crackling fire looked warm, much of its heat dissipated before reaching the bed.

Clean and dry, she felt much better. When her mother picked up the old silver-handled hairbrush and began to draw it through Lisa's hair in long, steady strokes, she sighed in contentment.

As Martha re-braided Lisa's waist-length tresses, she said, "I know you probably shouldn't be out of bed, but since it is Christmas, I thought we might ask Ben or Mr. Tanner to carry you down to the sofa in the parlor for dinner, if you feel up to it."

Lisa whipped her head around, almost yanking the braid out of her mother's hands. "Mr. Tanner? Is he still here? Mama, have you invited him to dinner, too?"

Martha gathered the loose plaits and returned to her task. "Of course, dear. It would have been inhospitable of me not to include him. He and Ben are downstairs. They spent the night in the hired hand's room because of the storm."

Lisa fell silent as her mother pinned her braids on top of her head. Jared Tanner was still in the house. He had slept in the room next to hers all night—a single wall separated the two beds. What if she'd had one of her nightmares? He might have heard her. She'd never cared if one of the hired hands heard her cry out in the night, but Jared Tanner was different. She couldn't put her finger on the reason, but his presence made her uneasy. She had half hoped she wouldn't have to see him again.

She didn't mind having Christmas dinner with Ben, of course. Martha had been inviting him to spend holidays with them for years. Ben was a kind, thoughtful man Lisa had known all her life. Widowed for the past ten years, he had been courting her mother since before the war. Lisa had thought there might be a second wedding in the family last spring, but Dan's death and her pregnancy had caused Martha to put her own wishes aside while she tended to her daughter's needs.

As fond as she was of Ben, Lisa wasn't comfortable with the idea of him carrying her anywhere clad only in her nightdress and wrapper. Besides, he was in his fifties and not a very large man. They might both go tumbling down the stairs. And she couldn't allow Jared Tanner to do it. After the intimacies of the day before, she needed to put as much distance between them as possible.

"I don't think I should go down the stairs yet, Mama. You go on without me. Andrew and I will be fine up here."

Martha looked disappointed. "I had hoped you'd feel strong enough. The parlor is so much cozier. But if you're sure, we'll eat up here with you. I wouldn't dream of leaving you alone on Christmas. I'll ask the gentlemen to bring up a couple of the smaller tables and some chairs."

The thought of entertaining Jared Tanner in her bedroom was even worse than eating with him downstairs. "Oh, no. You're right. The parlor is much warmer and cheerier. I'm sure I can make it on my own if I'm careful. Perhaps Ben would carry Andrew in the cradle."

"I know he'd be glad to, dear, but I still don't like the idea of you on the stairs."

"Mama, I'll be fine."

Martha pursed her lips. "All right. But wait 'til Ben comes upstairs so he can help you down." She glanced at the clock on the mantel. "I think dinner will be ready in about an hour. If you don't need me, I'll get back to work."

"Go ahead. We'll be fine."

Lisa watched her mother hurry out of the room. Mama always wanted everything to be perfect when she entertained Ben, who wouldn't notice a pig dancing on the dining table when he was with her. Ben thought the sun rose and set with Martha, and Lisa enjoyed watching her mother transform into a blushing teenager in the glow of his open adoration.

She felt a brief twinge of envy when she thought how nice it would be to have a man feel that way about her again. Dan had been very attentive before he'd left for war, but of course, they'd both been mere children then. She was centuries older now.

Andrew stirred and fussed, and she fed him again before he fell back to sleep. At eleven o'clock, the muffled sounds of boot steps and masculine voices drifted up from the front hall. If she wanted to be decent, she'd better get out of bed and get some more clothes on. Still feeling weak, she stood and made her way to the wardrobe to get her dark red velvet wrapper and slippers. The wrapper had been a Christmas present from her mother several years earlier, and Lisa had always loved the way the garment's rich hue complimented her dark coloring.

When she opened the door of her room, Ben and her mother had just reached the top step of the broad, curved staircase. Jared Tanner followed and towered over them as he stepped onto the landing. This morning his thick black hair was still damp from washing, and he was clean-shaven, but the shadow of his beard darkened his rugged jaw and cleft chin. Lisa was shocked to realize he was a dangerously handsome man. Yesterday, she hadn't noticed anything as superficial as his looks. His expression was unreadable, and she shifted her attention to Ben.

"Lisa, you look radiant. Martha tells me you're doing well enough to have dinner downstairs with us." Ben smiled his congratulations as he took her hands and planted a swift kiss on each cheek.

Lisa smiled. He might be balding and downright ordinary, but there was no denying Ben's warm sincerity had a certain charm.

He released her hands and grinned at Martha. "Now let's see your new grandbaby."

"He's right over here." Martha proudly led the way to the cradle.

As they stood together gazing down at the sleeping infant, Ben took her mother's hand and give it a squeeze. She stood behind them watching the interplay and wondered how much longer they were going to put off the inevitable. Her father had been gone over fifteen years, and Martha was still a young woman.

Ben cocked his head toward her. "Shall we bring this young man down to join us?"

"By all means."

He bent and lifted the cradle in both arms, allowing Andrew to slumber on undisturbed.

Lisa was moving to follow her mother and Ben out of the room when Jared stepped forward, placing a restraining hand on her shoulder. "Mrs. McAllister, you shouldn't try to go down those stairs by yourself."

She had hoped if she ignored him he might disappear. She shrugged off his touch. "Mr. Tanner, I'm sure I am capable of walking downstairs." She tried to brush past him through the doorway, but her feet left the ground as a pair of strong arms swept beneath her knees and shoulders and lifted her effortlessly.

Cradling Lisa against his chest, Jared explained in a matter-of-fact voice, "You left me no choice."

She twisted to face him, and a sharp stab of pain shot through her. She bit her lip in response, which only made her angrier. "Mr. Tanner, put me down this instant."

Jared adjusted his hold and headed toward the stairs, careful not to jostle her. "Sorry, ma'am, but I can't."

She tried another tactic. "Please...this is very awkward."

His arms tightened. "Feels fine to me, and since you won't listen to reason, I have to make sure you don't overexert yourself."

She wasn't happy, but she didn't want to start an argument. She was grateful for the very real help he had given her the day before, so she settled back and allowed him to carry her to the parlor without comment. If she could tolerate him for an hour or two, he would go away and she could put him out of her mind. Her focus now had to be on making a new life for herself and her son.

Martha and Ben were waiting in the parlor when Jared set Lisa on the pile of pillows her mother had arranged on the sofa.

Martha turned to Ben. "If you and Mr. Tanner wouldn't mind keeping Lisa company in here, I'll bring dinner in directly."

"I'd love to, Martha, honey, but I can't let you carry those heavy things all the way from the kitchen by yourself. If you'll just tell me what to do, I'll carry everything for you."

Ignoring Jared, Lisa smiled at the pair. Ben was

not a Southerner by birth, but something about Martha's delicate, ladylike air turned all men into Southern gentlemen in her presence, despite the fact she was strong enough to have raised two children and run the farm on her own for years.

Lisa covered her mouth and gave a slight cough. "A person could starve to death while you two decide who's going to serve dinner."

Martha looked startled then smiled. "We'll do it together." She glided out of the room with her half-crinoline swaying beneath her skirt and Ben following in her wake.

Lisa was left alone with Jared and her sleeping son. Since Andrew required no attention at the moment, and she didn't want to start a conversation with Jared Tanner, she leaned back against the pillows and surveyed the parlor while she waited for Ben and Martha to return with dinner. It displayed most of Martha's best things, brought overland from Kentucky or shipped up the Missouri River, including an enormous piano, twice as wide as it was deep, and two pairs of elaborate brocaded draperies that had been a wedding present.

Everything about this room, and indeed the whole house, was shabbier than it had been when she was a little girl, but she still loved the place with a fierce protectiveness. She loved every one of the soft pink bricks of the house and outbuildings. Each brick had been made by hand on the property by the slaves who had been freed years ago. The same protective feeling welled up inside her every time anyone or anything threatened her home or her place in it. And now that she had Andrew, she was more determined than ever to preserve it for him. Her father had built this house, and it was the only legacy she would be able to give her son.

Lisa gazed into Andrew's face in the cradle beside her and watched his little pink rosebud mouth work up and down as he sucked his tongue. Martha and Ben interrupted her reverie when they returned bearing plates heaped high with wondrous-smelling holiday fare. Three places were set at a large round table in the center of the room, in front of the sofa and fireplace, and Lisa's silverware and napkin had been arranged on the small table to her right. With a flourish, Ben produced a bottle of wine, which he had somehow obtained despite its scarcity, and proposed a toast.

"To us all. May the new year before us bring peace and joy." He lifted his glass in the direction of the cradle. "We have already been blessed beyond measure."

As the others joined in the toast, Lisa noticed the glimmer of a tear in her mother's eye, and Ben's voice sounded none too steady. Her own throat tightened as her heart echoed Ben's wish for the year to come. Joy. For Ben and her mother, for Andrew and herself. Perhaps it was possible after all.

She savored the meal of smoky home-cured ham, steaming yams, and angel biscuits with apple butter and listened to her mother strive to keep the conversation flowing around the larger table. Martha had a gift for letting others feel she was genuinely interested in them and what they had to say. That was more than enough to get most men's tongues wagging. However, while Ben chatted happily, Jared hadn't said more than two words during the whole meal.

"So, tell us more about yourself, Mr. Tanner. Of course, Ben has told me a little about you, but I'd like to get to know the man who's helped us so much. I'm sure Lisa would, too."

Martha smiled at Lisa, but she returned her attention to her plate. She had no desire to learn anything more about Jared Tanner. Of course, she couldn't say so—not in front of her mother.

"There's not much to tell, Mrs. Culpepper."

"Please, you must remember to call me Martha."

"If you wish, ma'am."

"Ma'am?" Martha prodded.

"Sorry, ma'am. I'll try to remember."

Lisa almost choked on a piece of ham trying not to laugh out loud. Jared was clearly unaccustomed to dealing with ladies like Martha Culpepper.

"I expect Ben told you I work for the stage company. I met the owner, Mr. Holladay, almost twenty years ago in California and have been working for him ever since."

"My goodness, so young! You couldn't have been more than a child."

"I was twelve." Jared's abrupt answer and tone closed the matter to further question, but a flicker of curiosity stirred in Lisa. What must his childhood have been like if he'd had to go to work at twelve?

"I see." A tiny frown appeared between Martha's brows. "I understand you've just come to town from Denver."

"Yes, that's right." Jared stabbed another chunk of the orange yams swimming in butter and brown sugar with his fork.

"Will you be in Weston long?"

Her mother was nothing if not persistent.

"As long as necessary."

Lisa smiled at Martha's sigh. Jared's lack of

cooperation was frustrating her mother's desire to know everything about everyone.

"And what is the nature of your work for the stage company?"

"You might call it security work."

"I see." She might not see, but Martha Culpepper would never resort to outright rudeness. She changed the subject, and the rest of the meal passed in pleasant conversation.

When everyone had finished, Jared insisted on carrying Lisa back up to bed. This time she made no protest—out of consideration for her mother and Ben, she told herself. She tried to ignore the safe, protected way she felt, clasped against his warm, solid chest with his strong arms holding her weight.

After Jared eased her onto the bed and stepped back, she began to fuss with the covers, unable to meet his dark gaze. She was anxious to dismiss him from her room and her life before she lost any more of the protective distance she'd been working so hard to maintain. As she rearranged the colorful quilts, she began the gracious little speech she had been rehearsing in her mind all the way up the stairs.

"Thank you again, Mr. Tanner, for your help. I doubt we will have further occasion to meet, so I wish you well in your future endeavors."

Jared shot her a sharp glance. "That's very kind of you, Mrs. McAllister, but since I'll be living in Weston for the foreseeable future, I don't see how we can avoid running into each other from time to time."

She feared he might be right. In good weather, the farm was less than a half hour from town, and she usually made the trip at least twice a week. She hoped she wasn't going to have to sneak around to avoid him.

She gave him a polite smile. "I guess we'll just have to see."

"I might want to check in on your son now and again to see how he's doing."

"That's quite unnecessary. I'm perfectly capable of taking good care of him. We won't be needing your assistance any further."

"You never know. Now get some rest." He turned and left the room, closing the door before she could protest further.

Lisa stewed over his words for a few minutes, but soon all thoughts of Jared Tanner melted away as fatigue overcame her, and her lashes drifted down to her cheekbones.

Two hours later, her peace crumbled when Clay Ferguson arrived.

Lisa first heard his voice from the front hall while she was giving Andrew his evening feeding. What could Clay be doing here now? He had been a fixture during her childhood, always hanging around Seth and Dan. When the older boys went off to war, Clay had stayed home and continued to show up from time to time at the Culpepper farm with the excuse of helping out with various chores.

When they were younger, Lisa had considered him nothing more than a pest. Ever since Dan's death, however, Clay's visits had become increasingly uncomfortable. His childhood crush had developed into something spooky.

She glanced at the baby still pulling rhythmically at her nipple. Andrew's eyes were closed and his little body relaxed as he prepared to fall asleep. If she disturbed him before he finished, he might awaken and scream. She didn't want to do anything to draw

Clay's attention. With luck, her mother could persuade him she wasn't well enough to receive visitors, and he would go home.

Luck was not on her side. Clay pushed open the door and stepped into the room. Wearing a long black duster and holding his battered brown hat in one hand and a small brown paper-wrapped package in the other, he ambled over to the bed.

Lisa quickly flipped the sheet up to cover Andrew's mouth on her breast and forced a smile. "Why, Clay, what brings you out on an evening like this?"

His eyes lit, and his lips twitched beneath the scraggly new moustache he'd started growing since the last time she'd seen him.

"I come to wish you a Merry Christmas."

"How nice. Merry Christmas."

Clay grinned. "Thanks. Yer ma said I could come up. I brung you a present." He thrust the package toward her.

Lisa slipped her right hand from around Andrew and took it.

"Here, let me open it for you." He snatched it back and tore open the paper, revealing a small blue leather box with a gold filigree design stamped around the edge. He opened the box and removed a delicate, gold-rimmed cameo.

Lisa frowned. Where had Clay come by the money to buy jewelry? He'd never had two nickels to rub together.

"What's the matter? Don't you like it?" He sounded hurt, but his voice also held the seeds of anger.

"Oh, no. It's lovely, but I can't accept it."

"Why not? Ain't it good enough for you?"

Now he sounded belligerent.

"Ain't I good enough for you?"

"What do you mean?"

Clay tossed the cameo on the bed. Then he seemed to notice Andrew for the first time. "I see you done it, huh?"

The baby had fallen asleep and let her nipple slip from between his slack lips. Lisa eased him away, quickly pulling her nightdress together.

"I had the baby, yes."

Clay stepped closer and peered down. "Kind of puny, ain't he?"

"He's beautiful."

Lisa kept her voice low, but it was laced with an unyielding thread of steel as she clutched her son to shield him from Clay's critical eyes. Andrew stirred in protest, so she laid him in his cradle and prayed he would go back to sleep. She had never seen Clay like this, and she sensed she would need her full concentration to deal with him.

"Whatever you say. I don't know much about babies." He scratched his head. "Well, he don't matter now anyway. Your ma can take him."

Her mother could take him? "What are you talking about?"

"I'm talking about us."

Us? She had to nip this in the bud before he got any more outlandish notions. She tried a stern, big sisterly approach. "Clay Ferguson, I don't know what you mean. There is no *us*."

He swooped down near her face. "Don't you take that tone with me, Miss High-and-Mighty. I waited for you all these years, and I aim to have you."

He reeked of whiskey. He must be drunk. He'd never spoken to her that way before. She shrank against the pillow to put as much distance between them as possible.

"I come to see how long it would be before you're ready," he said.

"Ready for what?"

"Ready for me. You're mine now. I'm going to be the only one to touch your pretty hair." He reached forward and stroked her hair with awkward fingers. "I'm going to be the only one to kiss your pretty lips. Soon you'll swell up with another baby, and it'll be mine." He leaned forward.

"Clay, it's time for you to leave."

He smiled.

"Clay, go home. You're drunk."

"Now that's a fact, but I aim to get me a kiss." He leaned forward further, his eyes focusing on her mouth.

Lisa pushed against his shoulders. "I said go home. Now."

Suddenly, his fingers gripped her head, holding it steady while he closed the remaining gap between them. He ground his lips into hers, and his tongue pushed against her teeth.

Panic gripped Lisa. Her lungs threatened to collapse. She forced her hands up between them and shoved hard. "Nooo!"

Chapter Three

Outside the door, Jared swore under his breath. He'd never been one to eavesdrop, but when Martha had motioned for him to follow Clay up the stairs, he hadn't hesitated. He didn't like anything about Clay Ferguson, from the weakness in his eyes to the swagger in his step. On top of that, the man smelled like a distillery. Jared couldn't stomach the idea of him being in the same room with Lisa and Andrew.

He'd forced himself to stay quiet and listen, fighting the growing urge to barge in. He tried to tell himself it was none of his business. This was not his house. Lisa was not his wife. Then she screamed and all restraint fled.

Jared burst through the door and jerked Clay away from Lisa, throwing him to the floor. He reached down and grabbed the younger man by the shirtfront, pulling him back up in one swift movement.

"Ferguson, get out now. Do you understand?" He shook Clay for emphasis then let him drop to his feet. "And don't try to see Mrs. McAllister or the baby again."

Clay straightened up and fixed him with a furious glare. "Who the hell are you?"

"My name's not important. If you have an ounce of brains, you'll get out of this house now."

"I'll do whatever I damn well please."

Clay's hands inched toward his hips, and Jared reacted. He'd seen that motion too many times. In a split second, before Clay had any idea what was happening, Jared had his adversary on the floor and a pair of new pearl-handled pistols in his hands.

"Now get the hell out of here before I give in to my better judgment and use these on you and make a mess all over Mrs. Culpepper's clean floor."

Clay grabbed his hat and scuttled out the door like a rat on the run.

Jared turned to Lisa. She was staring at the guns with a look of horror on her chalky face.

"It's all right, Mrs. McAllister. Ferguson's gone. He can't hurt you."

"Get those out of here," she whispered.

He lowered his hands to his sides. "It's all right," he repeated, trying to reassure her. "You're safe now."

"No. You don't understand. Get them out of here." Her whole body was shaking.

Why was she so agitated? Surely she didn't think he would harm her. Just then Martha and Ben hurried into the room.

Jared handed the guns to Martha. "You'd better keep these. You never know when you might need them."

Martha's brows shot up. "I can't believe Clay wore guns into this house. He knows better. Please take them away. We don't need them."

Jared took the guns. "I think you're making a

mistake, what with all the riffraff around these days."
He glanced towards the door. "Right now, you'd better
tend to your daughter. I think she needs you. Ferguson
shouldn't be back to trouble you any further."

Martha hurried to the bed, and Ben and Jared
stepped into the hall.

Ben turned to Jared. "What was that all about?"

"The man's a foul-mouthed drunk. He was trying
to kiss Lisa when she screamed. I had to pull him off
her." Adrenaline pumped through Jared's veins just
thinking about it. "I should have shot him on the spot
with his own gun." He found himself craving the
release such an act would provide.

Ben regarded him with speculation. "It's just as
well you didn't. Lisa's mighty skittish around guns.
Always has been."

"I noticed. She looked at me like I might shoot
her."

"She's been afraid of them as long as I can
remember. Even Martha's not sure why, but they don't
keep guns in the house and haven't since Lisa's father
died."

Jared drew a deep breath and released it in an
effort to calm his racing pulse. "Ben, I don't know how
soon you and Martha were planning to get married,
but I think you should speed up your plans to take
both women and the baby into town. I don't think
Ferguson will be back soon—he's too much of a
coward—but it raises my hackles to think of them out
here all by themselves, especially now."

Ben nodded. "I'll talk to Martha about a date as
soon as I get a chance."

Jared glanced at the closed door of Lisa's room. He
couldn't quit worrying about her. He wondered how

she was doing, if she was still frightened. No woman should have to go through an experience like that, especially one who'd just had a baby. He fought a sudden irrational urge to rush back in, wrap his arms around her, and assure her no harm would come to her.

But he knew she wouldn't appreciate the gesture. She'd made a point of telling him she could take care of herself and he had no right to interfere in her life. And she was right. What had gotten into him? He couldn't go around trying to save every woman in distress who crossed his path. He and Lisa would both be better off if he kept his distance.

****

Lisa refused to tell her mother what Clay had said. She insisted it was nothing—that he had just startled her, but she was afraid her mother would notice the rapid rise and fall of her chest and the slight tremor in her hands. She was more shaken than she cared to admit. She couldn't be sure if it was the guns or Clay's threats, but it didn't matter.

Martha sat on the bed and held Lisa hands, tracing soothing circles with her thumbs.

"There, there, dear, don't you worry about a thing. You'll never have to see Clay again. Ben and I will take care of you. Everything will be fine. You'll see. You and Andrew will be safe in town with me and Ben."

Lisa sat up straighter, drawing away. "In town?"

Martha nodded. "Ben has been after me to marry him for the longest time, and I've finally agreed."

Lisa gave her a shaky smile. "That's wonderful. But I don't see what it has to do with Andrew and me."

"Well, dear, after the wedding, I'll be moving into Ben's house."

"Of course." Lisa nodded.

Martha drew her brows together in exasperation. "Well, you and Andrew will be coming with me. You certainly couldn't expect to stay out here alone."

"I don't see why not."

Her mother's voice rose a notch. "You can't stay out here all alone with a baby. It wouldn't be safe for either of you. What if something happened? How would you get help? And how would you be able to manage the place by yourself? The only sensible solution is for all of us to move to town together."

Instead of being swayed by her mother's logic, Lisa was more determined than ever. "I've lived here alone with you for years, and nothing has happened."

"Yes, but we're two adults, not an adult and an infant. It's hardly the same."

"Andrew and I will be fine. I can do most of the work myself, and I can hire help at harvest time, just like we always have."

"Lisa, you've never tried to do all that work and take care of a baby at the same time. You have no idea what's involved."

Tears pricked Lisa's eyes. "Mama, you know how much I love you and Ben, and I don't want to worry you, but I can't leave my home. I won't."

Martha rose and patted her hand. "You're tired and upset. This is not the time to be making important decisions. You get some rest, and we'll discuss it later."

"I won't change my mind."

"Goodnight, dear."

****

Dr. Hutchins stopped by two days after Christmas and pronounced Lisa well on the road to recovery, provided she stayed in bed for at least the next two weeks. She might have enjoyed following his advice except her abused parts were now itching as they healed, which made lying in bed maddening. On top of that, Andrew had decided to wake up and join the household in a big way. He was very vocal about his needs and discomforts, particularly when neither his mother nor grandmother could figure out what they were. He confused night and day and seemed happy only when Martha walked the floor with him or when he was nursing.

The third day after his birth Lisa's milk came in, which, in addition to being uncomfortable and messy, gave Andrew the ammunition he needed to soak through flannel diapers with amazing speed. Lisa could only lie in bed trying to avoid touching her breasts, which were enormous, tender, and rock-hard, and watch her noisy son run her mother ragged. She wished she could help but guiltily dreaded the day she would be well enough to do so.

This was not what she had pictured when she'd happily contemplated motherhood during the lazy summer days of her pregnancy. And, as if all that weren't enough, she was still so fat! She began to despair she would ever feel normal again.

The first few weeks after Andrew's birth passed in a blur of sleepless nights and exhausting days. Lisa felt like a sleepwalker, moving numbly through time, scarcely noticing the passage from one day to the next. And then things began to sort themselves out. Andrew cried less and slept more, and at more convenient times. By February, Lisa was starting to feel like a person again. She had time for small, personal things, like taking a full, hot bath and arranging her hair in some way other than simple braids.

Another encouraging change was the rapid return of her figure. The exercise of carrying the baby up and down the stairs at least a dozen times a day, often with piles of laundry on her other arm, combined with the demands of nursing, served to whittle the extra weight off her waist and hips like magic. The only place not shrinking was her breasts. They were still very full and strained the seams of her dresses. However, it was a small price to pay when the rest of her felt so much better.

The main irritant in her life was the frequent presence of Jared Tanner. Ben seemed to bring him along every time he visited the Culpepper farm, which was often. The man didn't do or say anything offensive, but his mere presence rubbed Lisa the wrong way. She couldn't look at him without remembering the gentle way his big, rough hands had cared for her and Andrew. They were strangers, yet the bond between them was unspeakably intimate. And the way his dark eyes followed her—watchful was the only way she could describe it—made her uncomfortable.

Oblivious to the tension, or choosing to ignore it, Ben and Martha went about making plans for their wedding, scheduled for the twentieth of March. Lisa knew they assumed she and Andrew would be moving in with them, although no one had mentioned the subject again. However, she was still determined to remain on the farm, and she saw no point in spoiling their happiness by bringing up the matter herself. The longer she put off any confrontation, the less likely they were to be able to dispute her decision.

****

The middle of February brought a welcome thaw, and Lisa decided to bundle Andrew up and drive to town to do some much-needed shopping. Because of her pregnancy and Andrew's birth, she'd been cooped up in the house for months and had scarcely seen a soul except her mother and Ben, and now Jared.

"Mama, I think Andrew and I will go shopping this morning. I could stop at Dr. Hutchins's and see if he has some tonic for your cold if you like. We're running low on flour, and I could use some more cloth to make Andrew some new gowns. He's growing like a weed."

Martha dabbed at her red nose with a handkerchief then smiled at her grandson sitting in the crook of his mother's arm while she ate her fried mush and molasses. "He is, isn't he? But do you think it's warm enough to take him out? You could always leave him home with me."

Lisa shook her head. *Grandmothers.* "He'd just catch your cold. If I wrap him in a couple of shawls, he'll never know he's been outside. And just feel the warmth of the sun coming through these windows. I haven't been out of the house in nearly five months except to go to the barn, and I'm about to go crazy."

"All right, all right. Go ahead. Just be careful."

Lisa laughed. "Yes, Mama."

Leaving Andrew with her mother, Lisa went out to the barn to harness Old Pete, the one horse the marauding Union soldiers had left them. When she attached the harness to the rickety old wagon, she wondered how much longer it could last. The wagon looked as though a strong breeze would reduce it to a pile of weathered kindling.

The two women had managed to take care of themselves and the farm reasonably well in the years since Seth had gone to war, but neither of them claimed any skill as a carpenter. And Ben could only do so much for them. His job as Express Superintendent on the eastern end of the stage line occupied most of his time.

Lisa sighed when she looked at the makeshift repairs she'd tried to make to hold the right front wheel to its rim. If only Dan... God knew the place could use a man's hand, but there was no point in dwelling on what might have been. She had only herself to count on now, and it was better that way. At least she wouldn't be wasting time and energy on foolish dreams.

She brought Old Pete and the wagon around to the back veranda by the kitchen door, and Martha bustled out carrying a pile of knitted woolen shawls in a willow laundry basket. It could only be Andrew.

"Mama, you're going to suffocate him."

"I don't want him to catch cold." Martha handed her the bundle. "Now snug him in and tuck these around him so he's good and secure."

Lisa settled her son in a cuddly cocoon on the floor of the wagon, snapped the reins, and the wagon lurched forward across the muddy yard toward the main road.

As they plodded along, she glanced down every few seconds to be sure Andrew was all right. The baby seemed to enjoy the rolling motion of the wagon and the crisp, fresh air of his first outing while she basked in the pleasure of being outdoors again. The sun warmed her face, and the air was rich with the smells of damp earth and wet leaves.

The trees had no leaves yet, but the snow from the Christmas blizzard had melted, and the land seemed to whisper the promise of spring.

Lisa loved spring. As she looked out across the steep-sided, round-topped hills of the orchard at the gnarled, black outlines of the apple trees, she could almost see the tender leaves that would sprout from those twisted limbs in two months' time. She never regretted for one moment that they'd had to sell off the tobacco fields after Papa's death. No field of tobacco could compare to the fragrance of the orchard in May or its leafy coolness in the heat of August.

The farm might only be a short distance east of the edge of town as the crow flies, but the crow didn't have to fly up and down hills the way earthbound people and animals did. Papa used to complain that if you stretched the road out flat, it would reach all the way to Liberty, or at least Platte City. But today, Lisa enjoyed every inch of the journey, past her neighbors' dormant fields and the big distillery run by the brother of the stage company owner.

When they reached the pockmarked blacktop of Main Street, she had to pay more attention to her driving. She wasn't sure which would be the greater catastrophe—if Old Pete stepped in a hole and broke a leg or if one of the wagon wheels hit a bump and splintered into a thousand pieces. Fortunately, neither calamity came to pass. She maneuvered the wagon to a spot in front of the mercantile, where she hopped down and tied Old Pete to the post out front.

It was wonderful to have the store open again. Last year things had been so depressed in the sleepy river town the residents had been forced to cross the Missouri River to Leavenworth to buy basic supplies. Since the war began, the whole town had suffered a decline in fortune that mirrored her own. The buildings on Main Street looked shabby, and half of the storefronts were still boarded up. Even the macadam paving, which had been the pride of the county when it was installed nearly fifteen years earlier, was falling apart for lack of funds to repair it.

Once inside the store, Lisa was beset by a gaggle of ladies. She forced herself to smile at the clucking and cooing over Andrew while she made arrangements with Mr. Cody, the proprietor, for the supplies on her list to be loaded into the wagon. Martha would have been in her element, but Lisa never enjoyed being the center of attention, particularly the attention of the group of her mother's friends that was growing by the minute. However, she was not too proud to enjoy the compliments being paid to her son.

"Lisa, he's beautiful! I believe he favors your father, don't you?"

Lisa smiled at Mrs. Ottsby, the rotund little wife of the largest remaining tobacco merchant in town. "I like to think so."

From over her left shoulder, she heard a low murmur. "How fortunate. It's hard to say who he'd look like if he resembled his own father."

Lisa gasped. She recognized the voice of Eliza Worthington, the spinster daughter of the Methodist preacher and town gossip extraordinaire. Eliza had been sweet on Dan all through school and bitterly jealous of Lisa. After he died, she'd spread rumors that because of his severe injuries, he couldn't have fathered Lisa's baby.

Lisa's ears burned. *The witch*! She'd been isolated on the farm so long she'd forgotten Eliza's malicious tongue. Someone should have put her in her place years ago. It was certain her well-meaning father never would. Lisa felt herself rising to the bait when Eliza's words caught her attention again.

"You've heard, of course, about the robbery yesterday."

All heads turned her way, and Eliza preened before going on, clearly enjoying the attention.

"No? Well, let me tell you, it was the most brazen thing. A dozen armed men rode right up to the bank in Liberty in the middle of the afternoon and robbed it, in broad daylight. They even shot and killed some poor man in the street."

Astonished murmurs rose from the ladies clustered around Eliza. Silas Gordon's Confederate guerillas had committed any number of outrageous crimes in the area during the war, but such behavior was unheard of in peacetime.

"And," Eliza continued, "they say the leaders were those James boys from over in Kearney." Her eyes pinned Lisa like an arrow from a bow. "Oh, and Lisa, dear, you won't believe what else I heard." Eliza's voice was silky with satisfaction as she relished her next tidbit.

"I'm sure I won't." Lisa raised one brow. A sensible person wouldn't believe half the things Eliza said.

"The bandits were wearing masks, but they say one of them bore a remarkable resemblance to Clay Ferguson. How is Clay anyway? I know he's always been a special friend of yours."

Eliza smiled like the cat that caught the canary, waiting for an answer.

Lisa's heart plummeted. She had tried so hard not to think about Clay for the past two months. She had tried to tell herself he hadn't meant anything he'd said, it was just the alcohol talking. He wasn't really a threat to anyone. But she'd never been completely convinced. There'd been the cameo and those fancy guns. Eliza's words brought back the specter of Clay's threats with an unwelcome jolt.

Lisa forced a smile and looked into Eliza's malicious little eyes. "I wouldn't know. I haven't seen Clay in months."

"Oh, really? Well, that's probably just as well."

Her nasty seed planted, Eliza turned her attention away from Lisa and back to the others. "Now, have you all seen the gorgeous new man in town?"

Lisa turned away from the group, grateful Eliza had moved on to another juicy topic. She had no interest in any man, particularly not one Eliza considered gorgeous. Her thoughts and emotions were in turmoil thanks to the suggestion that Clay might have become a bank robber, possibly even a murderer. As she ran her fingers unseeingly across the gouges in the scarred wooden counter and tried to snare her whirling thoughts long enough to make sense of them, a name pierced her consciousness.

"...Jared Tanner..."

She straightened and strained to hear what was being said behind her.

Eliza was babbling on. "...and they say he's a hired gunman who's killed twenty-six men."

Lisa had always wondered about the identity of the mysterious *they* who always seemed to be willing to tell Eliza everything about everyone in town.

"Mr. Holladay sent him here to ride shotgun on some of the westward runs out of Atchison where they've been having so much trouble with stagecoach robberies. I just know a man who looks like that, so dark and dangerous, will take care of those outlaws in no time. I don't know which is more exciting, the man or his job."

By the time she finished, Eliza was flushed and tittering breathlessly.

Lisa was fed up with Eliza's foolish prattle. It was bad enough to have to listen to her comments about Clay. Lisa had no interest in hearing another word about Jared Tanner. "Eliza Worthington, what would your father say to hear you carrying on that way in public? Why the very idea of describing a strange man as *gorgeous*."

Stung by the rebuke, Eliza pulled herself up to her considerable, albeit scrawny, height and lifted her nose a notch. "Oh, and how proud will you be, Lisa McAllister, after your mama marries Ben Wainwright and you and Jared Tanner are living under the same roof? Or perhaps you're looking forward to it."

Several ladies gasped at Eliza's crude innuendo. Lisa stepped forward, her palm itching for the feel of Eliza's cheek. Then she hesitated. If she gave in to temptation, word would be all over town in no time. She couldn't embarrass her mother by getting into an altercation in Mr. Cody's store. And of course, there was Andrew to consider. What would Mama do in a situation like this?

Lisa wrapped Andrew in his shawls and cast her gaze on Eliza's spiteful face. "I'm so sorry about your manners, Eliza. I shall convey my condolences to your father the next time we meet." Then she turned her back and walked out the door, her skirts swaying behind her like a giant bell. Her mother would have been proud.

When she reached the wagon and settled Andrew, she released a pent-up breath and sank down on the seat. Martha never seemed to mind what she referred to as a "spirited discussion." In fact, arguments energized her. But Lisa had always hated confrontations. She never felt comfortable with the verbal sparring her mother found so stimulating. Besides, she had other, more important, concerns about the events of the morning. What if Clay really had robbed the bank? And what if he came back to act on his drunken threats?

****

The next afternoon, Lisa was in the kitchen folding Andrew's clean laundry. She had taken advantage of the break in the weather to haul the heavy iron laundry kettle out to the backyard. Leaning over the steaming brew of hot water and lye soap, she had pounded out all her fears and worries on the innocent mass of dirty diapers and gowns. Nothing was resolved, but she felt a little better afterwards.

Suddenly, she heard the sound of hoof beats and looked out the window across the side veranda to see Clay careening into the yard astride a huge black horse she'd never seen before. It was a far cry from the broken-down nag he'd been riding for the past several years. Her sudden inhalation drew Martha's attention from the pot she was tending at the fireplace. They were expecting Ben for supper, as usual.

"Who is it, dear?"

"It's Clay." Both Lisa's voice and hands were shaking.

Martha set her big wooden spoon aside and stepped over to the window. Lisa had told her about the robbery the day before, including Eliza's conjectures about the identities of the participants.

In spite of Eliza's prodding, Lisa had done a

creditable job of putting Clay out of her mind again. It wasn't that she hated him or was afraid of him — she was just so much more comfortable when she pretended he didn't exist.

"Damn."

Lisa turned in shock at Martha's murmured response. Her mother never swore. Never.

Before either of them could utter another word, Clay stepped into the kitchen. He wore the same long duster he'd worn the last time they'd seen him but had on a new hat with a silver band and new boots of elaborately tooled leather. He was grinning and strutting like a peacock in his finery.

"Clay," Lisa said.

His grin widened through his sandy stubble of beard. "Howdy."

"What are you doing here?"

"Is that any way to welcome your future husband and breadwinner?" At her tiny snort of disbelief, he dropped the grin and glanced at Andrew sleeping in his cradle near the warmth of the fire.

Lisa edged over, hoping to block Clay's view. "What do you want?"

"I don't want nothing from you, not yet anyway."

"Then why are you here?"

"I brung you some money."

"I don't want your money. Where would you get money, anyway?"

"Feeling spunky, are you?" Clay's grin twisted. "I don't have to account to you for nothing. I just happened to get lucky, and I want to share my good fortune with my wife-to-be. Here." He tossed a wad of bills on the table. "Buy something pretty for yourself. No woman of mine is going to be dressed in rags like those." He gestured to Lisa's worn work dress.

She clenched her fists as hot blood rushed to her face.

Martha had remained silent throughout their exchange, but now she stepped forward, straight as a poker and just as unyielding. "That's enough, Clay Ferguson. You are no longer welcome in this house. Get out now, and don't come back."

Clay snorted. "Don't make me laugh, old woman. I go where I want." But Lisa could see the telltale signs of unease as he shifted his weight back and forth on his shiny new boots.

Martha took two steps forward. Her voice resonated with soft steel. "I said *get out*, and I meant it."

Clay backed up. "I'm leaving now, but I'll be back whenever I want." The defiance in his voice had a hollow ring.

"I don't think so." Martha took one more step.

Clay backed up again then spun and stomped out the door and across the porch to his horse tied to the railing.

Neither woman watched him ride off. Lisa barely registered the sounds of his departure. Her attention was on her mother.

"Mama, how could you do that? He was probably armed again."

"Maybe," Martha replied, "but what was he going to do, shoot me in my own kitchen? I don't think he's that far gone yet. He's nothing but a bully and a coward, and the only way to deal with him is to stand up to him."

Lisa shook her head. Clay might not have sunk to the level of shooting unarmed women, but he had crossed some kind of line, judging by the money on the kitchen table. There might be some other explanation for it, but in her heart, she feared Eliza's gossip was true.

"Mama, what are we going to do with this money?"

Martha eyed the stack of bills. "I'm not sure. Heaven knows we could use it, but we can hardly profit from ill-gotten gains, which those appear to be. Then again, we can't walk into the bank and return it without having to explain how we came by it. And we can't be absolutely certain this is from the bank robbery." She tapped her lower lip. "Clay has presented us with a number of problems here."

She walked back to the pot she had been tending, which hung over the coals from a big iron hook, and lifted the lid, giving the chicken stew a stir. "I think I will discuss this with Ben and Jared when they arrive. They should be here any time now."

Lisa groaned. "Not Jared Tanner again, Mama. I told you what Eliza said about him being a hired gunman. She might not be right about much, but it looks like she was right about Clay, so she could be right about Jared, too."

Martha kept stirring, stopping to take a small taste and add salt. "I think to say he's a hired gunman is an exaggeration in the least. Jared is a friend of Ben's, and I trust Ben's judgment. He will be welcome in my house unless he proves himself unworthy."

"But, Mama, a man who makes his living shooting people..."

"I know how you feel about guns, but Jared doesn't strike me as a violent man, in spite of his occupation. He's always been a perfect gentleman in my presence." Martha turned her head and looked Lisa in the eye. "Has he ever treated you roughly?"

Lisa shifted her gaze to the baby clothes she was folding. "No, I'm just uncomfortable having a stranger so involved in our private affairs."

"I'm sorry, dear," Martha said. Then she added softly, "Because I'm afraid Jared Tanner may soon become even more involved in our lives." A small smile played around her lips. "In fact, he may be the answer to several problems."

Lisa narrowed her eyes. "Mama, what are you plotting?"

"Oh, nothing. Now we'd better get the table set; the men should be here any minute."

Martha breezed out of the kitchen, humming under her breath before Lisa had a chance to question her further. Not that it would do any good. Her mother was obviously hatching some scheme, and wild horses couldn't drag it out of her before she was ready to tell.

She glanced at her brown calico dress with its assortment of baby stains on the shoulder, bodice, and skirt and put a hand up to touch her bedraggled hair. She hadn't worried about her appearance when she'd thought Ben was going to be their only guest, but she couldn't let Jared see her this way. Every time she looked into his knowing black eyes, she was reminded he'd seen her at her most vulnerable and disheveled, and she was anxious to erase that image from his memory. If she hurried, she might be able to make herself presentable before he arrived.

Chapter Four

By the time Lisa had washed, donned a simple day dress of dark green calico dotted with tiny white flowers, and re-pinned her braids in a tidy coronet, male voices had been drifting up from the family parlor for twenty minutes. She cast a quick glance at the mirror on the back of her wardrobe door. Although she wasn't wearing a corset because she was still nursing, her appearance was acceptable. Quite good enough to receive Jared Tanner.

She rarely bothered with a half-crinoline at home, but her petticoats fluffed her skirt nicely, and she attempted to emulate Martha's elegant sway as she made her way down the stairs to join the others.

Ever since the awful Christmas scene with Clay, Lisa had sensed an undercurrent of pity in Jared's demeanor, and it infuriated her. She might, on rare occasions and only in the middle of the night, give in to the temptation to feel sorry for herself, but she refused to allow anyone else to feel sorry for her, ever. Especially Jared Tanner.

When she entered the room, conversation halted.

Three pairs of eyes stared until Martha beckoned her.

"Come in, dear. We were just discussing the choices you and I are facing."

A chill gripped Lisa as she took the seat next to her mother on the sofa. "Mama, I'm sure this is neither the time nor place."

"Lisa, the decisions we must make now are very serious, and Ben and Jared are hardly strangers. I know how thoughts of leaving this house distress you—"

A rush of heat replaced the chill. "I can't—"

Martha took her hand and patted it. "I know, dear, but, now more than ever, I am convinced for safety's sake you and Andrew must move into town with Ben and me. In fact, we are so concerned Ben and I have decided to move the wedding date up. We will be married next Sunday."

Sunday. Lisa stared straight ahead at the leaping flames in the fireplace, trying to make sense of it. Sunday was too soon. She wasn't ready. What was she going to do? She forced a wavering smile. "I'm happy for you both, but as I told you, Andrew and I are staying here."

Martha sighed. "I had hoped you would be reasonable and consider Andrew's well-being above sentiment."

Lisa rose and began pacing, too agitated to sit still. She had to make her mother understand. She stopped in front of the fireplace, took a deep breath, then turned. "I am considering his well-being. It's important for him to grow up in his own home, on Culpepper land. It's all I have to give him."

Ben leaned forward. "Lisa, honey, you and Andrew are family to me. You know you'll always have a home with your mother and me."

She winced at the hurt in his loving eyes. "I know you love us, but you're used to a nice quiet house. You have no idea how disruptive a baby would be with all the noise and extra activity. Besides, you and Mama will be newlyweds. You deserve some privacy."

"Now don't you go worrying about us."

A speculative gleam came into Martha's eyes. "There is one other alternative. Jared is looking for a place to live after I move in with Ben, and I would be happy to give him room and board here in return for help with the chores and the protection he would provide you and Andrew. He could sleep in the hired hand's room. It would be a great comfort to me to know you weren't out here all alone."

Lisa's glance darted from her mother to Jared in disbelief. He nodded, his face solemn and the expression in his dark eyes unreadable. Her mother must have taken leave of her senses.

"Mama, you can't be serious! What makes you think we would be safer with a...a...hired killer in the house?"

At her words, Jared's posture stiffened and his jaw flexed, but he didn't speak.

Martha was unmoved by her daughter's argument. "I assure you, I am perfectly serious. I have spoken with Jared at length, and I'm convinced he will do whatever is necessary to ensure your safety."

Lisa's mind reeled. This was madness. She couldn't live in the same house with a man she barely knew, a man who made his living with a gun, a man whose presence raised every defense she possessed.

Martha rose and crossed the room to join her, resting her hand against Lisa's back. "As much as we may wish to deny it, it appears Clay is now an outlaw.

Jared has shared with me some of the things he said to you, and after the way he behaved the last two times he came here, I must make sure he never returns to find you and Andrew defenseless."

Lisa refused to turn around, and when she replied, her voice was tight with the effort to sound reasonable. "But, Mama, even if someone else were living here, they wouldn't be around all the time. Andrew and I might still be alone if Clay came back. Besides, I don't believe he'd actually hurt us."

"I'm not so sure. And think of the risk he might expose you to." Martha's voice held a note of panic "He may have a price on his head soon. What if he decided to come here for shelter with a posse after him? Do you think for one moment he would hesitate to use you and the baby as hostages if he were surrounded?" A delicate shudder rippled through her body. "It doesn't bear thinking about. Besides, if it were well known around town that Jared was living here, I doubt Clay would have the courage to show his face."

Lisa had to agree. Clay would be unlikely to worry about anyone else if his own safety were at risk. But Jared Tanner, here in the house? Every day? No, it was impossible. Perhaps if she tried another approach...

"Mama, we couldn't have a single man living out here alone with me. What would people say? It wouldn't be decent."

"Nonsense. You're a respectable widow. Having a man living in the hired hand's room is no different than taking in a paying boarder. Since the war, lots of women have had to do that."

"But, Mama—"

Before she could say another word, Martha cut her

off. "I won't hear any more objections. My mind is made up. You have until the wedding to decide whether you will be sensible and move into town or Jared moves in here next Sunday evening."

Resentment coiled in Lisa's breast at her mother's ultimatum, but she remained silent. She would not be prodded into acting like a child. She'd made her position clear, and there was nothing more to be said.

"I just want to protect you, dear," Martha added. "I can't help it. I'm your mother."

"I understand, but I have to do what I think is right. I won't change my mind." Lisa gathered her battered pride and prepared to make a dignified exit. "If you will excuse me, I'm afraid I've lost my appetite."

She glanced at Martha, Ben, and Jared in turn, but the bold challenge in his eyes caught her off guard. It was as if he were daring her to stick to her decision, a decision that would make him a daily fixture in her life. The gall of the man! She gave her skirts an angry swish and stalked out of the room.

Upstairs, Lisa paced back and forth across the braided rag rug beside her bed. Both alternatives her mother had presented were unpalatable, but what was she going to do? She had to think of something in the next few days or she would lose by default, and Jared Tanner would move into her house.

After tossing aside every scheme she concocted, she heard Andrew's cries along with the sound of footsteps coming up the stairs. She glanced at the clock with a pang of guilt. It was past his normal suppertime, and he must have awakened hungry. The steps were too heavy to be her mother's. Ben must be bringing the baby up so she could feed him.

The door opened, and Jared stepped into the room, cradling the wiggling, crying infant with both hands as if he might break. He thrust his tiny charge toward Lisa, careful not to loosen his grip. "I think he's hungry."

Lisa crossed the room and snatched her son. She turned her attention to the child, hoping if she ignored the man he would go away. However, Jared appeared to have no intention of leaving. He ambled over to one of the chairs by the tall front windows and stretched his long frame out on it.

She pressed her lips tightly together. "Mr. Tanner, you may leave now. I need to feed Andrew."

"I know, but I want to talk to you, and if you're feeding the baby, you can't get up and walk out. Walking out seems to be your favorite way of dealing with uncomfortable situations."

He was goading her. And she was furious at herself for not being able to ignore him. Her eyes narrowed. "Are you calling me a coward?"

His face softened into a look that could almost have been mistaken for tenderness if she hadn't known he was a cold-blooded killer.

"No. After being with you for Andrew's birth, I'd never accuse you of cowardice. I think once you accept reality, you face it head on. Your problem is the accepting. Now go ahead and feed him, or we'll never get any peace."

The baby's plaintive cries had increased to lusty squalls in spite of Lisa's attempts to quiet him with crooning and bouncing. She glared at Jared.

He nodded. "Go ahead. I won't look." He turned in his chair and made a show of staring out the window.

She considered going into her mother's room across the hall, but he would just follow her. She grabbed her heavy rocking chair with one hand and dragged it across the floorboards as far from him as she could, facing it toward the opposite wall. Then she sat and unbuttoned her dress. She wasn't sure she would be able to relax enough to let her milk down with Jared in the room, even though she didn't believe he would go back on his word and spy on her. But since Andrew was rooting around like a starving piglet, she had to try.

Then she noticed the spare flannel diaper she sometimes used when burping the baby hanging across the arm of the chair. If she draped one end over her shoulder and let it hang down, it would cover both her son and her breast. She would feel more comfortable if she weren't exposed, even if Jared did stay on the other side of the room. She tried it, and, satisfied with the result, settled back to let Andrew eat his fill.

For a few minutes the room was silent except for the soft smacking sounds of the baby suckling, and Lisa grew more irritated as she waited. She had nothing to say to Jared Tanner, so she wasn't about to begin a conversation with him. This whole thing had been his idea. Why didn't he get on with it? Finally, annoyance and curiosity got the better of her. "Well?"

"I wanted to give you two time to get settled."

She fought the temptation to turn her head. It was disconcerting talking to someone behind your back. "Mr. Tanner, you obviously feel we have something to say to each other. Please get to the point."

"First of all, you might as well start calling me Jared if we're going to be living together."

Her head whipped around despite her best intentions, and the motion jerked the nipple out of Andrew's mouth. At his howl of protest, she turned back. "We are *not* going to be living together."

"So, you've decided to be sensible and move into town?"

"No." She disliked the sulky sound of her own voice.

"Lisa...damn, this is awkward, talking to someone you can't see."

She agreed but made no response. She heard the chair creak and the sound of footsteps pacing back and forth in front of the windows.

"You've got to understand, this is for your own good," he said.

"I understand everyone is using threats to try to force me to do something I don't want to do."

"And I'm the threat?"

"You know the answer."

"Clay is a much bigger threat to you than I am." His voice grated with exasperation.

"I don't agree," she replied. "I don't believe Clay would actually harm us, while you're nothing but a hired gun."

Jared spun around and strode over to stand in front of her chair. Lisa sucked in a quick breath and tightened her grip on Andrew under the cloth, but Jared focused his angry dark gaze on her face.

"You don't know me at all."

She glared back. "That is precisely the point."

"I'd never hurt you or the baby." It was a flat statement and a promise.

"Why should I believe you? Are you a killer, or aren't you?"

He waited a moment before answering, and she thought she heard him counting under his breath.

"I've killed before—I won't deny it. But those men were thieves and murderers who deserved to be killed, men who made a living robbing stages without regard for who might be injured or killed in the process." His eyes dared her to dispute him. "I've shot men to protect innocent lives, and I don't regret it. I'd do it again if I had to."

The implication was clear, and it was one Lisa couldn't accept. Although a small, hidden part of her longed for the luxury of the strength he offered, the price was too great. She might wish Clay gone, but she couldn't bring herself to wish him dead.

She drew herself up as straight as she could in her chair, still balancing Andrew on one arm. "Mr. Tanner, the man you are so cold-bloodedly considering shooting may be misguided, but I have known him all my life. He will not hurt us. Now please leave at once."

"I'll leave, but that won't change a thing. You've got three days to make up your mind. You forget I heard what he said to you. I know what he wants. I saw what he did. And next time it will be worse. If you refuse to move to town with your mother and Ben, you can expect to see me back here Sunday night and every night after that."

Tears of frustration stung her eyes, but she dashed them aside with the back of her free hand. "Why are you doing this? You don't even know me. None of this is your problem."

The look in his eyes softened, but he remained implacable. "The *why* isn't important. I'm going to do what needs to be done for you and your son, so you'd better find a way to accept it."

****

By Sunday morning, Lisa still hadn't found an answer to her dilemma. She hadn't said another word to her mother about it, but while she helped Martha pack clothes and personal things to take to Ben's house, it was obvious Lisa wasn't packing anything for herself or Andrew. If Martha noticed, she made no comment.

The wedding was held at the Weston Baptist Church at three o'clock that afternoon. The service was lovely and simple, and Lisa fought to suppress her tears as she stood beside her mother. Martha's face radiated happiness, and Ben was bursting with pride. The ceremony was marred only by the presence of Jared Tanner. Lisa couldn't imagine why Ben had asked Jared, a newcomer in town, to stand up with him. Ben had lived in Weston for nearly twenty years and had many friends who'd have been proud to do the honors.

After the wedding, the Ladies' Sunday School Guild hosted a supper in the church hall, and Lisa made the most of her reprieve. She wanted to postpone going home as long as possible. She dreaded the prospect of walking into the house and facing the hollowness of her mother's absence for the first time in her life. She sat and chatted, occasionally nibbling at the food on her plate and holding Andrew so a steady stream of ladies could admire him.

It was a large gathering. Most of the town was there, including Eliza Worthington and her father, as well as many other unmarried young ladies. The war had been hard on Platte County, like most of the rest of the country. Many young men had gone off to fight and never returned, and many young women were left to worry about their futures with so few potential husbands available.

Lisa soon noticed a cluster of local belles surrounding Jared's tall figure. He stood head and shoulders above the soft cloud of femininity fluttering around him and looked decidedly ill-at-ease. Eliza Worthington hung on his left arm, her jaws moving furiously as she chattered. As if he felt Lisa's gaze, Jared glanced across the room straight at her with a pained expression that was almost pleading. She couldn't restrain the smile that tugged at her lips. Let him suffer. She wasn't about to rescue him.

Late afternoon rolled into evening, and she realized most of the guests had departed or were gathering up their things to head home. Ben and Martha had long since disappeared. She should go home, but the prospect seemed so lonely. Suddenly a towering form materialized beside her, and a deep voice said, "Are you ready? Let's go home."

"Oh!" She started. Then she realized who it was and glanced up. "It's you."

Jared frowned. "Yes, it's me. Are you ready?"

"Well, yes. But do you have to come with us now?" She had been hoping against hope there was a way to postpone this moment, but now that it had arrived her mind went blank. All she could think was she wasn't ready.

His eyes narrowed. "You knew what to expect. Now let's go." His abrupt tone suggested patience worn thin.

Lisa found herself and Andrew being hustled out to the waiting wagon before she could protest further. She noticed Jared had already loaded his few belongings into the bed of the wagon and tied his horse to the back. He must be planning to drive them back to the farm.

Then she remembered she couldn't drive the wagon and hold the baby at the same time. Martha had held Andrew on the ride to the church, and Lisa had forgotten to bring his basket. The realization left her momentarily chagrined. Living alone would require more concentration. If she hoped to prove to her mother she was capable of managing on her own, she would have to attend to every detail. She wouldn't allow herself to accept that Jared Tanner's presence was anything other than temporary.

The drive home was silent and strained. Jared concentrated on keeping Old Pete from breaking a leg in the darkness on the muddy and rutted road, while Lisa busied herself plotting ways to get rid of him.

When they reached the Culpepper barn, he climbed down and reached for the baby without a word. She tried not to notice the strength in the hands that guided her to the ground. Murmuring a thank you, she wrapped Andrew's shawls tighter against the wind and hurried across the dark yard toward the house.

She climbed the four steps to the back veranda and let herself in through the kitchen door. Andrew was starting to fuss at being bundled so tightly. She fumbled around for a lamp so she could see to stoke the fire and warm the cold room. When the flame flickered and she replaced the glass globe, she was unprepared for the scene of destruction that met her eyes.

Every utensil in the room had been jerked from its proper place on the shelves or in the cupboards and flung to the floor. The flour sack had been slashed, and the furniture and floor were dusted with white. The half-eaten remains of a loaf of bread and a joint of ham lay on the kitchen table next to an empty whiskey bottle.

A horrible combination of outrage and fear clenched her vitals. She couldn't think, she could only feel. She screamed. And she didn't just scream. She screamed a name. "Jared!"

Seconds later, he bounded across the porch, his steps thundering on the elevated boards, and burst through the door. His appearance frightened her almost as much as the state of her kitchen. His gun was drawn, his black eyes flashed, and everything about his posture suggested a taut readiness for deadly action.

In a split second he surveyed the room, searching for the source of danger. As soon as he determined the three of them were the only occupants, he reached for her with one arm and drew her hard against his side, never relaxing his vigilance or his grip on the pistol.

Lisa clutched Andrew to her breast and closed her eyes. The sight of the gun in Jared's hand sent a cold shiver through her body, yet a tiny part of her sought sanctuary in the solid mountain of strength he represented. Soon the initial shiver was followed by another, and then she began to shake all over. Bloody images flashed through her brain leaving only an intense impression of fear.

He tightened his grip and swore in words she couldn't quite hear. "Stay here. You'll be all right. I have to search the rest of the house." He loosened his hold and sat her on a kitchen chair.

She stayed where he put her, only vaguely registering the sounds he made as he moved through the rest of the house. What had happened? Why? And who would have done such a thing? Her frenzied brain could find no answers.

A few minutes later, he returned, his gun holstered under his coat. "There's no one here."

She nodded. The fear was receding. The trembling had almost stopped. As if sensing it was safe at last, Andrew began to wail.

Jared dragged another chair around to face her and sat down. "Well?"

"Well, what?" She had her hands full with Andrew, who had begun struggling in earnest.

Jared cast his gaze around the room. "Now you know why your mother didn't want you here alone."

Lisa's fears were retreating, thanks to his commanding presence, and the knowledge disgusted her. She'd played right into his hands by hanging on him the way she had, but she couldn't help herself. Now she would have to undo the damage and work even harder to persuade him and her mother she was capable of taking care of herself and Andrew. "You don't think Clay did this, do you? Any drifter could have come in here. I never lock the door. For all I know, you could have done this after we left this afternoon to try to persuade me to see the error of my ways." She didn't believe it, but the defiance felt good after the weakness she had allowed him to see.

A tiny muscle flexed in his jaw. "That is the stupidest thing I've ever heard you say. When will you get it through your head that I..."

He broke off and stared at his boot for a few seconds before returning his eyes to her face. "Look, Martha told me Clay was pretty mad when he left the other day." He gestured to the debris around them.

"This looks like the work of an angry child who wants to prove he can do something he's been forbidden to do. A drifter might have eaten your food, but why make all this mess?"

She lifted her chin. "That doesn't prove anything."

"No, but it makes you think, doesn't it?"

She turned her gaze to Andrew. Jared might be right, in fact he probably was, but she couldn't admit it. Where would that leave her? She refused to accept she needed his protection or anything else he might offer.

"I need to feed Andrew and put him to bed," she said, intending to put an end to the conversation.

Jared stood, scraping his chair across the wooden floor. Irritation hardened the lines of his rugged features. "Fine. You take care of him. But you can't deny what's happened here by trying to ignore it. One of these days you're going to have to grow up and face the truth. Pretending isn't going to change anything."

Why did he have to scold her like a child? Lisa's pulse increased as her anger mounted, but she remembered her mother's training. She would be ladylike if it killed her. "I don't know what you're talking about. Now, I really must go upstairs. I assume you can settle yourself in the hand's room. I'm sure you remember where it is." With that, she left the room.

"I can take care of myself," he called after her. "But can you?"

She stiffened further at his challenge but continued down the hall and up the stairs. What an infuriating man. She'd show him how much she needed him.

Andrew was so worn out by the day's excitement he fell asleep before he finished nursing. She kissed his soft dark hair before tucking him into the low wooden cradle next to her bed. Then she sank down on the bed and leaned back on her hands trying to ease the soreness in her shoulders. She was bone-tired, drained by the happenings of the day, first the wedding and then the scene in the kitchen.

The kitchen. She groaned. She really should clean up the mess. It would be even harder to face in the morning. But what if Jared was still down there? She didn't have the energy to indulge in any more skirmishes. She had to think of some way to get him out of the house for good, and soon.

The house was dark and quiet as she made her way down the stairs with a lamp in her hand. When she stepped into the kitchen, her breath caught. Everything was back in place, as if she had imagined the whole ugly picture. Dishes and pots were neatly stacked on the shelves of the cupboards, the chairs were tucked under the table, and the floor had been swept clean. The flour had even been transferred to a new sack and returned to the pantry. She knew who was responsible, but why? Was he trying to hammer home her need for a watchdog and keeper?

Her nose began to twitch, and she turned toward the fireplace. *Unbelievable*. The man had even made a fresh pot of coffee and left it on the warming trivet for her. Well, she wasn't such an ingrate as to refuse to drink it, not in the state she was in, and particularly since he wasn't here to see her. Then she had a sudden thought—where was he? She had neither seen nor heard him since coming downstairs. Was it possible he had acceded to her wishes and left?

Before her mind could deny that unlikely possibility, the floor creaked twice above her head. So, he had gone to his room. She poured herself a cup of steaming coffee and sat at the kitchen table. She took a long, slow drink, savoring the smell and the warmth as much as the flavor. What was she to make of this man? A hired gunman who appeared to be ready to protect her and her son with his life, yet would clean up her kitchen, brew a pot of coffee, and leave her in peace to enjoy it, knowing his presence would only upset her.

Jared Tanner was a more complicated man than she had realized, and he seemed determined to compound the baffling turmoil in her life. She needed him to leave so she could begin the process of setting up an orderly, independent life. But first she would have to squelch the burgeoning seed of comfort growing in her heart as she listened to the muffled sounds from the room above her. She tried to tell herself she was just lonely without Martha, and that any human presence would have served the same purpose, but she didn't fully succeed.

Hours later, a scream pierced the night. Blood. Blood was everywhere, on her hands, on the man's head. She rubbed her hands furiously against her clothes, but the blood wouldn't come off. The man's head, her father's head, loomed before her. Only the whites of his eyes showed, and his forehead was misshapen. Half of it was missing, with a pulpy red mass where skin and hair should have been. She screamed again.

"Lisa. Lisa, wake up." Big hands shook her shoulders. "You're dreaming."

Her mind struggled to surface through the haze. The horrible image faded and disappeared. A different face, healthy and whole, replaced it. As her eyes adjusted to the dim moonlight, the square jaw and tousled black hair of Jared Tanner came into focus.

"What are you doing here?" she asked, confused and half asleep.

"You screamed. I had to make sure you were all right."

She blinked, hesitating. "I...I'm fine. It was just a dream, a bad dream."

His hands rested on her shoulders, and his voice was gentle. "Do you have nightmares often?"

"Not any more. I did when I was younger."

"Do you want to talk about it?"

Talk about the terror and blood? Talk about the beloved face made monstrous?

She shook her head. "No. No. I'm fine, really." The terror would pass. Her pulse would return to normal. It always did.

"Do you want me to stay with you until you fall asleep?"

She was almost weak enough to give in, but not quite. After the dream, her mother always sat on the side of the bed and stroked her hand or sang until she fell asleep. But her mother didn't live here anymore. She would have to learn to deal with it on her own.

"I'll be fine."

Jared dropped his hands and stood. "If you're sure..."

"I'm sure."

He left and she was alone again in the dark. Why did she have to have the dream again tonight of all nights? Why did he have to be the one who offered comfort? And why did she have to be so tempted to accept it?

Chapter Five

Over the next few weeks, Lisa pondered the problem of how to remove Jared Tanner from her house and her life. Not that his presence was oppressive. He was gone quite a bit riding the stages west out of Atchison, which was over an hour's ride across the Missouri River and to the north. He could have ridden the train to Atchison, but its fixed schedule was inconvenient, and Jared said he preferred a horse with four legs to one with iron wheels and a smokestack.

When he wasn't working for the stage line, he spent most of his time caring for the livestock or working in the barn. Lisa was busy with Andrew and the housework, and she didn't want Jared to think she was interested in what he was doing, so she rarely ventured out to check on him. However, from the house she began to notice things like broken boards replaced by new ones and listing fence posts that snapped to attention overnight. The supply of firewood beside the back steps never diminished, and one day the huge, sagging barn doors magically pulled themselves into square.

She knew it wasn't magic. Jared was steadily transforming the farm into the place she remembered from her childhood, the place she had dreamed of ever since. She should be grateful, and she was, but she resented her gratitude. She wanted to be the one to bring the farm back through her own efforts, but she didn't have the time or strength. So, although she knew she should thank him, she kept quiet.

She rarely saw him except at mealtimes, and then only on days he wasn't riding a stage. Meals were silent, hurried affairs, and she had to admit the tension was mostly her doing. She had rebuffed his attempts to make conversation until he gave up and ate in silence.

After the first week, she had second thoughts about the wisdom of the silent treatment. Although he kept his thoughts to himself, Jared's haunting black eyes never left her from the moment he walked through the kitchen door, still damp from his cold wash-up at the pump in the yard, until he pushed his chair back from the table, nodded his thanks, and went upstairs to his room. He was so watchful, as if he were giving her time to adjust to the situation before forcing her to acknowledge him. The problem was, only he knew the deadline. He put Lisa in mind of a big mountain cat, crouched and waiting to pounce on its prey. Sometimes she wanted to scream and throw something at him to provoke the inevitable.

The only thing that lessened the intensity of his focus on her was Andrew. Jared had taken a real shine to the baby and was surprisingly good with him. Suppertime was Andrew's fussiest time of the day, and he fretted in his cradle while Lisa was trying to cook unless she dropped everything and picked him up.

Since that was impossible, she had to grit her teeth and ignore his plaintive demands.

But when Jared walked in, he headed straight for the cradle, picked up the irritated infant, and Andrew quieted. Jared would bounce the boy in his arms and croon nonsense to him in a resonant rumble that replaced the tears with an unblinking stare from the baby's round, brown eyes. Lisa was torn between gratitude for his help and jealousy for the special bond he had formed with her son.

Perhaps as payback for her cold, impersonal treatment, Jared insisted Lisa comply with the terms of his agreement with Martha to the letter. He was to be served three hearty meals a day when he was available, and his laundry was to be done once a week, without exception.

Of her household tasks, Lisa despised laundry above all others. The harsh lye soap burned her hands, and she ended up soaking wet by the time she had stirred the clothes with the big wooden paddle, wrung them out, and hung them on the line to dry. And the man produced so much laundry. She had never seen anything like it. He must change everything from the skin out every day. On top of that, he expected the sheets on his bed to be washed every week. She was sure he was doing it just to spite her; she had never known a man so bent on cleanliness.

But she was determined not to fall down in any of her obligations. Dirty clothes and a few missed meals might drive Jared out of the house sooner, but it was a matter of pride. She refused to let him think she couldn't handle anything he dished up. Besides, he might complain to her mother. Then Martha would have additional ammunition in the battle to force her to move into town where she wouldn't have so much work. Lisa took Andrew to visit her mother and Ben at least twice a week, and Martha never failed to ask how she was managing on the farm. The pressure was subtle but unmistakable.

****

Toward the end of March, after a month of escalating tensions, a sudden warm spell brought spring to the countryside overnight.

"Lisa, are you home?" The high-pitched feminine call was preceded and followed by a persistent rapping on the big brass knocker on the front door. "Lisa!"

She was in her bedroom struggling to change Andrew. He had learned to grab his toes and stick them in his mouth, which was especially fun to do when he wasn't encumbered by bulky clothes. She was trying to fasten a clean cloth around his plump little bottom when she heard the commotion from the front porch. Snatching him up, she hurried from the room and down the curved staircase, trying not to trip. The voice sounded familiar through the thick panels of the door, but it couldn't be...

She flung the door open. "Jessamine Randall! All the way from Philadelphia!"

Five feet two inches of auburn-haired feminine dynamite wrapped in mauve silk burst through the doorway and straight into Lisa's arms, nearly knocking her and Andrew over. "Lisa, it's so wonderful to see you again, and is this your baby? Your mother said you had a new baby. He's so cute! He looks just like you. What's his name? May I hold him?"

Lisa laughed and held up her hand to stem the rushing tide of words. Jessy Randall had always been a bundle of energy, and it hadn't diminished in the four

75

years since they'd last seen each other.

"Jessy, Jessy, slow down. Come in, please, and let's sit in the parlor like the dignified, grown-up ladies we're supposed to be."

Jessy looped her arm through Lisa's, and they walked into the main parlor. "Can you believe how old we've become? You're a mother now, and I'm a confirmed spinster. Why, the last time I saw you, we were barely out of the schoolroom."

Lisa led the way to the gold satin sofa. "I wish your parents hadn't insisted on sending you away from Missouri after the war started. I know they wanted you to be safe, but it was so lonely after everyone left."

Jessy squeezed her friend's hand. "I'm so sorry about Seth. I'm sure you and your mother still miss him something awful."

"Yes, we do."

They were quiet for a moment, then Jessy spoke. "Your mother also told me about Dan. How are you getting along? I remember how fond you were of him."

Lisa looked into her friend's sparkling green eyes, as warm and open as ever. This was Jessy, her staunchest childhood ally. It would be wonderful to have someone to share her thoughts and troubles with again. "Oh, Jessy. I'm so glad you're here."

"I'm glad, too. Do you want to talk about it?"

Talk about it? Lisa hadn't been able to share her true feelings with anyone since Dan's death. She couldn't tell her mother she'd been wrong to marry him. She couldn't admit her guilt over her lack of genuine grief. She couldn't share her fears about Clay or even voice her complaints about Jared without inviting more pressure to move to town.

"You know you can tell me anything," Jessy prodded. "In fact, I insist. Now what's wrong?"

"Just about everything."

Relief lifted her spirit as she unburdened herself, knowing her friend would neither judge nor scold but would only accept and support her. Lisa had always counted on Jessy for that, and it was reassuring to know some things hadn't changed.

Jessy didn't let her down. She listened while Lisa shared her conflicted emotions about Dan but made no attempt to hide her reaction to Clay's behavior.

"Lisa, that is abominable. I shudder to think what he might have done or might do in the future. What do you plan to do about it?"

"There isn't much I can do."

"Nonsense. You can't just live in fear, worrying about when he'll show up or what he might do next."

"I don't live in fear. I haven't seen Clay in weeks, and he may not come around again, not with Jared here."

Jessy lifted one auburn brow. "Who's Jared?"

"You mean my mother neglected to mention my *watchdog*?" Lisa explained her mother's ultimatum. "So, until I can think of some way to get rid of him, I'm stuck with him, living right here in the house."

"Your mother thinks you're safer with a hired gunman in the house? That doesn't sound like the Martha Culpepper I remember."

"No, it doesn't. Personally, I think she's lost her mind."

They were interrupted by a loud thumping from the back porch to the kitchen. "Lisa," a deep voice boomed, "Where's supper? I'm starved."

Lisa pressed her lips together. "Well, now's your

chance to meet him." She glanced through the windows at the darkness that had settled while they'd been talking. "I didn't realize it was so late. Would you mind holding Andrew while I fix supper? It sounds like Jared is in a foul temper."

Jessy glanced toward the doorway. "I'd be glad to. Is he always like this? I can't believe your mother would subject you to such a difficult man."

Lisa was already on her feet as Jessy hoisted Andrew to her shoulder. "Truthfully, no. He usually has very little to say. But the stage line has been attacked by bandits twice in the last week, and Jared hasn't been on the right coach at the right time to catch them, so his temper's running a little high. Come with me and you'll see what my mother has saddled me with as punishment for not seeing eye-to-eye with her."

They found Jared rummaging around in the kitchen. When they entered, he looked up from the loaf of bread he was slicing.

"Oh, there you are. I was hungry."

"So I gathered. I'll have your supper ready in a few minutes if you can restrain yourself."

He took a bite from the slice in his hand, chewed, and swallowed. "I think I can manage." Then he turned his attention to Jessy. "And who is this lovely lady?"

Lisa expelled an exasperated breath. "Don't bother trying to charm her. She heard your bellowing all the way in the parlor."

Jared smiled at Jessy. "I didn't bellow, did I Miss...?"

Jessy looked flustered. "Randall, Jessamine Randall. And I really couldn't..."

"See." He turned back to Lisa. "Miss Randall says I didn't bellow."

Lisa threw up her hands. "Oh, for heaven's sake. Will you get out of this kitchen? I'll bring your supper into the dining room when it's ready. Jessy and I will eat in here, where the atmosphere is more civilized."

Jared took another bite and strolled toward the dining room. "Whatever you say. Good evening, Miss Randall."

Jessy stared at his broad back and long, powerful legs as he sauntered from the room, then turned to Lisa and whispered, "Why didn't you tell me the truth about him? He's magnificent."

Lisa returned her attention to the wooden bowl where she was mixing cornbread. "Don't be ridiculous, he's nothing of the sort. And Jessamine Randall, I can't believe you said that. I always gave you credit for having more sense than the rest of the fluff-brained girls around here who are only interested in snaring a husband."

Jessy sat down with Andrew on her lap and handed him a wooden spoon to gnaw. "Well, you're right about one thing. I have no interest whatsoever in finding a husband."

"Oh? What are your plans? I never got a chance to ask what brought you back to town and if you plan to stay." Lisa bustled around the open hearth, filling various pots while they talked.

"I certainly do. I'm here to open a new Freedman's Bureau School."

Lisa whipped around, and the ladle in her hand fell to the brick hearth with a hollow clang. "You're what?"

"You heard me." Jessy grinned.

Lisa retrieved the ladle and wiped it clean. "I heard you, but I have a hard time imagining the daughter of the august Judge Randall being allowed to organize and teach at a school for former slaves. What do your parents think about this?"

"They're doing their best to be enlightened about it, but I'll admit it's an uphill battle, especially for Mama." Andrew banged his spoon on the table and chortled when Jessy tickled his tummy.

Lisa wrapped a dish towel around the handle of the cast iron skillet and lifted it off the fire with both hands. "It must be quite a shock for your mother to have her daughter turn into a reformer. I doubt she's ever done anything more radical than donate used clothing to the poor box at church."

Jessy held Andrew's middle and bounced him up and down, making him laugh again. "She'll have to get used to it. I became involved with the abolitionist cause in Philadelphia, and now that the slaves are free, there's an enormous need for schools for them. Last night, Papa was telling me half the people left in Weston after the war are former slaves."

Lisa stopped to consider. "It's possible. So many white men were killed in the fighting, and most of the slaves in town stayed after emancipation. After all, it's the only home they know."

"Yes, and it won't do the town any good to have half the residents illiterate. So, I plan to open a school for the children of former slaves as soon as possible."

"You sound like you're committed to this."

Jessy nodded vigorously. "I am. So, you can see why I have no interest in a husband. I don't expect I'll ever marry. A husband would only try to prevent me from doing what I know is right."

Lisa could see the fire of a zealous reformer in her friend's clear green eyes and hear it in her ringing voice. Jessy had never been one to embrace anything halfway. "But aren't you worried it might be dangerous? You know most of the folks around here supported the Confederacy, and many of them weren't too happy when the state legislature freed the slaves last year. They might not take kindly to you or your school."

Jessy shrugged. "I'm not worried. I'm determined to succeed, no matter what."

Lisa retrieved a plate from the cupboard. "I'm sure you will. I've never met anyone who could successfully stand up against you when you set your mind to something." With a big spoon, she mounded food on the plate. "Now, I'll take this to the hungry bear in the dining room, then we can talk some more."

Jessy rose to her feet. "I'd love to stay, Lisa, really I would, but I have to get home. Mama will worry, and besides, there's a meeting of the Town Council tonight, and I have to present my plans for the school."

Lisa glanced out the window and frowned. "It's awfully dark. Are you sure you can get home by yourself? I could ask Jared to take you after dinner. I'm sure he would agree. He enjoys his role as the protector of helpless women."

Jessy laughed. "Although I'm tempted, I'm hardly helpless, as you well know. I really must go now."

"If you're sure. I'll drop this plate off in the dining room on the way to the door."

Jessy followed Lisa into the spacious yellow dining room where Jared sat alone at the big mahogany table with a disgruntled look on his handsome face. As soon as he saw Jessy, his expression changed.

"Miss Randall, are you leaving so soon?"

Lisa set the plate in front of him with a ringing thud. "Yes, she is. She has to go home right away, and she doesn't need any help. Now eat your dinner." She grabbed Jessy by the elbow and pulled her out of the room.

Jessy flashed a smile over her shoulder as she passed into the hallway. When they were out of earshot of the dining room, she whispered, "Lisa, what's come over you? I've never known you to be so rude to anyone before, and he doesn't seem all that bad to me."

"You don't have to live with him."

Jessy flashed an impish grin. "More's the pity. All I know is he sure does stir you up."

"That shows how much you know." Lisa stuck her tongue out the way she had when they were ten years old, and both girls laughed. "Now give me my baby."

At the front door, Jessy pulled on her mauve kid gloves and wrapped her black knitted shawl around her shoulders. The two friends embraced.

"I really am glad you're back, Jessy."

"So am I. You must come into town and visit me soon. I'll tell you all about my plans for the school."

"I'll do that." Lisa watched Jessy walk down the steps and untie the reins of her horse. "Goodnight and be careful."

"I will." Jessy waved from the seat of her smart little buggy and set off into the darkness.

Lisa shivered in the chill of the early spring evening before she pulled the heavy front door shut. Following Jared's strict orders, she turned the key in the lock until she heard the solid click. She shifted

Andrew to her other arm to ease the ache forming in her shoulder.

Sometimes she envied Jessy. Her friend was always so full of enthusiasm. Life had been good to Jessamine Randall. She had indulgent parents who allowed her the freedom to do anything she liked, as well as complete financial security. But none of it had spoiled Jessy. She had always stood up for anyone who needed a champion, and apparently, she intended to keep right on doing so.

For a moment, Lisa jealously longed for the luxury of energy to spare for other people's problems. Then she chastened herself for indulging in self-pity. She had a comfortable home and a beautiful, healthy son, and she was truly grateful. The war had stolen those things from thousands of other women. Now, if she could just rid herself of the guardian in her dining room...

"Lisa!"

Now what could he want?

She sighed, switched Andrew back to her other arm and started down the hall. It had been a long day, and she was tired. Andrew might be only three months old, but he was heavy, and the constant carrying had taken its toll on her back and shoulders.

By the time she walked into the dining room where Jared was finishing his meal, Lisa's good mood from Jessy's visit had evaporated. "What is it?"

His lips compressed. "I was going to suggest you join me for dinner. I could hold the baby while I eat my pie."

She examined his face. Lines of fatigue fanned out from his eyes and bracketed his chiseled mouth. He looked as tired as she felt. It had been a long day for him, too. Yet he still offered to help her with Andrew.

Her immediate reaction was to refuse. But at that moment Andrew seemed to gain fifty pounds, and his weight pulled her down, compressing her spine. Besides, for some reason, the baby loved sitting on the big man's lap, tucked into the crook of one arm. He would giggle and coo and delight in kicking Jared's solid thigh with both feet.

"All right." She walked over, slid Andrew into Jared's waiting hands, and picked up his empty plate. "I'll bring you a piece of pie."

Her feet felt as though her shoes were made of lead as she made her way to the kitchen. She glanced at the clock on the cupboard—it was nearly seven. She would be glad to collapse into bed as soon as she got Andrew to sleep. She fixed herself a small plate of beans, salt pork, cornbread, and greens and sliced a large wedge of dried apple pie for Jared. As an afterthought, she added a generous topping of sweet, fresh cream.

Now why did I do that, she wondered. He's like a stray cat—if I feed him too well, he'll never leave. Even as the words formed in her mind, a tiny thought blossomed. What if Jared didn't leave? She squelched it; she couldn't allow herself to think such a thing. Of course, he would leave. Why wouldn't he? She'd have to keep her guard up against dangerous notions like that.

"Here's your pie." She plunked it down in front of him.

****

"Thanks."

Jared ate in silence for several minutes. Only Andrew's happy babble filled the room. When he finished, he set his fork down across the plate and pushed it out of reach of the baby's questing fingers. Then he studied Lisa while she ate. She scarcely had the energy to chew her food. He wasn't sure he should tell her about his suspicions, but he had to impress on her the need for extra caution. Maybe his news would make her realize she should follow her mother's wishes and move to town.

But even as he thought it, a flash of revelation struck. He didn't want Lisa to move in with Martha and Ben. He wanted her to stay here, in this house, with him and Andrew. The notion shocked him. Where had that come from? They couldn't continue to live together this way. The situation was only temporary. It had to be. He would finish this assignment and move on, just as he always did. There was no room in his lonely life for a woman and child.

He collected his scattered thoughts. "I spent most of the day chasing those bandits again."

"Hmm," Lisa murmured as she chewed.

"There were four of them this time. I managed to fight them off, but one took a bullet in the shoulder."

"Did you kill him?"

"I don't think so. And why do you say it that way? You make me sound like a bloodthirsty murderer."

"Well, aren't you?"

He fought to control his temper. He was fed up with her attitude toward him and his occupation. "I'm not going to apologize for my job."

"Nobody asked you to."

He closed his eyes and prayed for patience. When he spoke, his voice was low and strained. "That's enough, please. I have something important to tell you."

She stared at him in defiance.

"The men wore bandanas over their faces, but I'm pretty sure two of the men were Frank and Jesse James. I recognized them from some pictures Ben received from Pinkerton's. They're investigating that bank robbery in Liberty."

"And why should that concern me?"

"I think one of the other men was Clay."

Her eyes rounded then narrowed. "I don't believe you. You're making it up."

Knowing of her suspicions from Ben and Martha, it never occurred to Jared she'd refuse to believe him. "Why would I do that?"

"I don't know. You've been listening to the gossip in town. You might be mistaken."

"It's possible, but I don't think so. And neither do you."

She set her jaw but didn't reply.

"Why do you keep defending the man? He's a thief and a coward who threatened you and broke into your house."

He noticed a glistening in the corner of her eye, and it made him angry — angry with her for refusing to accept the obvious and angry with himself for causing her tears.

"You don't know that," she countered.

"He threatened you. I heard him."

"I'm sure he didn't mean it. He's just...oh, I don't know what he is."

"Well, I do."

"You'd love to shoot him, wouldn't you?"

"Lisa, I don't *love* shooting anybody. And besides, the next time it might not be me. It might be a bank guard or a sheriff or a railroad agent. Believe me, it's going to happen sooner or later. A man who takes up that way of life can count on coming to a bad end."

Lisa covered her face with her hands, driving her fingers into her hair. Her gesture sent a shaft of guilt straight to his heart. She had looked so tired. All he wanted to do was ease her burden, but he'd ended up adding to it.

"Do you care about him that much?"

He reached out and stroked her back. She flinched then her taut muscles relaxed to his touch. He continued to glide his hand up and down her spine, waiting for her answer.

"Care about him? Care about Clay?" She paused and lifted her head. "I suppose I do, but not the way you think. I'm just tired, tired of all the fighting, tired of all the dying." She pulled away from his hand and stood. "I just want to be left alone to raise my son in peace." She reached for Andrew, who had fallen asleep in Jared's lap.

"Lisa, it's not that easy, and you know it."

"It can be. Just go away and leave me alone."

"I can't do that."

"Of course, you can." Her voice was bitter.

"Lisa..."

"Just leave us alone."

He watched her back as she left the room. It was the loneliest sight he had ever seen.

Chapter Six

The next morning, Lisa arose before dawn. She was going to town and wanted to be out of the house before she had to face Jared again, with his hard accusations and soft caresses. She told herself she wasn't running away from anything, she just needed to escape for a little while. She tiptoed around her room being careful not to wake Andrew and struggling to open the big doors and heavy drawers of her wardrobe without a telltale creak. She dressed simply and swiftly and listened for a long moment. Satisfied she had not awakened the man on the other side of the wall, she lifted her sleeping son from his cradle and crept downstairs.

With luck, Andrew would sleep until she got to her mother and Ben's, and she could nurse him there. Martha would be thrilled to see them, and it would give Lisa one more chance to persuade her mother to get Jared out of the house. She could also use the quiet time alone in the wagon to think. Everything had become a tangled mess, and she craved the return of order and certainty.

Lisa left Andrew sleeping in the kitchen in his willow laundry basket padded with towels while she slipped across the yard to the barn. The sky was still dark, but dawn was close, and its rosy promise gave her enough light to find her way without a lantern. The air in the barn was warm from the heat of the animals' bodies and pungent with their smells mingled with the sweet scent of hay from the loft.

Several heads lifted when she entered the barn, hoping her arrival meant an early breakfast. She only took the time to feed Old Pete, however, and allowed him to eat while she readied the wagon. She needed his cooperation if they were to make a silent exit.

When everything was ready, she opened the heavy double doors, straining not to let them bang against the walls of the barn. As she hurried back toward the house to retrieve Andrew, she spared a glance at Jared's window. Still dark. She loaded her sleeping son and his basket into the wagon and settled it between her feet.

By the time they reached the Wainwright's house, the sun's rays had reclaimed the sky and a few people were up and stirring. Lisa shook her head. She had turned the situation over and over in her mind until she felt dizzy. She was certain of only one thing, Jared had to go. She would never have any peace in his presence. And it couldn't happen a moment too soon. She could already sense the hole his departure would leave.

She pulled Old Pete to a stop in front of Ben's house and tied the reins to the ringed post. Smoke rose from the kitchen chimney in back, so her mother must be up. The house was really more of a cottage, a charming, single-storied structure of red brick with white trim and a seamed tin roof. The rooms had such low ceilings Lisa wondered how Jared had been able to stand inside. It was much more modest than the faded grandeur of her own home, but she knew her mother was happy here. In a couple of months, Martha would fill the front gardens with hollyhocks, marigolds, and snapdragons and the large back garden with vegetables of every kind.

Lisa climbed down and reached up to lift Andrew from his basket. This time he woke. He blinked in surprise at his surroundings but didn't howl. However, she knew he would be hungry, so she wrapped him securely and hurried up the short flagstone walk to the front door.

After a minute or two, Martha answered dressed in her wrapper and nightdress. Her light brown hair still hung in its long braid. "Lisa! What are you doing here at this hour?"

Lisa smiled and tried to keep her voice cheerfully casual. "Hoping to get some breakfast. May we come in?"

"Of course, of course." Martha ushered them through the parlor and dining room to the kitchen. "You warm yourselves here by the fire, and I'll have the bacon and grits ready in no time. Ben will be out in a minute."

Lisa unwrapped their shawls and sat down with Andrew on the chair her mother had pulled over for her. "Thank you. I think I'd better feed him now." She propped her elbow on the arm of the chair, arranged Andrew, and unbuttoned her dress. While the baby nursed, she sat back and watched her mother's smooth, practiced movements as she prepared breakfast. It was almost like being at home again, the way it used to be.

Lisa sighed. It was a soft sound, but Martha turned her attention from the bacon sizzling in the skillet. "I hope you can stay longer today, since you've come so early. I must confess I've been missing you."

"Oh, Mama, we've missed you, too." Lisa meant it with all her heart. Sitting in a kitchen watching her mother cook, she could almost pretend none of the events of the past three months had ever occurred.

"How are things at the farm?"

There was that question again. Lisa grimaced and turned her head to peer through the small kitchen window at the naked hawthorn tree in the yard. "We're fine."

"You never mentioned it, but Jared told Ben what happened the night of our wedding. I was hoping you'd be ready to join us here by now."

"I'm sure he made more of it than it was." Lisa tried to suppress the shudder that shook her at the memory of the devastated kitchen. "Besides, you and Ben don't have room for two more people, even if one of them is pretty small."

Martha wiped her hands on her apron and turned. She rested a hand on Lisa's shoulder and rubbed it gently. "You know there will always be room for you wherever I am. If that's the only thing holding you back, I know Ben would be glad to add on another room."

Lisa reached up with her free hand and placed it over her mother's. "No, Mama. You and Ben need time together, and I'm old enough to make a life for myself now. I want to. I need to."

Martha squeezed her daughter's shoulder and then withdrew her hand. She walked back to rescue breakfast from the fire. "I don't know why you want to make life harder for yourself than it has to be."

Lisa watched as Andrew took his last few pulls then wiped his mouth and re-buttoned her dress. "Sometimes, it's the best way, the only way." She hesitated. "Mama, I want you to ask Jared to leave."

Martha didn't look up from turning the bacon. "I don't think so, dear."

"I'm serious. I don't need him and he...he makes me nervous."

"Why is that? What does he do?"

Lisa tightened her jaw in frustration. How could she explain it? "It's not so much what he does. He's just...there."

"That's the idea, dear."

"Well, I don't want him to be."

"I'm sorry, but it's for the best, and if you weren't so stubborn, you'd admit it."

Lisa beat back the urge to scream. "Mama, I didn't come here to argue with you."

"Good, then eat your breakfast." Martha set the plates of food on the well-worn kitchen table. "Afterwards, you can do some shopping, and Andrew can stay here with me."

Before Lisa could argue further, Ben strolled in adjusting his suspenders, his face and hair damp from his shave. He walked up behind his wife, wrapped his arms around her waist, and planted a lusty kiss on the back of her neck below her left ear.

Martha turned and shoved him playfully. "Ben Wainwright, behave yourself. Can't you see we have company?"

"At this hour?" He whipped his head around. "Lisa! What are you doing here?"

Lisa couldn't help but smile at his flush of

embarrassment. "It's nice to see you, too, Ben."

Martha reached up and steered her husband by the shoulders to the bench opposite Lisa. "Sit down and eat. Lisa brought Andrew to visit us. I'm hoping to persuade her to let me watch him while she goes shopping."

Lisa gave up. There would be no changing her mother's mind today. "I could use a few things from the store. I won't be gone long."

Martha reached for the baby. "Take all the time you need. This young man and I will have a wonderful time, won't we, sweetheart?"

Lisa sighed and picked up her fork. Her mother was already completely engrossed in Andrew. Neither of them would notice her absence. As soon as she finished breakfast she retrieved her shawl. As predicted, no one spared her a glance.

Once outside her thoughts returned, unbidden, to Jared. She had to prod herself to stir up her usual antagonism. She couldn't be certain what he felt for her, but it wasn't indifference. His over-protectiveness baffled and irritated her, but his presence was also comforting in a way she couldn't accept, ever. To accept him would be to admit her weakness, her neediness. She couldn't allow that to happen. She had to find a way to make her mother see reason.

It was a beautiful spring morning. The sun shone brightly, burning through the cool mist remaining from the night before. Here and there the lovely dark pink of redbud and cheery yellow of forsythia peeked through the leafless trees. Birds chirped and flitted between branches, and squirrels raced around trying to remember where they had buried their nuts months before.

She didn't need much, so she decided to leave the wagon and walk the rest of the way to the mercantile. She paid close attention to her footing as she descended the steep road. All around her the hills were dotted with other houses, some as small as Ben's and others much grander.

When she crossed the narrow bridge to the main part of town, more people filled the streets, on foot, in wagons, and on horseback. She made her way to Mr. Cody's store to pick up a few small items before returning to collect Andrew. Remembering her last trip to town, she was glad it was still so early. She didn't relish another encounter with Eliza Worthington. She was delighted to find some soft yellow yarn for a spring bunting for Andrew without meeting anyone she knew.

While she paid for the yarn, her eyes kept straying to the jars of penny candy Mr. Cody kept on the counter next to his ornate brass cash register. She remembered coming into the store as a little girl before her father died and being allowed to choose a few pieces to take home. How long had it been since she'd eaten store-bought candy? Ten years? Fifteen? Suddenly the urge to treat herself in this small way overcame years of enforced thrift. What could it hurt? She deserved it after everything she'd been through lately and everything she had yet to face before her life could be put in order.

She spent fifteen precious cents on chocolate drops and peppermint sticks even though she couldn't afford such an extravagance. She still had the money Clay had left, but she couldn't bring herself to touch it. Her mother had given her last year's apple money, and she would have to make it last until she could sell some honey this summer and harvest the main crop in the fall. Oh well, she would do without something later. Right now, her spirits sorely needed a lift.

Sucking on a peppermint stick as she strolled back up the hill, she felt quite cheerful. It was amazing how a single small luxury could distract one from the weightier issues in life. When she reached the Wainwright's house, she found her mother and Andrew sitting in the sun on the front porch. Martha was singing an old nursery song that stirred faint memories from Lisa's own childhood.

When Lisa opened the front gate, Martha looked up from her cooing grandson. "Hello, dear. Did you get everything you needed?"

"Right here." Lisa patted the parcel of yarn and the small brown paper bag with the candy.

"Can you stay for lunch?" Martha was obviously loath to relinquish her charge so soon.

"Oh, no, I couldn't. Jared will be mad enough about not finding his breakfast on the table as it is."

If she had hoped to gain sympathy for her plight, she was sorely disappointed. Martha shrugged her shoulders and replied, "I guess you'd better be going then."

Lisa frowned at her mother's refusal to back down and send Jared away. If Jared were gone, the main source of tension would be gone from her life. She shied away from the pang of loneliness that struck when she thought of the house without him.

****

Back at the farm, Jared paced the kitchen like a caged mountain lion. Where was that fool woman? He'd watched her leave in the pre-dawn darkness and wondered what she was up to. Since she hadn't taken anything with her except the baby, he knew she couldn't be going far, so he'd let her leave. Now he doubted the wisdom of his decision. Where could she be going that she had to sneak out of the house before the chickens were up? Did she feel such a need to escape him? He winced at the thought.

He was well aware of the tension his presence created. Martha had told him she was counting on the conflict to motivate her daughter to act sensibly and leave the farm. However, he wasn't sure Lisa's mother was fully aware of the nature of the tension between them.

Yes, his presence irritated Lisa. It was a constant reminder that no one thought she was capable of running her own life. But there was more. Whether she admitted it or not, a wick of attraction smoldered between them and threatened to explode into flames at the slightest provocation. And he was feeling plenty provoked.

Every day it grew harder to look at her, to listen to her voice as she played with her son, to smell her unique fragrance as she brushed past him, yet not be able to reach out and touch her. He was locked in an intimate tangle with a beautiful, desirable woman, but she wasn't his. She cooked his food and washed his clothes. He chopped her wood and took care of her animals. But in the evening, when they were both tired from the exertions and frustrations of the day, they couldn't turn to each other for solace. He couldn't hold her against his chest and stroke the silken waves of her hair while her body relaxed against his. That comfort taunted from the other side of an invisible line neither of them dared cross.

Every night, he lay in the darkness on one of the

lumpy single beds in the hired hand's room and conjured up images of Lisa alone in her big bed on the other side of the wall. He wondered what she was thinking. She never gave him a sign she found him anything other than an exasperating nuisance dumped on her by her mother. But he would never forget the first night after the wedding, when she'd stepped into the kitchen and screamed his name. He could still feel her arms clinging to him and the surge of energy it sent to every nerve ending in his body. He'd known then what he'd suspected before, that he would protect this woman with his life. It made no sense, but there it was.

Those feelings and frustrations served to fuel his anger rather than temper it as he paced the kitchen floor. Just when he had decided to ride to town to look for her, Lisa and the wagon passed the window on the way to the barn. Relief washed over him, starting in the center of his chest. She hadn't left after all. Then anger quickly replaced it. Where the hell had she been before the crack of dawn? And where did she get off scaring him like that?

****

Andrew had fallen asleep in the laundry basket on the ride home, so Lisa lifted him out carefully after returning Old Pete to his stall in the barn. She took her time walking back to the house, wondering what was in store for her inside. Jared's horse was in the barn, so there was no chance of avoiding him. He would be waiting, and he would be angry.

If there was one thing that man required, it was to be fed on time. He would probably demand to know where she'd been. Well, she didn't need an excuse to visit her mother whenever she wanted. If he didn't like her going into town so early in the morning, too bad.

With that attitude planted firmly in her mind, she opened the back door and stepped into the kitchen.

Jared stood before her, a tower of barely restrained fury. His black eyes flashed, and every muscle in his body tensed, ready to fight.

As soon as she saw him, she took a tiny, involuntary step backwards and held Andrew tighter. The man seething in front of her was more intimidating than a riled bull and just as dangerous.

"Where the hell have you been?" he roared.

She had expected a show of bad temper, but she had never anticipated such rage.

Andrew awoke with a start at Jared's bellow and began to cry. Lisa frowned and tried to soothe him. Her son's wail banished her fears and rallied her maternal instincts. She turned on Jared.

"Now look what you've done, you big bully. You woke him and scared him to death."

Jared frowned and reached for the baby. "Here, give him to me."

Lisa glared and held Andrew tighter. "I'll do no such thing."

Jared paused. When he spoke, his voice was tightly controlled. "You know he always calms down when I hold him."

"I'm not about to hand my son to a madman who flies into a fit of rage just because his breakfast is late."

"This has nothing to do with breakfast, and you know it."

"No? Then what are you so upset about?"

He ran the long, blunt fingers of one hand down his black-stubbled jaw. "Lisa, sit down."

"I will not."

"Please."

In spite of his gruff tone, she had caught a lightning-swift flash of something in his eyes that was startlingly like a plea. She couldn't help herself—she sank down onto one of the chairs and waited for him to continue.

Jared didn't look at her as he resumed pacing in front of the fireplace. "I'm sorry I yelled at you, but when I saw you leave this morning—"

"You watched us leave?" She'd been so careful. She could have sworn she hadn't awakened him.

Now he turned and pinned her with a hard gaze. "Yes, so don't ever think you can get away with something like that again."

Her only answer was a stubbornly set jaw, so he continued. "Anyway, you didn't take anything with you, so I didn't think you'd be gone long. When you didn't come back, I got...concerned."

Lisa digested his statement for a moment. What did he mean by *concerned*? Was he trying to say he'd been worried about her? That was as ridiculous as it was unlikely.

"Why?" she challenged.

He rubbed his jaw again. "Why? How should I know?" He threw both hands in the air in a gesture of defeat. "Because any sane man would. Although I'm not sure I qualify on that count anymore."

Then he stalked out of the kitchen and headed for the barn. Still without breakfast.

The rest of that day and all the next, they barely spoke. She made sure to have his meals ready on time, and he mended the ladder to the hayloft and rode out on a stage run to Topeka. Things between them were changing, and Lisa could only react to the unsettling hints emanating from Jared's silence.

He had always been watchful, but now whenever they were in the same room, his gaze bored into her. Even when he held Andrew, Jared's attention was focused on her. Sometimes his look was an ebony velvet caress, sometimes a sharp, steely jab that made her shiver with an emotion she couldn't name. Either way, she was living on a precipice, and any wrong move would send her sailing into the abyss below.

By the afternoon of the third day, she was so preoccupied with her own worries she failed to notice the arrival of visitors until the loud hoof beats and shrill whinnies of horses in the yard broke her concentration. Andrew was upstairs napping in his cradle, Jared was somewhere outside, and she was in the kitchen laboring in sweaty solitude over one of her least favorite tasks—ironing. She glanced up from the calico dress spread before her on the board and set the heavy flatiron on its rest.

Good Lord in Heaven, it was Clay. And he had three other men with him. Whether to bolster his nerve or intimidate her further, she didn't know.

As if they were paying a formal call, the men tied their horses in front and stood together on the porch while Clay banged the knocker on the door. Lisa hurried to answer it, her mind flying faster than her feet all the way down the hall. What could he want, and how could she get rid of him before Jared saw him? She disliked confrontation, and any meeting between the two was bound to be ugly. She hated to think of anything happening to either of them, regardless of her feelings about each man individually.

Clay stood before her grinning like a jackal. The other men stood behind him, silent and unsmiling. Lisa forced her stiff lips into what she hoped resembled a smile. "What can I do for you, gentlemen?"

"Ain't you going to invite us in?" Clay asked, still grinning.

Lisa refused to be baited. "What do you want, Clay?"

"I just want my friends to meet my intended."

"I am not your—"

Clay pushed past her, ushering his companions into the parlor as if it were his. He sprawled across the sofa, dirtying the pale satin with his muddy boot. The other three remained standing. Their looming presence spooked her. She desperately wanted all four of them gone.

"Can I bring you gentlemen anything?" she asked, hoping to hurry them along.

"No, ma'am," answered one of the strangers, a slender blond with a short, prickly beard and the most hypnotic pale blue eyes she had ever seen.

"Bring us some whiskey," ordered Clay.

"I don't keep spirits in the house."

"I bet I can find something." Clay levered himself up. "Be right back, boys."

Lisa followed him as he sauntered out of the room and crossed the foyer to the family parlor. On a sudden impulse she said, "If you're looking for the bottle I found in the kitchen a couple of months ago, it's gone. It was pretty much empty anyway."

Clay's eyes drifted, then seemed to focus. "Oh, yeah."

So, Jared was right. The marauder had been Clay.

"I hear you got yourself a man living here now."

Lisa had an uneasy thought. Had her mother been wrong? Was that what everyone in town thought, too? "He's only a boarder."

Clay ran his gaze appraisingly down her body. "I don't aim to have no boarder trying out what's mine."

Heat suffused her cheeks. She wished he would vanish from the face of the earth and take his friends with him.

"What the hell's going on here?"

Jared stood in the doorway, shirtless, the heavy muscles under the curling black hair on his chest as taut with tension as a coiled snake. His guns were strapped low across lean hips with his right hand poised above one handle. Jessy had been right—he was magnificent. And terrifying.

Lisa hesitated, trying to force herself to concentrate on the man, not the guns. The memory of another man, a beloved man, with a horrible, bloody hole in the side of his head flashed into her brain and nearly stilled her heart. She had to stop this. She couldn't bear to consider the possible outcome. She rushed forward with her hands out. "Put them away, please. It's nothing. It's all right."

Jared turned part of his attention to her. "I don't think so." His right hand dropped to the handle of his gun. "Ferguson, I told you once before, and I won't tell you again. Get out of this house, and don't come back."

Clay grinned. Three silent forms appeared in the hall behind Jared, prepared to ensure the safety of their comrade. "Don't go getting riled, company man."

Jared drew one gun from the holster. He didn't aim it or cock the hammer, but threat shimmered in the room.

Lisa swayed against the rock-solid bulk of his chest, and her hands grasped his arms to restrain him. "No," she whispered urgently. "Please."

Jared kept his eyes on Clay. "Take your friends

and get out."

Clay grinned wider. "You might like to meet my friends. They've got their guns aimed at your back right now."

Jared wheeled around, swinging Lisa behind him.

Clay moved to stand with his associates. He pointed to a lean young man of above average height with sandy brown hair and hazel eyes. "This here's Morgan Bingham, and these two are Frank and Jesse James." He waited for his words to take effect.

Lisa peeked around Jared's shoulder. Frank James looked dark and mean, but his brother Jesse, the man whose pale eyes had so fascinated her in the parlor earlier, was as compelling as he was frightening.

Jared narrowed his eyes as he regarded the men. "I believe we've already met. Yesterday. I never forget a face, even if it's hiding behind a bandana."

He stared and they stared back, each side daring the other to act first. Then Jared tipped his head toward Lisa. "Have you finished with him?" He jerked his chin toward Clay.

She nodded. "Yes." And it was true. She could truthfully say she hoped she never saw Clay Ferguson again.

"Good." Jared turned back to the four men who waited in silent readiness. "Gentlemen, it seems your business here is finished." He raised the barrel of his gun a fraction.

Clay wavered, as if tempted to press his numerical advantage, but Jesse made the decision for the group.

"Seems you're right." He placed his battered beige hat on his head with finality. "Come on, boys."

Clay shrugged and followed the others toward the front door without a backward glance. When the door slammed, Lisa shivered and instinctively sought the shelter of Jared's arms. For a few long seconds, she closed her eyes and allowed herself to absorb the comfort he offered while attempting to banish the image of the gun in his hand aimed at Clay. With her face buried against his chest, she breathed in the scent of him—a reassuring blend of sawdust, leather, sweet hay, and the intoxicating musky smell of the man himself.

When she realized what she was doing, she pushed away. "You'd better get washed up. It's almost supper time."

His fingers still encircled her wrist, and he pulled her back into his arms. Silently cursing her own weakness, she went.

"I wouldn't have let them hurt you." One big hand stroked her hair while the other cradled her against his chest.

"I know."

He eased his hold enough to look down into her face. "Then what were you so scared of?"

"Don't you understand? You might have killed Clay, or those men might have killed you."

"That wasn't likely. Clay's a coward, and the others aren't fools. Over the years I've learned to read men pretty well. I won't let anything happen to you or Andrew."

"That's not the only thing I worry about."

"It's the most important thing. You've got to trust me."

"How can I? I don't really know you."

"Don't you?"

She thought about it. In some ways she knew him well. In others he was a complete mystery. "I've got to fix supper."

"Lisa, you can't dismiss this that easily."

"Dismiss what?"

"Everything. Clay's coming here, the things he said, your fears." His eyes softened and his voice took on a husky edge. "The way you feel in my arms."

She jerked away. "That was a mistake. It won't happen again."

"It probably shouldn't, but it will."

She shook her head. "No, it can't." She couldn't let it. They were playing with fire. She had felt the strength of Jared's need in his arms and seen it in his eyes, and on some basic level she had responded to it. If she became more deeply involved with him, she couldn't bear to let him go. And he would go, one way or another. He had to go. She needed him to go. She just couldn't face it quite yet.

She reached for his hands. She had to make him understand, to agree. "Promise me...promise me you won't..."

"Won't what?"

"Won't press this any further."

"You know I'd never hurt you."

"You keep saying that, but I can't believe it." If she let him get close enough, he would hurt her. She knew it.

He dropped her hands and his lips tightened. "I give you my word. I won't force any unwanted attentions on you."

"Good. I'm glad that's settled. Now I'll go fix your supper." She turned and walked down the hall toward the kitchen.

If only she could be confident about the *unwanted* part.

Chapter Seven

After Clay's visit, Lisa found herself looking at Jared through new eyes. He had thrust himself between her and the threat of the outlaws' guns. She could no longer summon her former impatience with his desire to protect her. On at least two occasions he had been right—she had needed him. And while she refused to admit it in so many words, she was grateful for his strength.

He fit into her life in so many ways. He had stepped so naturally into the role of man of the house that her imagination kept plaguing her with images of him fulfilling other, more intimate, duties of a husband as well. The visions frightened her as much as they tantalized her. What was the matter with her? She didn't want that. She couldn't want that. She could barely remember being with Dan, and Clay's threats and innuendos repulsed her.

But Jared was not Clay. He showed her she could trust him time and again, day in and day out. He was uncommonly good with Andrew, and he put far more effort into the rehabilitation of the farm than she had any right to expect.

One weekday morning toward the end of April, he surprised her by asking if she wanted to bring the baby and drive to town with him. Lisa and Andrew could visit her mother while he picked up some things he'd ordered at the mercantile. She was glad to abandon the menacing pile of laundry waiting to be ironed in favor of an excursion in the bright sunshine.

When Jared returned to Ben and Martha's to collect Lisa and the baby, the back of the wagon was filled with kegs of paint. She asked what he was planning to do, but he just smiled. The next day when she went outside to call him in for lunch, Lisa almost fell over. The barn was blushing. A deep, fresh red was rising to cover the aged and fading boards, and the doors and window frames sported a crisp new white.

When Jared came around the side of the barn with a bucket in his hand, she covered her surprise by pouncing on him. "What do you think you're doing?"

He frowned. "Painting, what does it look like?"

"I can see that, but who told you to? I can't afford to pay for all that paint."

"Maybe not, but I can, and it needed it."

She couldn't deny the truth of his assertion, but she didn't like the idea of being financially beholden to him. It was just one more thread in the web he was weaving around her.

"There's no need for you to spend your money around here. Your agreement with my mother called for room and board in exchange for your presence and help with a few chores."

He studied her before answering. "Why not consider it a broader interpretation of the term?"

"You never discussed it with me," she protested.

"It's my barn. Suppose I wanted to paint it green, or blue, or even purple?"

He remained silent, but his eyes sparkled. As she watched him, the image of a purple barn made the corners of her mouth twitch. Finally, she couldn't contain her smile any longer. Her smile turned to outright laughter, and he joined her. In a few minutes, she had forgotten the cause of her earlier irritation.

****

May brought the warm days and lush greening that made it Lisa's favorite month of the year. Almost overnight, the orchard burst into a sweetly scented fairyland of pink and white blossoms. She struggled to tear herself away long enough to tend to the basic chores in the house. Every morning, as soon as she had made the beds and washed the dishes, she carried Andrew and a blanket out to the orchard. She spread the blanket on the lumpy, moist ground and allowed the baby to play while she raked and clipped and tidied after the winter.

One of her first tasks as soon as the trees were in bloom was to set out the hives. The flowering trees drew plenty of bees, and those bees made gallons of honey which she sold in town to supplement her income as well as saving some for herself. Few things tasted better than apple blossom honey drizzled over fresh, hot cornbread or biscuits.

During the winter, the hives were stored in a small shed at the edge of the orchard. Her mother had always helped her with this job, and Lisa wasn't sure she would be able to handle it alone. The tall wooden boxes were awkward and heavy when all the screens were in place.

She tried moving the hives but gave up after

dragging the first one a few feet and setting it down on her foot. Jared was around somewhere. She would have to find him and ask for help. She knew if he'd known this job needed doing, he would have done it already. He took so much upon himself, she wondered he didn't collapse face first into his dinner every night from exhaustion. But he rarely looked tired and never complained. When he set his mind to something, the man was relentless.

She walked up to the open door of the barn. "Jared!"

"Around back," came the answer.

She walked around the side of the barn and found him squatting on his heels in the mud of the pigsty, slowly running his hands over the distended belly of the huge sow. The sow was due to farrow any day, and Lisa was hoping for a large, healthy litter. She could keep a few piglets and sell the rest for some much-needed cash.

"I think she'll deliver soon." Jared rubbed his hand over the sow's belly.

"I hope so, but how can you tell?"

He glanced up. "I do have some experience with this."

She flushed furiously. "I hardly think it's the same." How dare he bring that up, and to compare her to a sow!

He lifted a brow and smiled. "I was referring to my experience with pigs. I spent a lot of time on farms when I was young."

She was only slightly mollified, but his comment made her think. Maybe that was the explanation for his desire to fix the place up. He missed the farm life he had known as a boy. "Was your father a farmer?"

"No." His answer was short and his tone clipped.

She'd hit a sore spot. She knew he didn't have any animosity toward farming, so the reaction must have been to her mention of his father. She changed the subject. "I came to see if you could help me set the hives around the edge of the orchard."

He tipped back on the heels of his boots and stood in one fluid motion, wiping his hands on his pants. "Sure."

He followed her to the edge of the orchard, where the hill began its slope down to the shallow valley. The apple trees were planted on the sides of two hills that flowed up and down, away from the higher knoll where the house sat. Lisa's father had said the valleys protected the trees from frost in the spring by permitting better air circulation and allowing the colder air to sink down and away from the trees on the rising hillsides.

When they reached the hives, Jared motioned her aside. "Just show me where these go."

"I can help, too. I've done it for years."

"Well, there's no need for you to do it now." His look and tone told her he would accept no arguments, so she pointed out the spots where the hives had always sat and went over to flop down beside Andrew on the blanket.

Jared puzzled her. Why was he so intent on proving he could do the work of at least two men? She had little experience with men, but none of the ones she'd ever known had worked as hard as he did. She barely remembered her father. Seth had been a feckless teenage boy when he'd left for war. And the hired hands had never done more than the bare minimum required to draw their pay. In comparison, Jared seemed driven.

Lisa lay back on the blanket and watched Andrew. He wasn't crawling yet, but he could roll himself over and was trying to push up on his chubby forearms. His silky dark hair had grown longer and now curled at the nape of his neck in soft swirls that tempted her fingers, and his bright, inquisitive eyes took in everything around him. Her heart contracted with love whenever she looked at him. He was such a precious treasure.

With nothing demanding her attention at the moment, she rolled onto her back and stared at the clear blue sky through the soft filter of white blossoms clustered on the gnarled black branches. The sky was still the pale, cloud-smudged blue of spring. In another month the heat of June would bring the deep, clear azure of full summer. It felt wonderful lying there, allowing her muscles to relax in the heavenly warmth that was not yet hot. She closed her eyes and drew in a deep, apple-scented breath.

Suddenly, something feather-light touched her cheek, then her nose, then her eyelids. She wrinkled her nose and swatted at the air. A deep masculine chuckle from above startled her upright. She opened one eye against the shower and saw Jared standing above her shaking a branch just enough to send a flurry of delicate petals down to cover her.

"What do you think you're doing?"

"Just trying to wake you up, sleepyhead."

"I wasn't asleep."

"Looked like it to me." His eyes seared her like live coals.

Surely she hadn't fallen asleep and let him see her with her defenses down. It had seemed like only a moment.

Without a word, but keeping his eyes on her face, he sank onto the blanket beside her. He stretched out his long legs and reached for Andrew, who chortled in delight when the big hands lifted him. Jared settled the baby low on his stomach and leaned him back against his own upraised knees, forming a seat. Like a prince on a throne Andrew sat, aided by one of Jared's hands, and surveyed the scene around him, enjoying his new perspective. Jared lay back, resting his head on his other bent arm and regarded the boy.

He cleared his throat. "I was wondering..."

"Yes?"

"It's such a nice day, how about having supper out here?"

"Here, in the orchard? On the ground?" Lisa was astonished. Was he suggesting a picnic? What had gotten into him lately? Maybe it was just a bad case of spring fever.

He glanced at her with a glimmer of challenge in his dark eyes. "Sure. Why not?"

"No reason. That would be nice."

Jared lifted Andrew, handed him to her, and rose to his feet. "Good. Call me when you're ready. I've got some more work to do." Then he turned and headed toward the barn.

She stared after him, taken aback by his sudden departure. Jared Tanner was the most confusing man she'd ever met. One minute he was gruff and guarded, the next warm and relaxed, and the next all business again. His moods were so mercurial it was impossible to figure out what he was thinking.

By suppertime her nerves were on edge. All afternoon she had tried to persuade herself this would be a meal like every other they had shared—it would just be served in a different place. But she had seen the flare of his hunger and felt a response deep within her own body that surprised and shocked her. No, this was not going to be an ordinary supper.

She wanted to keep the atmosphere as casual as possible, without any evidence of special effort on her part. However, at the last minute, she was unable to resist the urge to mix up a quick batch of apple fritters using part of a jar of the applesauce she'd put up last fall. She had always enjoyed fritters. The fact the sweet, round doughnuts were a special favorite of Jared's was inconsequential.

She needed to feed Andrew before supper or he would spoil the meal with his fussing. He was starting to experiment with table food and would probably like the fritters, but he needed his milk first or he would be a very unpleasant little fellow. When everything was ready to take outside, Lisa sat down in the kitchen, unbuttoned her dress and settled the baby in the crook of her elbow. She had been bustling around so much it took a minute or two to relax enough to let the milk flow, but when it came she took advantage of the sense of calm nursing always gave her and leaned back in her chair and closed her eyes.

Outside in the yard, Jared finished washing up and decided to check and see how Lisa was coming with supper. When he stepped into the kitchen, his breath stilled in his chest. Before him was the most compelling sight he'd ever seen. A tiny voice told him not to look, he was intruding, but he couldn't tear his eyes away from the woman and child. Gilded by a dusty sunbeam, Lisa's face was relaxed and peaceful as her son pulled steadily at her rosy nipple, his tiny fingers splayed against the creamy fullness of his mother's breast. Jared's throat went dry. He hadn't been a part of any kind of family for years. Now, beyond reason or understanding, he wanted this woman and her child more than he had ever wanted anything in his life.

Lisa's lashes drifted upward. It took long seconds for her eyes to focus on him standing in the doorway. Neither of them moved or spoke, but a tiny shiver, barely visible, passed through her. Still they stayed frozen, gazes locked.

Eventually the baby released her, and she re-tied the ribbon on her chemise and began to button her dress. Her movement broke the spell, and Jared felt the blood return to his limbs. He walked toward her and reached for Andrew. "Here, let me hold him for you."

She allowed him to take the baby. "He needs to be burped."

"What should I do?"

"Just hold him up to your shoulder and pat his back, but you'll need this towel —"

"Too late." Jared twisted his head to see the gloppy white mess Andrew had discharged across his shoulder and down the back of his shirt.

Lisa started to laugh. "Here, give him to me. And give me that shirt, too. You'd better go and change or you'll start to smell pretty sour after a while."

Jared kept his grip on the baby, turning him so he could look into the big, innocent brown eyes. "Not so fast. This is men's business." Then he glanced at Lisa. "I think I'll take this little fellow up with me to change, so he can appreciate all the trouble he's putting me to. We'll bring the shirt back when we're done. You can get everything ready, and I'll carry it outside when we get back." He headed upstairs with the baby.

Lisa shook her head with a smile. "Suit yourself," she called after him.

Andrew was so content to be held in Jared's arms, and Jared was so good with her son, she couldn't object. It amazed her how comfortable the man was with the baby. Most men, even Ben, acted like babies were marvelous alien creatures at best and terrible nuisances at worst. Not Jared. He had a natural affinity for Andrew. He would make a very good father someday.

Some day? He made an excellent father now. She rushed to banish the unwanted thought, but the image remained.

When the two returned to the kitchen, Jared handed Andrew to her and grabbed the handle of the big basket full of food. "After you." He swept his free hand toward the door.

She carried the baby with one arm and draped the blanket over the other as she led the way to the orchard. The sun was low on the horizon but had not set, so the air was still comfortable, although the cool breezes of evening were starting to stir. She spread the blanket, put Andrew down on his stomach, and sat beside him. Jared joined them with the basket, and she laid out the food. Soon they were munching away. Andrew divided his attention between a fritter in one hand and a deviled egg in the other and managed to cover his face with a remarkable combination of both, to his mother's frustration and Jared's amusement.

The earlier tension in the kitchen had dissolved into a magical domestic harmony Lisa was loath to dispel. It was so perfect and new, sitting outside under the fragrant trees and watching the sun set while

Andrew chuckled as Jared tickled his bare toes. She studied Jared, thinking she had never seen him so at ease. Gone were his usual intense expression and the habitual creases between his brows. He looked younger and less forbidding.

She was definitely seeing a new side of the man. That reminded her how little she really knew about him. Now she found she wanted, no needed, to know more.

"Jared?"

"Hmm?"

"I've been wanting to ask you something?"

He rolled over and looked at her. "What's that?"

"Why do you always work so hard around here?"

He let out a snort of laughter. "Is that a complaint?"

"No, of course not. But it isn't necessary, and I want to know why."

He rolled back and went to work stroking the sole of Andrew's foot with a blade of grass, which made the baby kick and giggle. "I like to."

Lisa knew she was taking a risk pressing him further, but she plunged on. "If you enjoy farming so much, why do you work for the stage company?"

For a long breath, he didn't answer. Finally, without diverting his attention from the baby, he said, "I've been on my own since I was twelve years old. Ben Holladay found me in California and gave me a job. Without him, I would have starved or been hanged for thieving. This is a job he needs done, and I figure I owe him."

"You've been on your own since you were twelve? What happened to your parents?"

"My father disappeared, and my mother died."

He stated it without emotion, but Lisa suspected the wound had never fully healed. How could it? All alone, and so young. Maybe that explained why he was so self-contained. At least she'd had her mother after her father died. She wanted to know more, but Jared's expression and tone told her he wouldn't welcome any further questions about his childhood. Besides, that still didn't explain his current occupation.

"Surely, after all these years, you've more than repaid any debt you owe Mr. Holladay. You could choose a life that suits you better."

He sat up and faced her. "It's a matter of loyalty, and up to now the life has suited me fine."

She didn't want to think about the possible implications of that statement. "I think it's time to go in now. It's getting cooler, and I don't want Andrew to catch a chill." As if on cue, the baby sneezed.

"Take him inside, and I'll clean up."

Lisa picked Andrew up and hurried into the house.

The rest of the evening, she remained upstairs with Andrew. She didn't even come back down to wash the dishes. That could wait until morning. She needed time away from Jared, time to think. She couldn't imagine him leaving now, but she didn't know how much longer she could bear to have him stay. They were like a pair of horseshoe magnets—if you turned them just right the attraction was mutual and overwhelming, but twist things a little and they shoved each other away like opposing poles.

Besides, Andrew's condition seemed to be worsening. What had started as an innocent sneeze had progressed to more sneezes, then a runny nose, and finally a fever. Throughout the night, she got up with him repeatedly as he fretted and fussed and struggled to breathe through his tiny, stuffed-up nose.

By two o'clock, the baby was listless and weak and could barely manage a pitiful cry. His hair was damp, and his cheeks were flushed. Lisa laid her hand across his brow.

Oh Lord, he was burning up! What should she do? Andrew couldn't die. She wouldn't let him. Her mother might know what to do, but Martha was fast asleep in her own bed a couple of miles away. Dr. Hutchins—that's who she needed. Jared could ride to town and get him.

Holding the limp baby in one arm, she banged on the wall connecting her room to Jared's with her fist. "Jared! Jared!"

Moments later, he burst through her door. His black hair was tousled and a thick growth of whiskers coated his square jaw. He had pulled on a pair of pants, but the top two buttons were still undone and his feet were bare. His pistol glittered wickedly in his right hand, and he looked ready to battle the devil himself. It was a sight that would have terrified her under normal circumstances, but relief and gratitude overwhelmed her fear.

He scanned the room for the cause of her distress, and seeing no one, lowered his gun. "What is it? What's the matter?" His voice was rough with sleep.

Lisa held up her cherished bundle. "It's Andrew."

Jared was next to her in a second, taking the baby from her arms. "What's the matter with him?"

"A fever. Feel him."

Jared carried the baby closer to the lamp. Lisa winced at the reddened and crusted nostrils and shallow breathing that raised and lowered the tiny chest in rapid pants.

"He might just have a cold, but I can't be sure," Jared said. "Do you want me to fetch the doctor?"

She huddled next to him in her long white nightdress, peering anxiously at the baby, her arms wrapped around her sides. She tried to think, but she had been awake all night, and fatigue and worry clouded her mind. "Yes...I don't know. No, don't leave me here by myself. Oh, Jared, what if he dies?" Her voice broke on the last word.

He reached around her with his free arm and drew her against his side. "Shh. He isn't going to die. I promise you. Everything will be all right."

She buried her face against the warm skin of his chest. The smell of him was intoxicating, like an elixir of strength. Surely no harm could befall her or her son as long as they remained in the safety of this man's arms. She shuddered and drew a ragged breath.

Jared eased his arm from around her and began to glide his hand up and down her back. She was naked beneath her gown, so there was nothing to impede the smooth passage of his hand across the soft fabric from the nape of her neck to the top of her hips. His long fingers stretched across her upper back and tightened when they reached her waist. He stroked with a gentle, but steady, pressure—sensual but not sexual, soothing but not arousing. His fingers drained the tension from her mind and muscles. Finally, she dragged herself away from the solace of his strength and stood upright. He made no effort to continue to hold her.

"What do you think we should do?" she asked in a steadier voice.

Jared studied the baby in his arms. "I think we can make him more comfortable if we bring his fever down and open up his nose a little. Then, if you want me to, I'll ride to town for the doctor in the morning."

She nodded.

He handed Andrew back to her, picked up a lamp and led the way to the kitchen. He suggested she bathe the baby in cool water until his temperature came down and his color returned to normal, being careful not to let him get too cold. While she did that, Jared built a fire, filled a large kettle with water, and hung it on one of the swinging iron hooks to boil.

After about twenty anxious minutes, she called to him. "I think his fever is down. Could you come and look at him?"

He held the lamp closer to Andrew's face to look at his eyes, and then plunged his hands into the water to feel the little body. The water had perked Andrew up. He was thrashing around and complaining vigorously.

"He feels cooler, and he's much livelier. I think you can take him out now. Be sure to wrap him up good after he's dry so he doesn't get chilled. Then we can take turns holding him under this cloth near the kettle. The steam should help his breathing."

Lisa sat down with Andrew on her lap in front of the brick hearth while Jared swung the kettle off the fire and held one of her mother's old tablecloths over their heads, creating a steam-filled tent. After a few minutes, she felt like a boiled crawdad, but Andrew did seem to be breathing easier. By the time she and Jared had traded places twice, returning the kettle to the flame each time to bring the water back to a boil, the loud snorts and snuffles had all but disappeared, and the baby's eyelids were beginning to droop.

"We may have to do it again tomorrow, but I think

he'll be able to sleep better now," Jared said.

She raised grateful eyes to his and smiled wearily. "I don't know how to thank you enough."

He didn't return her smile. "Let's just get him upstairs and see if he'll settle down for the night."

Andrew was still awake and stirring restlessly when they reached Lisa's room. "I think he may be hungry," she said. "He didn't eat much earlier because he was having so much trouble breathing."

"Then feed him."

She sat down in the rocker next to the baby's cradle and began to unfasten the row of buttons on her nightdress with wavering fingers. Jared made no move to leave. He sat down on the bed opposite her and regarded her intently. She said nothing but kept her eyes on Andrew as she bared her breast and guided the swollen nipple to his greedy mouth. She was self-conscious, but not really embarrassed. Jared was no longer a stranger or an outsider. Tonight, he had earned the right to be there with them at that moment.

Andrew fell asleep before he finished completely at the second breast, and Lisa laid him gently in his cradle, afraid the least movement would wake him again. But as she stood looking down at him, he never stirred. He slumbered peacefully, his slow even breathing broken only by an occasional soft snuffle.

She heard the bed ropes creak and sensed Jared's presence behind her, but she didn't turn. His arms came around her from behind and crossed loosely against her ribs, cradling her in an undemanding embrace. She went still for a moment, then relaxed against him, and his arms tightened to hold her there.

"He's better," he said in a low voice over the top of her head.

"Yes." She turned in his arms and leaned back to look up into his face. "He's better, because of you. Thank you."

"You don't have to thank me." He stroked her cheek with rough fingers, continuing to hold her close with the other hand. "I care about him, too."

"I know."

For a long moment, they gazed into each other's eyes. "Lisa." The word was so low and deep it sounded more like a rumble in his chest than her name. "There's something I want, badly."

Her eyes asked the question, but she already sensed the answer.

"I want to kiss you. I've wanted to all day...for weeks really. Please don't pull away."

The plea in his voice tore at her. That a man like Jared, who could take whatever he wanted, was asking permission touched her. He was giving her the power to grant or refuse. He would never force her. But she couldn't deny his need. It mirrored her own. She couldn't help herself—she nodded without looking away.

Fierce satisfaction swept across his face before he lowered his mouth to hers. His lips were firm and deliberate as he worked to coax a response from her. She moved her mouth, but she wasn't sure exactly what she was supposed to do. Before he'd left for war, Dan's kisses had been the tentative caresses of a teenage boy. This was completely different. Jared was a man, and beyond her experience.

"Open for me. Please." He nudged at her lips to show her what he wanted.

She was dizzy with the new sensations and did what he asked without hesitation. Immediately, his grip tightened and one hand slid up her back and buried itself in her unbound hair. He used that hand to hold her head steady as he slid his tongue into her mouth.

The action shocked her, and she started to draw back, but his hand tightened.

"No," he murmured raggedly.

She was overcome by a longing to give this man what he needed. She stopped struggling and forced herself to relax in his embrace. Soon the novelty of the kiss wore off, and a fire began to burn deep inside her. She discovered her arms had wound themselves around his broad, bare back and her hands were every bit as busy as his. Her tongue refused to remain passive and wove itself around his in an ancient mating dance.

He made a low noise deep in his throat and slid his right hand slowly down her back until it cupped the fullness of her buttocks. Then, as if he could stand it no longer, he pulled her hard against him and let her feel the force of his desire.

She knew immediately what she was pressing against, but instead of feeling frightened or disgusted, a breathless excitement gripped her. She rubbed against him. The sensations were so thrilling and so new she lost herself in the pleasure of it.

Finally, he dragged his mouth away and released the pressure on her hips. She collapsed against his chest, and they stood, holding each other until their heartbeats slowed and their breathing returned to normal.

Jared was the first to speak. "I'm not sorry."

She remained silent.

"This doesn't change anything," he said.

She pulled back and looked up, shaking her head. "It changes everything."

"No, it doesn't. The feelings were there before, and they'll still be there whether we act on them or not."

She didn't try to deny it. "But we can't, and it will be so much harder now."

"That's true. Now you know how much I want you, and I know you want me, too. I don't know where this is going, but we have to find out."

"I don't want to find out." But a small voice inside denied the words. Part of her had to know.

"I think you do, and I know I do. I'm not going to offer to leave, even though it might make some things easier, not unless you can convince me you really want me to go." He cupped her face in both hands and searched her eyes. "Do you?"

Lisa knew she should say yes and remove the unbearable temptation of his presence, but she couldn't bring herself to speak the lie. She shook her head. "No."

His lips moved in a tiny smile, then his serious expression returned. "I can't tell you I'll never kiss you again, or touch you, or that I won't want to get even closer to you, but I promise I won't press you for anything you don't want to give. I'd never do anything to hurt you. You know that, don't you?"

She nodded.

"Good. Now it's time for you to get some sleep." He led her to the bed and tucked her in, his hands lingering as he smoothed the quilt across her. Then he leaned over her, his expression rigid and deadly serious. "I want you to know leaving you tonight is the hardest thing I've ever had to do. But I want more from you than one night in your bed."

He closed the remaining gap between them and captured her lips in a kiss filled with frustrated desire and a promise of things to come.

Then he was gone.

Chapter Eight

The next morning, Andrew's nose was stuffed up again and he was still cranky, but his eyes were clearer, and his fever was gone, easing Lisa's fears. She had been awake most of the night listening to his every breath to reassure herself he was still alive and felt as wrung out as an old dishrag by the time she got up to start breakfast.

She had also spent those dark, lonely hours replaying the scene with Jared over and over in her mind. How could she have lost control of herself that way? She was shocked at her own abandon. But not too shocked to recall every detail. The kiss had opened her eyes to a whole new range of sensations and possibilities. Every tiny hair on her body stood at attention at the memory of his hands on her body and his tongue in her mouth.

She had to shake those thoughts right out of her mind. They could only lead to heartbreak. As it was, she didn't know how she could face him again. He was sure to feel she'd given him license to take even bolder liberties. He'd said as much last night, hadn't he? She couldn't be sure, because her passion-stirred senses had registered the effect of his words more than the words themselves.

When she reached the kitchen, there he was, sitting at the table, waiting for his breakfast as if nothing unusual had happened. As soon as she stepped into the room, he glanced up.

"How's he doing this morning?" He nodded at Andrew.

"Better, I think. But I'll need to steam him again. He's still pretty congested." On cue, Andrew snuffled loudly.

Lisa was relieved that so far Jared was only interested in the baby. She wasn't ready to discuss the other events of the previous evening.

"Do you want me to ride to town to get Dr. Hutchins?"

"I don't think that will be necessary."

"Well, think about it, because I won't be here to help you with Andrew if he gets worse."

An invisible hand gripped her chest and squeezed. Was he leaving? It hadn't occurred to her Jared might feel guilty about last night, too. For weeks she had wanted him to leave, but now her whole being rebelled against the thought, even if her mind told her it would be best if he just got it over with and left now, before she lost more than she already had.

"Why not?" She was half afraid to hear the answer.

"I should have told you—I have to go on a run to Denver today. I'll be gone for several days."

"Oh." Her breath flowed again, and the constriction eased. He wasn't leaving permanently, only for a few days. Maybe the separation would give her time to sort out her feelings and get a firmer grip on her emotions.

His eyes told her he had followed her thoughts as clearly as if she had spoken them aloud. She flushed and looked away.

"And when I get back, you and I are going to talk," he said. "Last night some very important things changed."

"I'm not sure I understand what you mean." She refused to meet his gaze. She was afraid her idea and his idea of the progression of their relationship were as different as a mule-drawn cart and a steam locomotive.

The legs of his chair grated against the floor as he pushed himself back from the table. "Lisa." He reached for her hand and drew her toward him between his legs until she perched on his knee holding Andrew in her arms.

"Look at me," he ordered in a husky voice. She complied. "We can't pretend it never happened, and we can't go back."

The heated emotions in his gaze seared her flesh, and she recoiled slightly. "Yes, we can."

His jaw squared, and his arm tightened around her waist. "No. We both want the same thing." He pulled her closer and pressed nibbling kisses down her tender neck.

Ignoring the seductive shivers racing through her, she shoved against his shoulders. "Are you sure? And what is that?"

"To be together."

Together. A word that meant everything, and nothing. She had to determine his true intentions before she could sort out her own response. "We live in the same house now. In what way exactly do you mean for us to be *together*?"

His brow furrowed. "You know what I mean, together."

"I'm not sure I do. Are you suggesting I live in sin with you? What about my mother? She'd never be able to hold her head up in town again."

"Why do you make it sound that way? It wouldn't be like that. We could go on the way we are, only closer. No one would be the wiser."

"People would soon figure it out. I might have another baby. Besides, that's not the most important thing. You would know. I would know. That's enough."

She waited, but he had no quick answer.

She continued to press him. "I've been married, and I have no desire to do it again. Do you?"

"What?" His brows rose.

"I didn't think so. Nothing can come of this...attraction, or whatever it is. You must see that."

"What I see is I want you and you want me."

She had to make him understand and accept their situation. So much was at stake. "Last night you said you wanted more from me than one night in my bed. What do you want? Several nights? How many? Five? Ten? Twenty?"

"Damn it, I don't know, but there's more to it than that and you know it."

"How much more can there be if neither of us wants to get married?"

"Lisa, we need each other. Can you say you don't want me?"

She was ready to scream in frustration. "Need. Want. That's all you talk about. But it's not what I need. It's not what I want."

"That's not true. I've felt it in you. Come here and I'll remind you." He tugged her toward him.

"No. That's enough." She jumped up from his lap. "You can take your needs and wants to Liberty. I understand they have a first-class bawdy house. I need a safe, stable life for my son. I want to be left in peace. That's what I need and want."

Jared stood, too, and ran a hand through his hair. "I don't have time for this now. I have to go."

"It might be better for both of us if you never came back." She hated the sound of the words but couldn't deny their truth.

"Maybe, but I will, so accept it. And think about what I've said while I'm gone. We'll sort this out when I get back." Then he turned and stalked out the door.

Lisa stood shaking in the kitchen as his heavy boot steps climbed the outside stairs then thundered around overhead as he gathered the things he would take on the trip. A few minutes later, he descended the stairs, clomped across the porch and into the yard without a word. She watched from the window as he led his horse out of the barn, mounted, and rode off without a single backward glance.

For the next three days, she threw herself into her spring chores and time flew by. She really needed to get her garden planted. She was a little late this year, but she tried to placate her conscience with the excuse that she had been more distracted than usual during the past few weeks. Between her worries about her mother, Andrew, Clay, and Jared, it was a wonder she had accomplished anything at all.

Andrew's cold improved, and long days outside in the sun speeded his recovery. With a bonnet shielding his delicate skin, he sat and pulled at the stubby grass while Lisa toiled and sweated, hoed and planted, poking the seeds for beans, onions, carrots, squash, and pumpkins into the dark, fertile soil. Jared had planted the potatoes, turnips, and spinach when he'd first moved in, and, although she'd resented it at the time, now she was grateful. She stood with her hands splayed against her lower back, trying to ease the deep ache seated there from hours of bending, and realized that running the farm single-handed was more of a job than she had anticipated. Not that she wasn't fully capable. It was just more work, that was all.

She finished her planting after lunch on the fourth day of Jared's absence. Settling Andrew for his afternoon nap, she congratulated herself on how much she had accomplished. And she had hardly missed Jared at all, at least not during the day. She ignored the fact she'd kept herself busy every single second to ensure that result.

It was the hours from suppertime to bedtime that dragged. She had never cooked for just one person before, and after two days of preparing the usual amounts, she had enough food to feed herself for the next three days. And the nights were so quiet. After Andrew had fallen asleep, only the loud, rhythmic ticking of the old mantel clock and the soft chirps of the crickets and hoots of the barn owls broke the silence as they went about their nocturnal business.

Jared had been gone before, but never for more than a couple of days at a time. Until this trip, she hadn't realized how he filled the house with little sounds just by walking into the kitchen in search of a late snack or rustling a newspaper in the parlor before going to bed. And most of all, she missed the reassuring sounds of his boots hitting the floor, one at a time, on the other side of the wall as he undressed, and the creaking complaints from the bed ropes as he climbed into bed.

Seeking to banish such unsettling thoughts, she took one last look at Andrew, and satisfied that he was sleeping peacefully, decided to walk back to the barn to check on the progress of her sow. That morning the sow had made herself a nest in the straw and, if possible, looked more lethargic than ever. Perhaps the birth was finally imminent.

She stopped at the back porch and exchanged her shoes for the pair of Seth's old riding boots she wore whenever she had any muddy work to do. Shoes were far too precious to ruin in the mud, but she had never been able to bring herself to work barefoot as so many farm women did.

Before she rounded the corner of the barn, she heard the grunts of the sow. They had a different intonation than usual, so Lisa pulled her skirt up between her legs, tucked the hem into the waistband to keep it out of the mud as much as possible, and rushed to the pen. There, four tiny pink piglets lay curled in the straw as the mother labored to push forth another. Lisa opened the gate and crouched near the sow. There wasn't much she could, or should, do as long as there were no problems with the birth, so she just watched.

The huge sow labored long and hard to bring forth her tiny babies, and in the end, eight had appeared. The last one was stillborn, and that saddened Lisa, but she was thrilled to have seven healthy piglets. She buried the dead piglet and waited until the other seven newborns were nursing successfully before returning to the house.

Upstairs, Andrew was awake from his nap and

hollering angrily. Lisa glanced at her hands and realized she was covered with mud, blood, and manure from her work in the pigsty. She called up the stairs, hoping the sound of her voice would reassure him, and rushed back out to the pump to wash with the bar of strong yellow lye soap she kept there. Then she hurried inside and up the stairs, talking loudly to Andrew all the way. "Mama's coming, sweetheart. Hush now. Don't fret."

Her skirt and blouse were still filthy, so she'd left them in the washtub downstairs. Wearing only her chemise and petticoat, she picked up her irate son. "There now, Mama's here. Everything's all right," she crooned.

Andrew looked skeptical through his tears but quieted down when she settled him on her lap in the rocking chair and offered him her breast. While he nursed, she talked to him companionably, something she found herself doing more and more often since Jared left.

"That's my good boy. Are you hungry? When you're finished, you can come downstairs and help with some chores. Then we'll see what we can find for supper. I think there are some biscuits left. Would you like one?"

As much as she enjoyed her one-sided conversations with her son, Lisa listened to herself and shook her head. She hated to admit it, but she missed Jared. She missed having someone to talk to who could talk back, even if he said things she didn't want to hear. What were they going to do when he returned? In spite of his departing orders, she had avoided thinking about their situation for the past four days.

There was no solution, at least none she could see.

She no longer truly wanted him to leave, and she doubted he could be persuaded to go now under any circumstances. But how could they maintain a decent, platonic relationship if he stayed? He had left no doubt as to his ultimate desire, and she questioned her own ability to hold out against the seductive force of his passion. The blood surged through her, heating her cheeks and causing strange throbbings in other parts of her body, when she remembered the way she'd felt in his arms, pressed up against his hard body, with his mouth hungering on hers.

Try as she might, she could think of no acceptable resolution to her problem. Her head told her to insist he leave, and right away, before they got any more deeply involved and risked heartbreak and scandal. But her heart cried out to keep him near, at least a while longer. Eventually, she gave up and took Andrew downstairs to find more mundane tasks to occupy her hands and mind.

That night, she was so exhausted after her long day in the garden and the pigsty she collapsed into bed at eight o'clock, right after Andrew had fallen asleep. Around midnight, she was jolted from a sound slumber by a loud banging on the back door and the sounds of men's voices on the back veranda. Terrified, her first thought was whether she had followed Jared's instructions and locked the door. Certain she had, she waited, huddled under her covers, for the men to give up and go away. After several minutes, during which the banging and shouting grew louder and more insistent, it became obvious that whoever they were, they weren't going to leave on their own.

She slid out of bed, shakily pulled on her wrapper, and fumbled in the dark with clumsy fingers trying to light the lamp beside her bed. Who could be out there at this time of night? Jared and her mother both had keys. But what if something had happened to Martha, and Ben needed her? He might not have the presence of mind to bring the key with him. With that possibility in mind, Lisa hurried down the dark stairs and through the back hallway to the kitchen.

A bright half-moon lit the porch so she could see the forms of at least two men who appeared to be supporting something bulky between them. Her first thought was that it might be Jared.

But what if it wasn't?

"Who's there?" she called, uneasy that they could see her through the window, lit by the lamp she held, but she couldn't identify them at all.

"Mrs. McAllister, it's Morgan Bingham. Let us in. We've got Clay, and he's hurt bad."

Morgan Bingham. That was the name of one of the men who had been with Clay the last time he'd come to the house.

She went to the window and held the lamp as close as she could, hoping to shed some light on the figures outside. She was able to make out two men, and one was indeed the man who had been identified as Morgan Bingham. She couldn't see the other clearly. They each had an arm around the slumped body of a man. His head hung forward, but Lisa knew by the sandy hair and shirt he was wearing that it was Clay.

She hurried to unlock the door, and the men pushed in, dragging Clay with them.

"Where can we put him, ma'am?"

"What happened to him?" The body of Clay's blue shirt was purple and black with blood, and his face was ashen and dotted with droplets of sweat. He appeared to be unconscious, and she wondered if he were still alive.

"He's been shot in the leg and through the shoulder."

Lisa glanced down and saw the fabric of Clay's pants had a gaping hole across the thigh. Darkened, oozing flesh swelled up through the hole. Her hand flew to her mouth, and she tried to force back the bile in her throat. It was a hideous sight, ravaged and inhuman. And it brought back memories she couldn't bear to face. The bloody face from her recurring nightmare rose unbidden before her.

"I can't help you," she whispered through her fingers. "He needs a doctor."

"No, ma'am. He can't have a doctor."

Her puzzled eyes asked the question, and she read the answer in Morgan Bingham's. Of course, these bullets were received during some illegal activity. The doctor would ask questions and expect answers. Then he would get word to the sheriff.

"We got the bullets out ourselves. Clay's strong. He just needs a safe place to heal and someone to watch over him."

"Why did you bring him here?"

"He kept calling your name before he passed out. We didn't know any place else to take him. Please, ma'am, you've got to help him. He's hurt bad."

As much as she wanted to, Lisa couldn't deny him. Clay had no family left. This probably was the only place he could find sanctuary. She couldn't send him away to die, no matter what he'd done.

"Do you think you can get him upstairs?" she asked.

"We'll try. Good thing he's out cold."

Lisa had to agree. She winced as the men lifted and dragged Clay's inert body up the curved staircase and into the bedroom across the hall from hers. The pain would have been excruciating if he were conscious.

She also noticed Morgan Bingham was favoring his left leg. Was she going to have two wounded men to tend? "Mr. Bingham, were you shot also?"

"No, ma'am, not this time." He grunted, shifting his hold under Clay's arms. "Took a ball above the knee during the war. Sometimes it reminds me, is all."

Clay and his companions might as well be Chinese, for all Lisa understood their way of life. The war was over, yet these men still chose to risk their lives every day, and for what? Could any amount of gold be worth the running, the fear, and the pain? She shook her head and tried to keep out of their way as they laid Clay on the bed and stepped back.

"We need to be going, ma'am. It wouldn't do you any good for us to be caught here."

She swung her gaze sharply from Clay to Morgan Bingham. "Are you saying someone is chasing you?"

"Likely so, ma'am."

"Aren't you worried they'll find Clay here?"

"I know you'll do your best for him, ma'am. We can't take him with us. He'd die for sure. We've got to go now."

She followed the men into the hall. "Will you come back for him when he's healed?"

Morgan Bingham turned. "If we can." Then they were gone.

She walked back into the room that had been her parents' and surveyed Clay's limp form in the middle of the bed. The most generous emotion she could muster for him now was pity. If he recovered, perhaps this brush with death would be enough to make him give up the excitement and easy money of his current way of life. She watched the rise and fall of his chest and decided that, although his color was bad and his breathing labored, he would probably live until she could get his clothes off and investigate the full extent of his injuries. If she could bring herself to look at them.

First, she worked on the boots, jerking and tugging. It was no easy task to remove a pair of tight, custom-made boots from an unconscious man. When she finally succeeded, she was damp beneath her cotton nightdress and her hair had formed vigorous curls around her face.

Next came the pants. The thought of pulling them down over the monstrous hole in his thigh was too much to contemplate, so she retrieved her sewing shears from the basket in her room and cut the pants off, taking the long underwear beneath, too. Clay's nakedness neither excited nor frightened her. Instead, she felt only disinterest mingled with mild disgust. However, it seemed indecent to leave him lying there exposed, so she draped a corner of the sheet over his midsection. Then she took a deep breath, swallowed twice, and forced herself to look at the actual wound.

At the first sight of it, she gagged and closed her eyes. Even with her eyes closed, she could still see it, red and pulpy and deformed. But it was no longer Clay's leg. The wound was in her father's head, and she was five years old, hiding in the play fort she and Seth had made in the woods from fallen branches. Her mother had given her strict orders not to leave the farmyard that day, but she'd been annoyed at being left alone when the men went hunting, so she'd sneaked off to play in the fort. She'd heard the shot, then her father's startled cry, and looked up in time to see him stumble to his knees. He'd been close enough for her to see the frozen look in his eyes and the gaping hole in his skull before he hit the ground.

She'd raced back to the barn to hide, sick with fear, until Seth found her hours later, and never told her mother what she'd seen. In all these years, she'd never told anyone. Eventually, her adult brain had come to accept what had happened, but her child's heart had never healed from the shock and pain of seeing the most important man in her life taken so suddenly and brutally.

And now another man lay bleeding, and possibly dying, before her eyes. Fear, vicious and snarling, rose inside and threatened to overcome her.

But she was no longer five years old. She might not have been able to help her father, but perhaps she could do something for Clay. She had to at least try.

Peering at the wound, she held the lamp as close as she dared without burning him with the hot globe. The bullet had penetrated the large, thick muscle of the thigh but had apparently not passed all the way through. Perhaps the bone had stopped it; there was no way to tell now. If Clay's companions were right, and they had indeed removed the bullet, they had made an incredible mess doing so. The mutilated flesh gave raw testimony to energetic gouging with a wide-bladed knife. He would be lucky to walk again, if the wound healed at all.

Next Lisa removed his shirt. The second bullet had passed clean through his shoulder, leaving a much smaller, neater hole that had bled profusely and still oozed. She was fairly certain the shoulder wound would heal once it was cleaned and bandaged, but she couldn't say the same for his leg. He needed a doctor, and right away. The men had been right, though—bringing in the doctor would be like giving Clay a ticket to his own hanging. And no matter how she might feel about him, she couldn't bring herself to do that. He would have to take his chances with her simple nursing.

After heating water in the kettle downstairs, she proceeded to wash off as much of the blood as she could. Some of it was dried and crusted and hard to remove, and she was grateful he never roused. When his shoulder was clean and bandaged with strips torn from an old muslin sheet, she began to work on his leg. The bullet must have nicked some major vessel, because when she gently wiped the area with the wet cloth to dissolve the dried blood and began to try to clean the actual entry wound, bright red blood gushed out like a fountain.

She froze for an instant in horror, certain he was about to die. Then a more practical instinct took over and drove her to grab a towel and press it down hard over the streaming cavity. For endless minutes, or hours, she pressed the steadily reddening cloth against Clay's leg. Finally, when her arms shook from the effort, she eased off. She was almost afraid to lift the towel, but when she did, she saw with great relief the flow had ebbed to a trickle. She threw the bloody towel into the basin, washed his leg again, and bound it with more muslin strips.

Her most pressing tasks complete, Lisa eased herself off the bed and gazed at the pale, still form beneath the sheet. He hadn't regained consciousness, but his occasional jerks and moans told her his body had suffered terribly from its ordeal, even if he wasn't aware of it. Since there was nothing more she could do for him at the moment, she gathered the basin and blood-soaked cloths and made her way back to the kitchen.

She had never been so tired in all her life, even after Andrew was born. Then, she had been on a plane above exhaustion, but now she felt as drained of her energy and lifeblood as the man in the bed upstairs. And she was filthy—sweaty and as covered with blood as a butcher. Even her fingernails were rimmed with scarlet.

When she reached the kitchen, she glanced out the window in surprise. The early summer dawn was beginning to lighten the eastern sky behind the black-peaked silhouette of the barn. She must have been working for hours. The prospect of the imminent arrival of a new day with all the troubles it would surely bring deflated her even further. She needed to sit down. She needed to sleep.

As she piled the soiled cloths into a basket to take outside to soak in the big laundry tub, she heard a noise on the veranda. Her heart froze, and her breath stilled in her lungs. Was it the posse Morgan had warned her about? She couldn't move Clay by herself, so there was nothing she could do to hide him if they insisted on searching the house. And how could she explain the grisly bloodstains down the front of her nightdress? While she stood frantically trying to decide what to do, the door opened.

****

Jared had been traveling all night, and he was exhausted to the marrow of his bones. The stage had been delayed and hadn't arrived in Atchison until three o'clock in the morning. If he'd had any sense, he would have staggered into the nearest hotel and collapsed for the remainder of the night. But a hotel held no appeal when home was just a couple of hours away down the pitch-black country road.

Home. That was how he thought of the place now, and it stirred his tired blood to see the familiar lines of the house appear on the rise past the distillery. Lisa would be there, still asleep in her big, soft bed. It would be heaven to drag his worn-out body up the stairs, shuck his clothes, and climb in beside her. He was too tired to do anything more than pull her into his arms and go to sleep, but he knew he'd sleep better in her bed than anywhere else. And a few hours later, nothing in the world would feel better than waking up with Lisa in his arms, warm and inviting, and making slow, delicious love to her. He'd dreamed of such a homecoming every night since he'd left, and the resulting lack of sleep was part of the reason for his current exhaustion.

He shifted in his saddle as he felt himself hardening again, just thinking about her. Damn, it was going to be difficult to be near her every day without giving in to his growing urges until he could come up with an acceptable solution to their dilemma. She'd mentioned marriage, but the idea was so foreign he couldn't even contemplate it. She'd said she didn't want it either, so there must be another answer. Whatever the answer was, it sure as hell didn't involve him leaving.

He settled his horse in the barn, walked across the lightening yard toward the back porch, and thought about Lisa again. Had she spent any time during the past five days thinking about him, and if she had, what conclusions had she reached? He knew she was attracted to him, but that could work against him as much as for him. She was a woman of strong principles, just the type to consider overcoming temptation a challenge and moral imperative. He had to find a way to make her see it was right for them to be together, not wrong.

With his mind on that problem, he was not prepared for the sight that met his eyes when he stepped through the kitchen door. "My God, Lisa! What happened to you?"

She stood in front of him with a heavy cast iron skillet in both hands, preparing to bring it down on his head. But he hardly noticed the pan. He stared in growing horror at her chalky face, huge, frightened eyes, and gory nightdress. A dozen gruesome possibilities flashed through his mind, each worse than the one before.

"Jared?" She blinked and lowered the skillet. Her eyes fluttered closed. The pan slipped out of her fingers and clattered to the floor with Lisa following behind.

When she began to sway, he rushed forward and caught her before she hit the floor. His heart raced. Had someone broken in and attacked her? And what about Andrew? Before he could decide what to do with her, she stirred in his arms.

"Jared? It is you, isn't it?" she asked, without opening her eyes.

She sounded frightened, yet hopeful, and he tried to reassure her. "Yes, sweetheart, it's me. I'm here now. You're going to be all right."

"Yes." Her eyes remained closed, but her face

relaxed.

He shook her. "Don't you dare fall asleep now. Lisa, you've got to tell me what's going on around here."

This time, she opened her eyes slowly. "It's Clay."

"Clay? Did he do this to you?" Jared swore he would kill the man. He cursed himself for leaving her alone.

She glanced down at her gown. "No...yes, well sort of."

"You're not making any sense." He scowled. "What the hell happened here?"

She struggled to sit up. "Last night, some friends of Clay's brought him here. He'd been shot."

"Was he dead?"

"No."

"And they expected you to take care of him?"

"There was no one else."

"Maybe, maybe not. But he's not your problem or your responsibility."

"No, but I couldn't just let him die, could I?"

Jared sighed and rubbed his aching eyes with one hand. "I suppose not. So, where is he? I hope you patched him up and sent him on his way."

"He was too badly injured for that. I'm not even sure he'll live."

Jared had a sudden suspicion. "Where is he?"

"Upstairs in bed in Mama's room."

He stood abruptly, dropping her to her feet. "Damn it, Lisa. You don't have the sense God gave a turnip. You can't keep him in the house. Don't you know a posse could come looking for him?"

She bristled and straightened her spine. "Of course. In fact, it's very likely, but there was nothing else I could do."

"You could have told those friends of his to take care of him themselves."

"He certainly would have died then."

"Probably." He was bone-tired and sick to death of Clay Ferguson. "And would that have been so awful?"

Lisa glared. "That's a terrible thing to say. You want Clay to die. You'd like that wouldn't you?"

"I promised you I wouldn't shoot him myself if I could avoid it, and I won't, but that doesn't mean I'm going to be sorry if somebody else does the job for me."

"What kind of man are you?"

Just then, Jared turned his head toward the front of the house and held up his hand. "Be quiet. I think I hear something." His voice was low and tense.

He listened intently. The sound was unmistakable — horses, several of them, coming toward the house.

Lisa glanced at him. "Maybe it's Clay's friends coming back to get him."

"Yes, and maybe it's not."

Chapter Nine

"Is there any place in the house we can hide him?" Jared asked.

Lisa thought for a moment. Then she noticed the trap door in the kitchen floor on the other side of the table. "The root cellar. I could pull the rug over it and no one would ever know."

"All right. I'll go up and bring him down. You keep them outside as long as you can." He sprinted off down the hall, and she heard him bounding up the stairs before she reached the front door.

She tiptoed into the parlor, pressed her body flat against the wall, and pushed the drapery aside just enough to peek out. Six heavily armed men were dismounting in front of the house and talking among themselves. One short gray-haired man seemed to be in charge, giving orders to the others, and shortly thereafter, two of the men slipped away around opposite sides of the house. Lisa prayed Jared could get Clay down the stairs before she was forced to open the door.

Behind her a board creaked, and she turned to see

Jared coming down the stairs in his stockinged feet carrying Clay's limp body wrapped in a blanket. He must have taken his boots off upstairs to avoid making any more noise than necessary. She marveled at the effortless way he cradled the unconscious man in his arms and carried him down the hall toward the kitchen.

A loud banging on the front door startled her, and she sucked in her breath to keep from crying out. How long would the men assume it would take her to wake up and come downstairs? She stood quietly in the front hall, counting to herself and listening for the sound of the root cellar door in the kitchen.

"Lisa."

She jumped when he whispered her name behind her back then turned, eyes wide.

"Get upstairs," he ordered in a low voice.

She frowned in confusion. The men were knocking harder. Shouldn't she open the door?

"You can't let them see you like that. Go get your wrapper."

She followed his gaze. She had forgotten her bloodstained nightdress. He was right—that would be difficult to explain.

With his hands cupping her shoulders, Jared turned her toward the stairs. "Hurry. I'll answer the door."

The banging continued while she raced up the stairs to her room. She snatched her wrapper out of the wardrobe and slipped out onto the landing clutching the soft red velvet around her. She peered down to the front hall. Jared nodded to her before opening the door to the insistent pounding.

"What is it?" he demanded of the group's leader.

The man stared for a moment. He seemed startled to be confronted by a disheveled giant in his socks.

"I said, what do you want?" Jared repeated.

The man cleared his throat. "I'm Sheriff Raymond Buford from Leavenworth County, across the river, and I'm here to see Mrs. McAllister. Who are you?"

"The name's Tanner. I rent a room from Mrs. McAllister."

"So, you're the boarder. I see."

Did he? His voice sounded suspicious. Was he suspicious about Clay or Jared's presence in the house?

"Where is Mrs. McAllister?"

"She'll be down in a minute."

Tension simmered in the front hall as the two men sized each up. Lisa hurried down the stairs to prevent a confrontation.

"Good morning, sir. I'm Lisa McAllister. What can I do for you?" Her insides quaked, but she was determined not to show it.

The sheriff doffed his battered brown hat. "Mornin', ma'am. I'm Sheriff Raymond Buford from Leavenworth County. I'm looking for Clay Ferguson."

"I'm sorry, I can't help you." She struggled to keep her voice steady.

"Ma'am, we think he was part of a group that robbed the bank in Oskaloosa yesterday. Two people were shot, and we believe one of them was Ferguson."

"I'm sorry to hear that, Sheriff. But what makes you think he would be here?"

"We have reports the men were seen riding this way, and we hear Ferguson's a special friend of yours."

Heat rose to Lisa's cheeks. Could Eliza's gossip have made its way as far as Leavenworth? "Well, you heard wrong. Clay and I were childhood acquaintances, nothing more."

"We have to search the house, ma'am."

She knew it would cause more suspicion if she tried to prevent them, so she acquiesced. "Go ahead, but tell your men to be quiet. My infant son is asleep upstairs, and I don't want him to be awakened."

"Yes, ma'am."

The sheriff turned and motioned the three men remaining on the front porch to come inside. They began to search the house, room by room, starting with the parlor. Lisa tried to maintain an aloof posture as she followed them, but inside she was crumbling. Couldn't they hurry up and leave? As they moved into the dining room, she had a sudden fear Jared might have forgotten to pull the rug over the door to the root cellar. Frantically, she looked around for him.

He was standing right behind her, where he'd been since the sheriff and his men had entered the house, acting as a silent guard. When her eyes sought his, he nodded and slid one hand around her waist, drawing her back against him.

She was surprised he would make such an intimate gesture in front of strangers, but perhaps he only meant to offer her comfort. When the arm stayed while the whole party made its way into the kitchen, she began to wonder. Was his protective and possessive behavior intended for her alone, or was it for the benefit of their unwanted visitors?

To make matters worse, the sheriff never took his eyes off them while his men searched the pantry, the back porch, and inside the cupboards. When they found nothing, the men headed upstairs with Lisa and Jared trailing behind.

First, they searched Lisa's room, opening the wardrobe and the linen presses in the wall beside the chimney. Miraculously, Andrew slumbered on in his cradle, oblivious to the turmoil.

When they were ready to move across the hall, Lisa got a tight, hollow feeling in the pit of her stomach. She hadn't had time to straighten the room, and frankly, she had forgotten all about it with the sheriff standing in the front hall. How could she explain the rumpled bed and bloody sheets?

When they entered the room, Jared squeezed her middle in warning. She was about to protest, then she saw what he had done. The quilt was pulled haphazardly over the sheets, suggesting the bed had been slept in and hiding all signs of blood. Jared's boots lay on the floor by the chair, and his saddlebags hung above them. Articles of his clothing and personal belongings were strewn about the room. He must have carried his saddlebags with him and done all this before bringing Clay down to the kitchen.

The sheriff turned to Lisa. "Ma'am, whose things are these?"

Jared squeezed her again, warning her to remain silent. "Mine," he replied, keeping his arm around her.

Sheriff Buford narrowed his eyes. "Yours, Tanner? I understood from the sheriff in Platte City that you rent a separate room in the back of the house."

"I did, but I've moved inside. To better protect Mrs. McAllister and her son."

"Mrs. McAllister, is that true?"

Lisa almost choked. Jared seemed to be implying to the sheriff that they were carrying on an illicit affair, but why? She glanced at him. His mouth was smiling lazily, but his eyes commanded her not to contradict his story.

She swallowed. "Yes, that's true."

After a pause, the sheriff motioned to his men. "I guess we're done in here. Now we'll search the barn and outbuildings."

"I'm sure you'll do your duty, Sheriff."

"Yes, ma'am." He snugged his hat down firmly on his head. "And Mrs. McAllister, if you should see Ferguson, remember it's a crime to conceal or abet a fugitive."

"I'll keep that in mind, Sheriff."

"You do that, ma'am. All right, boys. Let's go."

Lisa and Jared followed the men downstairs and watched from the veranda while they made their way through the barn, the chicken coop, the smokehouse, the springhouse and even the outhouse. When they finally walked back to the front empty-handed, mounted up, and rode off, she drew her first free breath in over an hour. Then she realized Jared still had his hand around her waist and pulled away in embarrassment.

"Thank God they're gone. Now you can explain the purpose of this charade."

"What charade?"

"You know what I mean, holding me like that and telling the sheriff you've moved into the house. You let him think there's something between us."

He frowned. "I don't want people to get the idea you're connected to Ferguson."

"And it's better they should believe I'm connected to you?"

"At least I'm not an outlaw."

"No, but did you think at all? Are you trying to make sure I'll never be able to hold my head up in town again?"

He reached out and caught her arms with both hands. "Stop it. I wouldn't do that to you, and you know it."

"You just have." She drew a deep breath as the events of the last several hours threatened to overwhelm her.

"Lisa, calm down. I let the sheriff believe what he wanted to believe because it seemed a lot less likely that we would be hiding another man somewhere in the house if you and I were carrying on a love affair. It was the best diversion I could think of at the time."

She wanted to believe he hadn't intended to harm her, but she wished he'd stopped to consider the consequences. "But what will happen to my reputation if word gets around?"

"If that happens, we'll deal with it. I don't think you have too much to worry about. The sheriff didn't look like a big gossip to me."

"Jared, this is serious."

He ran his hands lightly up her arms from her elbows to her shoulders and back, leaving goose bumps in their wake. If he intended the gesture to calm her, it failed. "Lisa, what's happened has happened. Right now, we have something more serious to deal with."

She shuddered at his touch. Was he referring to the unsettling conversation they'd had before he left? "This is no time for that kind of discussion."

"Probably not, but don't you think we ought to get Clay out of that hole in the ground before he suffocates?"

Clay! How could she have forgotten him? She slid from Jared's grasp and ran to the kitchen. She dragged the rug away and began tugging on the iron ring, trying to lift the heavy door.

He brushed her aside. "Let me do that." He swung the door up and back, then hopped down into the shoulder-deep cellar and squatted to lift Clay.

When he stood again, Lisa looked at Clay's face in cold dread. He was white as a corpse, and she couldn't see any sign of respiration. "Is he—?"

"Dead? Not yet. Let me get him back upstairs where I can take a look at his wounds."

Jared carried the unconscious man up the stairs and waited while Lisa changed the sheets on the bed. If Clay was going to die, she didn't want him to do it surrounded by such filth. She suspected Jared felt no such compunction but was surprised by his gentleness when he laid Clay's body on the bed and unwrapped the blanket.

"Get me some hot water and towels, and some more of these strips for bandages." Jared scanned Clay's pale body and the dark stains on the white cloths.

Lisa didn't hesitate. She returned with the supplies and stood aside as Jared set to work. He made no comment while he soaked off the old bandages and surveyed the wounds.

"You did a fine job." He pointed to the shoulder wound. "This one should heal quickly." Then he turned back to the gaping hole in Clay's thigh. "But I don't know about this one. There's not enough skin left to stitch together. We'll just have to keep a pressure bandage on it for a few days and hope for the best."

He sounded like an expert. She remembered his calm competence during Andrew's birth and had a sudden thought. "Do you have some sort of medical training?"

"I've tended my share of gunshot wounds." His words were terse, yet bespoke years of hard experience.

She ran her gaze down his body. Had some of those wounds been his? In his profession, it was a very real possibility. In an instant, her mind substituted Jared for the man on the bed and imagined his blood flowing and the hideous blackened holes being in his flesh. The picture made her ill.

A loud, complaining wail from across the hall broke into her morbid imaginings. Andrew was awake and ready to eat. Lisa glanced out the window and realized in amazement that it was only about seven o'clock in the morning. So much had happened in the past seven hours. She left Jared to finish re-bandaging Clay's wounds and went to change Andrew into dry clothes and feed him.

When she had finished nursing Andrew, she carried the baby into the room across the hall to check on Jared and Clay. Jared had finished, and Clay was now resting peacefully under the quilt. His color had improved, and she felt for the first time in hours that he might survive.

But when she examined Jared in the growing light, she grew concerned. He looked nearly as bad as Clay. His face was gray with exhaustion, and his eyes red-rimmed. Even his formidable strength seemed to have deserted him.

"You need some sleep."

He rubbed his hand across his bristly jaw. "Yes. But first I need food."

He'd shared much of the ordeal of the past few hours with her and probably hadn't had any sleep since the night before. Feeding him was the least she could do. "Would you like me to bring your breakfast up to your room?"

"No, I'll come down. I need to wash. And then I'll come back up here. I can sleep in the chair or on some blankets on the floor."

Jared was planning to take care of Clay? She must be suffering from sleep deprivation, too. Nothing made sense this morning.

"That's not necessary," she protested. "I can take care of him."

"You can't take care of a baby and an injured man at the same time. And besides, I'm the one with the experience, remember?"

"You would do that for him?"

Jared grimaced. "I wouldn't do a damned thing for him, and you know it. I would do it for you. And for me. I want him out of this house, and since you won't send him away until he's better, I'll have to make sure he heals as fast as possible."

After breakfast, she heated some water, and Jared washed and shaved in the kitchen before going back upstairs. Together they hauled the spare blankets and quilts from the linen presses and made as comfortable a bed as possible on the floor. After checking Clay one more time, Jared crawled into the pile of bedding and fell asleep in an instant.

The next day, Clay regained consciousness. At first, Lisa was relieved, but only briefly. He had developed a fever that sent him soaring in and out of a frightening delirium. When she and Jared changed the dressings, the shoulder wound seemed to be healing, but the hole in Clay's leg was swollen and suppurating.

Jared surveyed the oozing mess. "He'll be lucky if it doesn't turn to gangrene. We really should send for the doctor."

"I know. But you know what will happen if anyone finds out he's here."

"Sheriff Buford would be back before nightfall." Jared paused, and added softly, "And that might not be such a terrible thing."

"You're not considering—"

"No, of course not." His tone was testy. "I'm just tired, and I want him out of here."

She turned back to their patient. "We'll have to do what we can for him."

"I may have to clean the wound again and cauterize it. If I do, it won't be pretty."

Lisa turned to him and clasped one of his hands between her two smaller ones. "I trust you to do whatever needs to be done to try to save him."

He pulled her into his arms. "I wouldn't do this for anyone else. You know that don't you?" The harsh edge in his voice echoed the roughness of his actions.

Being in his arms again sent shock waves through her body. She swallowed hard. "I think you're kinder and more generous than you want to admit."

"No, I'm not."

Before she could read his intent, his head came down and his lips captured hers in a searing kiss. A blaze of raw energy flashed through her body from her head to the tips of her fingers and toes. Her hands came up to his shoulders to help support her wavering legs. Under her fingers, his muscles stretched and flexed over the bone beneath as he gathered her closer.

Ragged breathing tickled her ear just before firm lips began to trace its outline. She shivered and gasped.

He growled under his breath before moving on to the soft column of her neck. The slight rasp of his beard sent delicious chills down her limbs and tightened the buds of her nipples beneath her chemise. She tipped her head back and bared her throat like a defiant doe to a victorious wolf.

At this sign of surrender, he pulled his mouth away and groaned aloud. "Oh, God, I've been thinking of this for days. If you had any idea how much I want you..." Then, as if unable to stay away a second longer, he returned to her lips with renewed force.

It was a branding kiss, marking her as his. And when he finally pulled his head back, she did indeed feel marked, as if anyone who looked at her would know of her shameless response to his passion. She clung to him with her face buried against the solidity of his chest for long minutes that passed like seconds. She wished she could stay there forever, protected from the truths and hard choices of real life. But that was impossible.

"So that's the way it is, huh?"

Jared spun around to face the intrusive voice, keeping Lisa enfolded in his arms. In the bed, Clay was awake and struggling to sit up.

"Yes, that's the way it is," Jared replied.

"Clay, how long have you been awake?" Lisa wriggled free of Jared's grasp.

"Long enough." He looked Jared over. "Guess I was right about you. You do want my woman."

Lisa bristled. "Clay, I have told you repeatedly, I am not your woman. And I'm not his woman either."

"I think the lawman here might have other ideas. I know I do."

She had had enough empty bravado. She was sure

that was all it was. "Stop it. You're in no condition to threaten anyone."

Her statement seemed to bring Clay back to the reality of his situation. "How'd I get here, anyway?"

"Two of your friends brought you. They'll come back for you as soon as you're well enough to be moved." She prayed it was true.

"Huh. Well, my leg hurts like hell. Somebody bring me a bottle."

"You shouldn't be drinking. You have an infection and a fever."

"I don't care. I got to have something for this pain. You got any laudanum?"

"No."

"Then bring me a bottle."

Lisa looked to Jared for assistance.

"There isn't any in the house, but I'll get you some as soon as I can," he said to the man on the bed.

Her mouth tightened. She disapproved of strong spirits, but if Clay drank himself into a stupor, maybe he would be easier to care for.

Unfortunately, they weren't that lucky. The next week was sheer hell for all the occupants of the house. Clay's fever came and went as his body battled the infection. When it was up, he moaned deliriously and thrashed around in the bed. Jared had to tie him to prevent him from tearing the wounds open.

Between periods of fever, Clay was nearly as difficult, whining and fussing and demanding more whiskey. Lisa was nearly ready to tell Jared to go ahead and send him away, anywhere, just to get him out of the house, but Jared was managing the bulk of Clay's care without complaining, so she decided if he could stand it, she could. Fortunately, Clay was enough of a coward he never had the will to defy Jared's orders and finally began to heal.

One afternoon, while Andrew napped, Lisa was outside washing another huge mound of laundry in the great black cauldron. With a baby and two men in the house—one of them sick—the laundry never diminished. At least it was a fine, warm day, and it gave her an excuse to get out of the house and away from Clay's incessant demands. How Jared could stand being around him without assaulting the man just to shut him up was a mystery to her. She admired his self-restraint.

While she was stirring the wet sheets in the steaming water with a big wooden paddle, Lisa heard a woman's voice call her name. *Oh, no, Mama*! Since Clay had been dumped on her doorstep, she had avoided any contact with her mother. She had been too busy for a trip to town, and she knew if her mother found out what had happened, she would have plenty to say about the situation. She would probably tell Ben, who might feel he would be doing them all a favor by notifying the sheriff. It was best to keep them out of it.

Lisa raised her hand to shade her eyes and was surprised to see the fashionable buggy and flaming tresses of Jessamine Randall bouncing up the hill toward the house. Jessy stood and waved before a jolt sent her tumbling back onto the seat. "Lisa!" she called. Lisa returned the wave.

When she reached the house, Jessy hopped down and draped the reins across the back-porch railing. Lisa had always thought it was a good thing Jessy's father saw to it she had exceptionally well-trained horses. Otherwise, Jessy would have been stranded many times by her own carelessness.

"Lisa, what have you been doing with yourself out here? I haven't seen you in town all spring, except at church. When you missed church this Sunday, I decided to ride out for a nice long visit."

"I've been busy; that's all." Lisa shrugged, trying to sound casual.

"It wouldn't have anything to do with that delicious man I met out here last time, would it?" Jessy's green eyes twinkled.

"Jessamine Randall, you are too much!" Then Lisa had a sudden flash of suspicion. "Did my mother send you?"

"Well...she did happen to mention at church it might be nice for us to get together for a good chat."

As fond as she was of Jessy, this visit had all the hallmarks of one of her mother's maneuvers.

"I'll just bet she did," Lisa muttered.

"Now, Lisa, your mother worries about you, and besides, she's right. And I have so many things to tell you."

Lisa couldn't help smiling. Her mother might have sent Jessy as a spy, but with luck, the lively redhead would be so wrapped up in her own concerns she would forget the original purpose of her mission. But where could Lisa entertain Jessy that she wouldn't hear Clay if he called?

"It's so warm this afternoon, why don't we sit out here on the veranda?" she suggested. "Besides, Andrew is inside taking a nap. This way we won't disturb him."

"But don't you need to be able to hear him if he wakes up?"

Lisa laughed. "Oh, we'll hear him. He's plenty loud when he thinks he's being ignored. Besides,

Jared's in the house. He'll pick him up if he cries."

"Jared helps you with the baby?"

Jessy looked as if she wanted to pursue what promised to be a fascinating topic. Lisa could have bitten her tongue. Now that little tidbit was sure to be passed on to her mother, and heaven only knew what Martha would make of it. Perhaps she could distract Jessy.

"Occasionally. Now, tell me your exciting news."

Her ploy worked. Jessy's face lit.

"It's about my school. It's been approved."

"That's wonderful. Have you opened it?"

"Not yet. I'm still getting things ready. And I'm afraid you were right—I'm having a bit of trouble with some of the less progressive elements in town."

"What kind of trouble?"

"Minor things. Little boys calling me names, some vandalism at the building I plan to use. Nothing serious enough to deter me."

"I never knew anything serious enough to deter you when you had your mind set."

"Sounds like a woman after my own heart," interjected a deep voice.

The startled women looked up to see Jared standing at the door from the kitchen. He was dangling Andrew away from his body, wearing a rueful smile.

"Good afternoon, Miss Randall, isn't it?"

"Yes, indeed, Mr. Tanner."

Lisa fought the impulse to tell Jessy to put her eyes back into her head.

Jared turned his attention to Lisa. "I think this young man needs a change, and I wasn't sure you'd trust me to give it a try."

Lisa stood and reached for the baby. "Here, I'll do

it. I'll be right back, Jessy."

"Let me come with you. I'd like to see how this is done. You never know when it might come in handy."

Lisa tried her best to dissuade Jessy, but her friend was unstoppable when her curiosity was aroused. As they ascended the main stairs, Lisa crossed her fingers and prayed Clay was asleep and that Jared had closed the bedroom door.

The door was closed, but as soon as her foot crossed the threshold to her room, Clay bellowed, "Lisa! Tanner! Damn it! It's hot in here. Bring me something to drink!"

Jessy jumped in surprise, but Lisa just sighed. "In a minute," she called back, then shook her head in disgust.

"Who is that?" Jessy stared at the door in amazed curiosity.

Lisa proceeded to change Andrew, ignoring the ruckus across the hall. "It's Clay."

"Clay Ferguson? What on earth is he doing here?"

Lisa finished diapering Andrew and began searching through the top drawer of the chest for a clean gown, using the activity as an excuse to avoid Jessy's question until she could decide how much she dared tell her.

Jessy, however, wasn't one to be put off when her curiosity was piqued. "Lisa, what is going on here? You can tell me."

Lisa bit her lip.

She had always trusted Jessy with every secret in her life, but this one was much more serious than the time she'd seen Mr. Merriweather's buggy parked outside the widow Norton's house early in the morning.

Clay's life was at stake if the news of his whereabouts leaked out.

She raised her eyes to Jessy's direct green gaze and decided to take the risk. Without her mother as a confidant, she'd had to hold too much inside during the past few months.

"Jessy, if I tell you, will you swear, cross your heart, not to tell anyone else, especially my mother?"

Jessy bristled. "When have I ever told your secrets?"

"Never. But this time it's not a matter of girlish mischief. I'm afraid this is deadly serious."

Jessy remained silent, expectant.

With one eye on the door, Lisa proceeded to tell her every detail of how Clay came to be recuperating from gunshot wounds in her spare bedroom—every detail except the kiss she had shared with Jared. She was too unsure of her feelings to risk discussing them with anyone.

When she had finished her recital, Jessy looked grim.

"Lisa, you've got to get Clay out of here."

"That's what Jared keeps saying, but how can I when he can't walk or ride? And besides, unless someone comes to take him away, I have nowhere to send him. I'll just have to keep him here for the time being, but it is nerve wracking, never knowing when someone might come to the house and discover him."

"Frankly, I'm surprised Jared hasn't turned him in. I wouldn't think he'd have much sympathy for a bank robber."

"He doesn't, but he promised he wouldn't call in the law, and I trust him."

Jessy peered at her closely. "You sound very sure

of him. Are you, by any chance, becoming fond of the man?"

Lisa hoped she looked properly shocked. How could Jessy suspect? "Of course not. He's just a boarder."

"I'm not suggesting any impropriety on your part, but it would be understandable if you developed feelings for him."

"I'm not even sure I would understand it."

"It's been over a year since Dan died, and Jared is so..."

"That's enough. I don't want to hear any more about him. Have I made myself clear?"

"Perfectly," interrupted a familiar voice from the door.

Lisa almost dropped Andrew. "Jared! How long have you been standing there?"

"Long enough. I came to tell you Clay's got a visitor."

Chapter Ten

Lisa's breath caught before she could speak. "The sheriff again?" The words came out in a hoarse whisper.

"No. It's Bingham."

"Oh." Tense muscles relaxed. "Ask him to come upstairs. I don't think Clay's ready to be moved yet, but perhaps we can discuss the arrangements."

Jared nodded and returned a moment later, followed by Morgan Bingham. As Lisa watched the men climb the stairs, she noticed that Morgan's limp seemed to have improved. Perhaps it was because his knee had only his own weight to bear this time.

When they reached the landing where she and Jessy waited, Morgan respectfully removed his tattered butternut slouch cap and nodded. His eyes lingered on Jessy for a moment, but he spoke to Lisa. "Good afternoon, Mrs. McAllister. I come to see how Clay's getting along."

"Physically, he's improving, but as you can hear, the same cannot be said of his temper."

Clay was now banging on the wooden headboard

of the bed with an empty whiskey bottle and bellowing his frustration for all to hear.

For the first time since Lisa had met him, Morgan Bingham smiled. It lightened his solemn features in a whole new way. "Sounds like he's getting his strength back just fine."

"Yes," she replied dryly. "Why don't you go in and see him. Perhaps that will improve his disposition."

Morgan went into Clay's room and closed the door.

"Who is that?" whispered Jessy, her green eyes alight with curiosity.

Lisa had seen the look before, and she dreaded it. It was typical of Jessy to become fascinated with anyone outside the normal ranks of polite society, so an outlaw would be doubly intriguing. She would have to nip her friend's interest in the bud, or it would be impossible to keep Clay's activities and whereabouts secret much longer.

"His name is Morgan Bingham. I believe he's a professional bank robber, and you can forget right now about trying to reform him, or adopt him, or whatever it is you do with the strays you collect. Your mother would have a fit of apoplexy."

Jessy made a disgusted face at the mention of her ever-so-proper mother. "You're right, of course, but it's so exciting! One doesn't get to meet a real live bank robber every day."

"Thank goodness."

"Oh, Lisa, sometimes you can be so conventional."

"And sometimes I think you thrive on being unconventional."

Jessy grinned. "Of course. It's so much more fun. It

would do you good to have more fun, you know."

"I have too many serious responsibilities to worry about fun. I have a son to raise, in case you forgot."

"Of course, I didn't forget, but you're only twenty-two. You're not a dried up old prune yet. You still have plenty of opportunities to have fun."

"Such as...?"

"Well, there's Jared, for instance." Jessy's eyes twinkled with mischief.

"Stop that right now."

"I'd make the most of it if he were living in my house."

Lisa opened her mouth to reply, but a sudden touch on her elbow stopped her. *Jared.* She had forgotten all about him. He must have been standing behind her during the entire conversation. Her cheeks flamed. Jessy must have been looking right at him the whole time. That would explain her provocative attitude. Jessy loved to stir things up.

Before she could react to Jared, the door of Clay's room opened, and Morgan Bingham stepped out. "Ma'am, I spoke to Clay, and if it's all right with you, me and Frank will be back to pick him up next Wednesday. If you could help him practice walking some in the next few days, I think he'll be ready to ride if we take it slow."

Relief flooded through her and pushed her pent-up breath out in a rush. Clay was leaving, maybe not today, but soon. She would have her house back, her life back. Then it struck her that she would also be alone with Jared again. Before, she hadn't minded being in the house with him in the same way. She'd been buffered by her determination to force him out. Now things had changed between them. She'd changed, though she didn't want to think about how, or why. She just knew it was going to be much more difficult living in the same house with him now.

An expectant silence intruded on her thoughts. Lisa realized Morgan was waiting for her response and pulled herself back into the moment. "Thank you for coming, Mr. Bingham. I'll try to have him ready to travel when you return."

"Yes, ma'am." Morgan nodded again and replaced his hat. As he passed in front of them toward the head of the stairs, Jessy stepped forward.

"Mr. Bingham, I'm Lisa's friend, Jessamine Randall." She held out her delicate gloved hand and smiled.

Morgan stared at her, frozen. He moved his hand tentatively toward her, but stopped, as if he couldn't bring himself to touch her, even through her soft glove.

Jessy dropped her hand but retained her bright smile. "Mr. Bingham, I was about to leave also, and I wondered if you would mind escorting me to my buggy?"

"Uh, no, ma'am. I'd be pleasured." He didn't meet her eyes, but offered his arm, and they headed down the stairs together. Over her shoulder, Jessy flashed Lisa a triumphant grin as she disappeared through the front door on the arm of the outlaw, leaving Lisa and Jared standing on the upstairs landing.

Lisa couldn't spare much time worrying about Jessy and Morgan Bingham. Clay was hollering again, and Jared's steady gaze held an intensity she didn't want to deal with. He looked ready to pounce on her the minute their visitors were out of sight. She chose the safer of the two men and, hefting Andrew onto her hip, hurried into Clay's room. Jared would be gone for the next two days, so maybe she would have a chance to think about things later.

Bright and early the next morning after Jared left, Lisa began working with Clay in earnest to get him ready to leave when Morgan Bingham and Frank James returned. He was difficult and obstreperous when she tried to persuade him to bear weight on his injured leg, loudly proclaiming to the world that she was trying to kill him. By the time he was able to cross the room on his own, Lisa found herself warming to the idea. She was relieved when Jared returned and Wednesday arrived.

However, when Clay's comrades showed up and helped him down the veranda steps to his waiting horse, an unbidden sadness swept through her. She knew with cold certainty she would never see him alive again, and in spite of everything he had said and done, she was unable to take any joy in the knowledge. Regardless of what he had become, Clay Ferguson had been part of her childhood, part of her past. It was sad to say goodbye to one of the last remaining pieces of her old life.

When the men were saddled up and ready to depart, Morgan tipped his hat. "Thank you for your help, Mrs. McAllister. Sorry we had to trouble you this way."

"Clay was an old friend."

Clay jerked his head around. "Don't talk about me like I was dead, woman. I'll be back. You can count on it."

Brave talk, so typical of Clay. She smiled a sad little smile.

The men rode slowly down to the main road with one on each side of Clay in case he started to topple.

When they were out of earshot Jared spoke. "He's riding to his death, and he doesn't seem to care." He shook his head.

"I know." Lisa stared at Clay's swaying back, and tears formed in her eyes.

Jared grasped her elbow and turned her to face him. "You can't feel sorry for him. The man's chosen his own life. He isn't worth even one of your tears."

"I'm not crying for him. I never cry." Other faces flashed before her, dear faces, familiar faces. "Oh, I can't explain."

"I think I understand."

She blinked and shook her head. "How could you? How could you understand and do what you do? You're part of it, part of the killing."

His features hardened. "Do you think you're the only one who's ever lost someone? Do you think I do what I do just to protect the boss's money?" He dropped his hands from her arms. "I risk my life every time I ride out to protect the drivers and passengers, to protect the public, people like you and Andrew." He turned and stalked across the yard toward the barn.

"I know," she whispered. "I know." And that was part of the problem.

****

One evening in late June, after a two-day absence, Jared stormed into the kitchen with a dirty handkerchief wrapped around his upper arm and a scowl on his face. Lisa had already put Andrew to bed and was drying the supper dishes when she heard his steps.

"I saved you some...what happened to you?" She dropped the plate and the dishtowel on the table and rushed across the room with no attempt to mask her concern.

"It's nothing, just a scratch." Anger mingled with disgust in his voice.

"Let me see." Ignoring his words, she untied the blood-streaked rag. Under the shreds of his shirt, she saw an angry, oozing welt with a deep gouge in the center.

"It just creased me."

"What creased you?"

"A bullet, of course."

"You can tell me what happened while I clean you up." As she crossed to the fireplace to fill a basin with hot water from the kettle, she hoped her demeanor gave no hint of the fear and turmoil she felt. A bullet wound. After nursing Clay, she had hoped never to see another one as long as she lived. And now Jared had been shot. This time the injury was minor, but next time it could be much worse.

She brought the basin and some clean rags back to the kitchen table. "Sit down and take off your shirt."

He grunted as he sat and let her help him remove the damaged shirt.

She glanced across his muscular torso before concentrating on his upper arm. He was so beautifully made, it pained her to see his flesh marred by a bullet. The wound wasn't serious, but it looked as if it would sting and throb like fury.

"All right, tell me everything." She began to cleanse away the blood and dirt.

Jared stared at the three-legged spider skillet on the hearth. "This time there were six of them. They rode up out of a wash shooting. I had to shoot three of them before they gave up and rode off."

Lisa's hands stilled. She was almost afraid to ask,

but she had to know. "Was it Clay and his group?"

He turned to face her. "Not this time."

She glanced back at his arm. "Did you kill anyone?"

"I don't know. They all rode away, but two of them were slumped over in their saddles."

"Doesn't that bother you?"

"Damn it, Lisa." He reached over with his good arm and circled her wrist with long, blunt fingers. "In spite of what you seem to think of me, I don't enjoy killing. Those men knew the risks when they started out, and some of them are bound to end up paying the price."

"I realize that."

"Then why do you keep needling me about it?"

"Because I don't like your being involved, that's why," she snapped. Suddenly aware of what she'd just said, she tried to jerk her arm out of Jared's grasp.

His eyes glittered with something other than pain, and he tightened his hold. "Not so fast. Why? Why don't you want me involved?"

"I don't know. I don't care what you do. Now, let go of me."

"Look at me." His voice was soft, but commanding. "Tell me the truth. Why don't you want me to do what I do?"

Her body was taut as a bowstring as she stared into his eyes. Finally, she wilted. "All right. I don't want you to get hurt or killed. Is that what you wanted to hear?"

"It's a start."

"Well, it's all you're going to get. Now, let go of me."

"Not until you tell me why it's important to you."

She wanted to hold out against his relentless prodding. It seemed important not to tell him what he wanted to hear, as if she would be committing herself by speaking the words aloud.

"Because I hate to see any living thing suffer," she prevaricated.

He smiled but didn't release her hand. "Not good enough. Why me? Be honest, Lisa."

"Please, don't do this. Don't make me say it."

His smile slid away and was replaced by a look of intense need. "You need to say it, and I need to hear it. Why would it matter to you if I lived or died?"

Unable to withstand him any longer, she gave in. "All right. It can't make any difference, but I care about what happens to you...very much."

Jared's dark eyes flashed. His Adam's apple bobbed. When he spoke, his voice dropped to a husky, seductive baritone. "You're wrong. It makes all the difference in the world."

He removed the bloody cloth from her hand and, with his hands on either side of her waist, drew her unresisting toward him. He showed no sign of pain from the crease in his arm.

"Show me how much." He pulled her to stand between his legs.

She stared into the velvety black depths of his eyes and was shocked to the core of her being by the emotion that welled up inside her. Her admission crystallized what she had been feeling for weeks, months even. She loved him. No good could come of it, but the feeling had a name, and she could no longer deny it. *Love.*

She placed one hand on each side of his face to hold it steady and bent toward him. Her eyes fluttered shut and her lips melted into his. He didn't take command of the caress. He let her show him everything in her heart, in her own time and her own way.

She was lost in the wonder of the first real kiss she had ever given. Her fingertips gloried in the thick satin of his hair, while her thumbs felt the rough texture of the scruffy new beard sprouting beneath his hard cheekbones. His lips were firm, but ever so soft, as he followed her lead, responding to her movements but never taking charge. She could feel his iron control, and she trusted it. He was giving her the freedom to push farther, to enjoy this gift of exploration in complete safety.

She nudged his lips with her own, and he cooperated by opening his mouth to her questing tongue. Shyly at first, then more boldly, she began to learn the taste and feel of him, the smooth sharpness of his teeth and the rough velvet of his tongue. She reveled in the opportunity he offered, the time to satisfy her own needs and curiosities without being overwhelmed by the force of aroused male passion.

As she increased the pressure of her mouth, the pace of his breathing increased, too. Then his fingers tightened at her waist. Suddenly he thrust her back to arm's length.

She regarded him for several seconds, suspended in time and place and fighting for breath. When he finally spoke, the husky rasp of his voice fanned the flames already burning in her.

"That's about all I can take right now, unless you're ready to go upstairs and let this progress to its natural conclusion."

She blushed and stared at the floor. She deserved

that. After the way she'd behaved, he had every right to believe she was willing to forsake everything for a few hours in his arms. And he was nearly right.

"I...I'm sorry. I never meant to do that, to lead you to believe I would..." Her voice trailed off as she searched for the words to explain.

Jared gave her a wry smile. "I know, sweetheart, and I'll survive the frustration. This time, anyway."

Lisa's gaze shot to his face. She placed her hands on his shoulders, in part to maintain the distance between them. She had crossed the line and could no longer trust herself. Her voice came out in an anxious rush. "But there can never be anything more between us." She had to persuade them both.

His smile dissolved. "After the way you just looked at me and the way you just kissed me, how can you honestly tell me it's going to stop there? You're not made of stone—I can feel it in you—and I'm sure as hell not either."

Her embarrassment faded in a quick flash of anger. "No, I'm not made of stone. But that doesn't mean I'm going to hop into bed with you."

"I don't expect you to, but I do expect you to be honest enough to admit your feelings."

Her feelings. She didn't want to want him. She certainly didn't want to love him. Things had already gone too far. And what of his feelings? He hadn't said anything.

"I'm not sure what you want from me. You said you're not interested in marriage, and neither am I. I want a safe, stable life for my son. That's all."

"You keep saying that, maybe because it's easier, but you're lying, lying to both of us. You want more. You know it. I know it."

She shoved against his shoulders. "You're wasting your time here. You should go find a woman who can give you what you want."

He dropped his hands from her waist. "I don't want another woman. I want you, and I don't give up when I want something."

"Neither do I."

Up in her room, Lisa sat in a chair by the front window, staring across the thick, green leaves of the tobacco plants in her neighbor's field and watching the summer sun sink below the treetops on the horizon. She thought about Jared and herself, and the impossible tangle their lives had become. Yes, she loved him, but she could take no joy in it. They had no future together. They weren't headed down the same road.

Why was he so determined to have her? He said he wanted her, but when she'd broken down and admitted she cared about him, he'd made no similar declaration. Was he only interested in a temporary physical relationship? If so, why hadn't he taken advantage of her passionate response when it would have been so easy? She flushed when she realized just how easy. Surely he had known.

The next day was Sunday, and, as usual, Jared drove Lisa and Andrew to the Baptist church in town. He never attended services with them but insisted on escorting them to the door and was always ready to pick them up when it was time to go home. As usual, Lisa and Andrew sat with her mother and Ben.

But today, when Martha invited them to Sunday dinner after church, as she always did, Lisa surprised her mother by accepting. For weeks, she had been so involved in her own problems with Jared and then with having Clay in the house that she had made some excuse or another. Today, in addition to not wanting to spend the rest of the day alone with Jared, she also longed for the comfort and companionship of her mother's company. It was the one thing she had always been able to count on, no matter what else happened, and she needed it more than ever.

As soon as they arrived at the Wainwright's, Ben and Jared retired to the parlor to entertain Andrew and talk business while Lisa and her mother went to the kitchen to start dinner. They rolled up their sleeves, tied on a pair of aprons, and set to work. Martha began to bread several thick pork chops and asked Lisa to shred a cabbage for slaw.

"Ben told me there's been more trouble on the stage line, serious trouble." Martha sprinkled the chops with salt and pepper.

"Yes, there was a shootout yesterday." Lisa had almost forgotten about it in her preoccupation with what had happened afterward. Now she shuddered in recollection of the event and how much worse it might have been. "Jared had to shoot three men, and one of them shot him in the arm."

"Oh, dear!" Martha dropped the chop in her hand. "Ben never mentioned Jared had been shot. But he looks fine today; it must not have been too serious."

"It was just a crease, thank heaven."

"All the same, I can't understand what the world's coming to. You'd think the war would have given these men enough shooting and killing to last several lifetimes."

"Apparently not. I've talked to Jared about giving up his job and going into something more peaceful, but he won't hear of it."

"Something like farming?"

"Well, yes." Lisa glanced up from her wooden bowl. "Mama, you'd be amazed at how much work he does around the farm, and he really seems to enjoy it. I can't understand why he's reluctant to quit shooting people and take up farming."

"I imagine he feels an obligation to Mr. Holladay, but I'm glad to hear he's such a help to you, dear."

She'd boxed herself into a corner this time. Now she could hardly deny it. "Umm, well...yes."

Her mother slid the chops into the cast iron skillet bubbling with melted lard and wiped her hands on her apron. She walked over to where Lisa was working at the table. "I don't mean to pry, and you don't have to tell me if you'd rather not, but are you beginning to develop feelings for Jared?"

The cleaver clattered from Lisa's hands. "Oh, Mama, first Jessy and now you." She kept her back to Martha and hoped she sounded lighthearted and unconcerned. She'd never been able to lie to her mother, and she knew this time would be no exception. Maybe Martha would let the subject drop.

No such luck.

"I just wanted to let you know I would understand if you did. In fact, I'd approve. Jared seems like a fine young man."

"I'm not looking for a fine young man, or any man."

"Lisa, don't be so stubborn. You're young. There's no need for you to go through the rest of your life alone."

"I'm not alone. I have Andrew."

"It's not the same, and if you don't know the difference, you should. Besides, haven't you ever considered that Andrew might deserve a real father?"

Lisa had thought of it more than once. She thought of it every time she saw Jared with her son. But the whole image was nothing more than a tempting illusion. "Jared doesn't want a family."

"How do you know? Have you asked him?"

"Mama, he's a drifter. He never stays in one place more than a few months. You've heard him say so."

Martha's eyes twinkled. "For the right woman, he might change."

"The subject is closed."

"Very well, but I only want you to be happy. I don't want you to waste as much time as I did."

Lisa glanced up. "You? Waste time?"

"I should have married Ben years ago."

"I always wondered why you didn't. I could tell you cared about him, and it was plain to everyone how he felt about you."

Martha put her arm around Lisa's shoulders. "After your father's death, I was afraid."

"I've never known you to be afraid of anything."

"Oh, but I was. I was afraid of the effect it would have on you and Seth if I remarried. I was afraid of what people might think. But mostly, I was afraid to love again. I was foolish. I looked happiness in the face for years and denied it. I don't want you to make the same mistake."

Lisa sighed. "It's not the same. I never had what you had."

Martha rubbed her shoulder lightly. "I know, dear. But you have the right to have it now."

"I can't—not with Jared."

"How do you know that?"

Lisa rubbed her forehead. The whole subject was

giving her a headache. "Mama, I really don't want to talk about this anymore. I have to do what I think is best."

"I know. I just hope you'll recognize it when you see it."

Lisa opened her mouth to reply, but her mother smiled and held up her hand. "I know, I know. I'll try to keep my advice to myself."

Lisa relaxed and smiled, too. "Thank you, Mama."

"Just remember that a few years from now when Andrew refuses the benefit of your wisdom."

When they sat down to dinner, Jared insisted on holding Andrew on his lap and feeding him bits of cornbread and pork chop, which the baby cheerfully attacked with his two new teeth. He also managed to eat his own dinner one-handed while keeping Andrew's questing fingers out of range of his plate.

"Lisa," he said, spooning a small bite of mashed potato into Andrew's wide-open mouth, "Ben tells me he and Martha are arranging a big party for Mr. and Mrs. Holladay in a couple of weeks. They're driving out from Washington in the special coach he had made for her. I'll have to show it to you. It's like a fancy hotel room on wheels."

Before Lisa could comment, Ben chimed in. "Yes, and your mother and I would like you to attend the party. Mr. Holladay instructed us to open his mansion for the event, and there'll be a dance with a real orchestra, so you won't want to miss it."

A dance. With an orchestra. Lisa had never been to such an extravagant affair. By the time she was old enough to attend grown-up parties, the war had started, and no one had parties after that. Besides, she was a widow, didn't know how to dance, and had nothing to wear.

"I don't think so. Besides, what would I do with Andrew?"

Martha passed her the basket of rolls. "Bring him along. Between the four of us, I'm sure we can keep an eye on him, and he goes to bed early. It would be such a help to me if you would come and serve as my assistant hostess, supervising the kitchen, seeing that all the guests are comfortable, and so on."

Obviously, they were determined that she attend the party, and Lisa wasn't sure she had the energy to fight the three of them. Besides, it would be fun to see everyone dressed up and hear the orchestra, even if she didn't participate in the festivities.

She sighed. "All right. If you need me, Mama, of course I'll come." Then she looked at her mother, Ben, and Jared, each in turn. "But I want it understood that I will be there to work, not to dine, or dance, or whatever else any of you might have in mind."

"Of course, dear."

Chapter Eleven

The afternoon of the party, Lisa was in a complete dither. Despite her mother's assurance she would be able to stay in the background, Martha had insisted on buying her a new dress. It was gorgeous, in a bright fuchsia-colored moiré, trimmed with intricate black braid. Her mother assured her the rich purplish-red color was stunning with her dark coloring, and Lisa hadn't protested too loudly when Martha paid for the dress and laid it, carefully wrapped, in the back of the wagon. The dress was the first grown-up party dress she had ever owned and the first ready-made dress as well. Fortunately, it had required very few alterations to look as if it had been designed and created just for her.

She'd decided to take the dress with them in the wagon and change at the Holladay mansion, where her mother would be able to help. Besides, she didn't want to risk soiling it on the ride to town. She doubted she would ever own such a fine gown again.

When it was time to leave, she was still bustling

around her room gathering all the articles of clothing and accessories she needed to take along.

"Aren't you ready yet?" Jared called from the front hall.

She rifled through her top drawer in search of her grandmother's dangling jet earrings. "Almost!"

"Well, hurry up. Your mother and Ben are expecting us in about five minutes."

Exasperated, she finally found the earrings and stuffed them into the small black reticule she planned to carry. Then, without bothering to go to the door, she called, "You could make yourself useful, you know. You could come up here and carry some of this."

"There's no need to shout."

She glanced up from the pile she'd made on the bed and saw Jared lounging in the doorway. The sight of him sent tiny waves of excitement racing through her. He was already dressed for the evening and presented a striking study in black and white. He wore a formal black suit with long, straight black trousers, a matching coat, snowy white shirt, black vest, and black string tie. With his black hair and eyes and flashing white smile, the warm tone of his skin provided the only accent of color. He looked like a dashing, sophisticated pirate who would be equally at ease at a formal state dinner as storming a clipper off the coast of Jamaica.

He shifted his weight from the doorframe and strolled into the room. When he reached the bed, he leaned down and plucked Andrew out of the mound of extra petticoats and stockings.

"What's all this?" He gestured to the jumble of clothing.

His question brought Lisa back to the present. "It's

everything I need for tonight, I hope."

"You want to cart all this to the party?"

"Yes. Now are you going to help me or just stand there like a decorative doorstop?"

He laughed. "I don't know. No one's ever described me as decorative before."

She was too anxious to feel playful. "And I'm sure they never will again. Now put Andrew down and help me wrap this dress."

With a smile lurking around his lips, Jared set the baby on the rug and went over to help Lisa. When they had finished bundling everything up to be taken downstairs, he leaned over and murmured near her ear, "You have nothing to worry about. You'll be the most beautiful woman there."

Her ears burned. He must be teasing her. Her features were too strong and her coloring too bold. No man had told her she was beautiful since her father died, not even Dan. "Nonsense. Besides, I'll be working. No one will be looking at me."

"I will."

Her heart took a little jump, but she could think of no appropriate response, so she ignored it. "I'll carry Andrew if you can manage the rest. We need to be going now. I'm certain we're already late."

Jared gave her a little bow. "Yes, ma'am." Then he picked up the carefully wrapped gown and the bag with the accessories and followed her out the door.

When they reached the stately brick mansion Benjamin Holladay had built in Weston fifteen years earlier, Lisa directed Jared to take her parcels into one of the small upstairs bedrooms. Then she and her mother closeted themselves behind the closed door and set to work.

She hadn't worn a corset in a year and a half, and she winced as Martha tightened the strings. "Mama, I'm not sure this is going to work. I don't think I can breathe."

Martha gave one last yank and tied the strings. "There, all done. The sacrifices we make for beauty... But you'll be the prettiest girl at the party tonight."

"I'm not a girl, and remember, I'm here to help you, not to enjoy myself." Lisa raised her arms so her mother could drop her skirt over her head. It rustled over the petticoats when she smoothed it into place.

"I don't see why those two things should be mutually exclusive." Martha helped Lisa into her bodice. "Besides, the Holladays brought so many servants with them I have a full staff in the kitchen and dining room. All you need to do is help me supervise. That should leave plenty of time for socializing. Now take a look. You're absolutely lovely."

Lisa turned to face the walnut cheval mirror in the corner. She hardly recognized herself. Her corseted waist looked tiny in contrast to the wide sweep of the crinoline, and the vibrant color of her gown was indeed the perfect complement to her dark brown hair and brows.

Martha had swept her hair into fashionable dove's wings on the sides of her head and pinned the rest of the rich, dark mass into an intricate knot in the back. Then she'd pulled several tendrils loose around Lisa's face to soften the severity of the style. The humidity of the warm Missouri evening had already caused those tendrils to curl, and Lisa loved the effect. She shook her head and set the shiny black earrings swinging.

Martha surveyed her daughter's image with a look of satisfaction. "He'll never know what hit him."

"Who?"

"Jared, of course."

"Mama..."

"Don't *Mama* me. I've seen him look at you. I can't wait to see his face tonight. Now let's get downstairs. We've got work to do."

Martha was only half right. There wasn't much work for Lisa. The servants needed little guidance as they went about their assigned tasks, so she mostly tried to stay out of their way. After the punch and the myriad of silver trays of food were set out in the dining room, Benjamin Holladay escorted his delicate wife down to the front hall to prepare to greet their guests.

Everyone who was anyone in Weston had been invited to the party, as well as a number of the host's business associates from Atchison and a complement of senior officers from Fort Leavenworth, along with their wives. Soon the house filled with partygoers, and they spilled out onto the porches and into the gardens. The strains of the small orchestra accompanied the guests as they delighted in the county's first lavish social event in more than five years.

Andrew stayed awake for about an hour after the guests began to arrive, but when he fell asleep in her arms, Lisa carried him upstairs to the room where she'd changed. She laid him in the center of the bed surrounded by pillows for safety. When she came back down, she scanned the crowded parlor for her mother to see if she needed help with anything.

"Lisa! Lisa!" A female voice trilled above the din.

Lisa turned and caught sight of a crop of vibrant red ringlets atop the animated face of Jessamine Randall plowing toward her through the crowd. Jessy seemed to be dragging a man in her wake, but Lisa couldn't make out who it was.

"Jessy, how nice to see you."

Jessy whipped out her lace-covered fan and waved it in front of her face. "Whew! I almost didn't make it across the room, but isn't this wonderful? I haven't been to a party like this in ages." Her green eyes danced with pleasure.

"I haven't been to a party like this ever." Lisa gave her a wry smile. "Don't you find it rather hot and crowded?"

Jessy laughed. "Of course, but that's half the fun." She yanked hard with her left hand and her male companion stumbled out from behind her back. "Lisa, you remember Morgan Bingham."

Lisa's jaw dropped in a very unladylike manner, but she couldn't help it. Neither could she help staring. She couldn't believe her eyes. Jessy was not only continuing to see the outlaw, but she had brought him to the Holladay's party. Her mother would faint dead away if she knew.

"Lisa." Jessy's irritated voice interrupted her thoughts.

"Oh...yes, of course." Lisa recovered herself. "How nice to see you again, Mr. Bingham."

Morgan Bingham didn't look any more comfortable with the situation than she was. His suit had clearly been made to fit someone else, and his gaze kept shifting around the room as if he were searching for danger in every corner. When his glance returned to Lisa he nodded. "Mrs. McAllister."

Please don't let him say anything about Clay.

He didn't. In fact, he didn't say anything at all. He just stood shifting his weight back and forth on his newly shined boots.

"Mr. Bingham, it's so warm in here, I wonder if I could prevail upon you to bring Jessy and me some punch. It's in the dining room."

Morgan looked relieved to be sent on the errand. He nodded again without speaking and disappeared into the crowd. As soon as he was out of sight, Lisa turned to Jessy and whispered, "Jessamine Randall, have you lost your mind? What are you thinking of, bringing a man like that here?"

Jessy stiffened. "Don't be such an old maid. Where's your sense of adventure?" Then her features softened. "Besides, Morgan isn't what you think at all."

Uh oh. That look spelled trouble. Jessy had always had a soft spot for society's outcasts, and now, apparently, had taken an actual criminal under her wing.

"Is he still riding with the James boys?" Lisa demanded. "Don't you know what they do? Hasn't my experience with Clay taught you anything?"

"Morgan is nothing like Clay." Jessy was emphatic.

"Surely your parents don't allow him to call on you." Lisa was aghast at the thought of Judge and Mrs. Randall welcoming an outlaw into their home as a suitor for their cherished only daughter.

Jessy shifted her gaze to the back of the head of the officer standing next to her. "Well, not exactly. He's more like one of my students."

"Your students are all much shorter. Don't try to tell me your parents haven't noticed the difference."

Jessy's expression was earnest when she turned back to Lisa. "I'm teaching Morgan to read, along with the others. Oh, Lisa, his family was so poor when he was growing up he never had a chance to go to school.

When I told him about my school, he started coming around during school hours. He said it was to look out for our safety since the school isn't very popular with some people in town, but I noticed right away how interested he was in the lessons. Finally, he admitted he couldn't read, and I've been working with him ever since."

Lisa could see how serious Jessy was, whether about the man or the challenge he represented she couldn't be sure, but this was more than just another of Jessy's whirlwind interests. She took her friend's hand. "But he could be dangerous."

Jessy's smile brimmed with innocent confidence. "He could never be dangerous to me."

Just then, Morgan returned with two cups of punch. Fine droplets of sweat dotted his brow and the freshly shaven skin of his face. His skin was pale, and his Adam's apple bobbed in his throat. But when his hazel gaze fell on Jessy, a new strength seemed to infuse him.

No, this man was not like Clay, despite their common occupation. There was a depth to him Clay had never had and never would. Lisa felt a sharp twinge as she watched the pair. Even the flighty Jessy seemed to be able to inspire deep emotions in a man.

At that moment, a big, warm hand closed around her upper arm, causing Lisa to whirl around and almost spill her punch. Jared was standing close beside her, his black eyes narrowed as he regarded Morgan Bingham. She hadn't seen Jared for a couple of hours and cursed the timing of his appearance. She closed her eyes. *Please don't let him give Morgan away, for Jessy's sake.*

"Bingham." The single word was heavy with

implied threat.

"Evening, Tanner." Morgan's eyes shifted, but he stood straight and tall next to Jessy.

"I know for a fact you weren't invited tonight. Did you come alone?"

"I'm here as Miss Randall's guest."

Jared glanced at Jessy, who lifted her little pointed chin and flashed a challenge of emerald fire from her eyes. "Then I assume we can trust you to see that nothing happens here tonight that could bring any harm to Miss Randall."

Morgan's spine stiffened, and his features took on a look of fierce determination. "I would never let anything hurt Miss Randall. You can bank on it."

Jared smiled, but the smile didn't reach his eyes. "Bank on it, interesting choice of words. However, since you're so certain of her safety, I'll leave her in your care. If you two will excuse us, Lisa promised this dance to me."

"I can't...I don't know how..." Lisa sputtered, but he had already swept her into his arms and was waltzing toward the French doors opening onto the back terrace.

An overflow crowd danced to the music of the orchestra wafting through the open windows. Officers in crisp blue uniforms with sparkling gold braid glided by in the moonlight with elegant, smiling ladies in their arms. Civilian gentlemen in their best attire escorted local ladies in new or artfully made-over gowns of every color. Everywhere she looked people were happily paired off. Two by two—wasn't that the way it was supposed to be? Who could there be for her, Jared? He didn't want strings, but she couldn't imagine wanting anyone else. Not now, not ever.

Loneliness gripped her until it nearly strangled her.

Suddenly, it was too much. She broke away and dashed through the dancers and down the steps. She could hear him calling through the noise of the crowd, but she didn't stop. He caught up with her on the back lawn, far enough away from the house to be out of sight and earshot of the partygoers on the terrace.

"Lisa, stop!" He reached for her and spun her around.

She faced him with tears streaming down her cheeks and anguish in her heart. "What do you want from me?"

"You're crying."

"So, what if I am? I have every right." She sniffed but made no effort to stem the flow of tears.

"Of course, you do. But why? And why now?"

She couldn't explain it, and she didn't want to try. She never cried, but now she couldn't seem to stop. Every hurt, every loss welled up and overflowed inside her. The only way out was through tears. She couldn't hold them back. She stood facing him, sobbing as if her heart would break.

He stared at her for a long moment, then muttered a curse and crushed her against his chest. With racking sobs, she poured out years of pain, soaking his shirtfront. When his hands roamed up and down her back, soothing her, and his deep voice murmured words of comfort into her hair, she made no effort to resist. She felt so hollow inside she greedily accepted the solace he offered.

For several minutes he seemed content to hold her, until there was no pain left and her body relaxed against his. Soon, however, his soothing hands became more purposeful, stroking, lingering at her waist, and cupping the fullness of her hips through the layers of clothing. Then they stilled. He drew a ragged breath and set her back. His eyes glittered in the moonlight with leashed passion, and the harsh shadows that fell across the rugged planes of his cheeks gave him the look of a ravenous panther.

She shivered and blinked back the tears clinging to her lashes.

"Let's sit down." His voice was rough as he gestured to a small stone bench half-hidden in a copse of birch trees at the edge of the garden.

She allowed herself to be led to the bench and sank down. Between her overheated emotions and the feelings engendered by his caresses, she felt as though her bones had turned to jelly. She stared across the dark grass silvered by the soft white light of the moon.

His voice interrupted her reverie. "Lisa, tell me what this is all about. Did someone say or do something to upset you?"

She sighed. That was Jared, ever the protector. She still didn't look at him but continued to peer out into the dark landscape, her gaze following the brief flashes of fireflies in the bushes.

Finally, she spoke. "I'm sorry. I don't know what happened. I haven't cried in longer than I can remember."

"Maybe you needed to."

"Maybe." She paused. "I know this will sound foolish, but I felt lonely all of a sudden in the midst of all those people." She laughed, but the sound was short and hollow.

He reached for her and drew her back, wrapping his arms around her. "That doesn't sound foolish. I've been alone most of my life. I know the feeling."

"But I have no right to feel that way. I have my mother and Andrew. I don't know what's wrong with me. For some reason, when I saw all those couples..."

"It's not the same, is it?"

She didn't answer his question, but kept talking, more to herself than to him. "Do you ever feel like there's somebody for everyone else in the world except you?"

He remained silent, so she continued. "When I was a little girl, my mother told me that somewhere in the world, everyone has a perfect mate. All you have to do is find that person. Sometimes I'm inclined to believe her. Even Jessy has found some kind of happiness with Morgan Bingham, as wrong as it may seem to us. But Mama never told me what happens if you don't find the right person." Her voice dropped to a whisper. "Or if you find them but everything else is all wrong."

Jared turned her toward him. "Look at me."

She resisted briefly, then surrendered to his demand.

"We can't control much of what happens in life, so we have to reach for every opportunity for happiness we're offered. You need to be loved, and not in the way your mother or your son loves you. That kind of love is wonderful, but it's not enough. You need to be loved by a man, a man you care about and respect. It's nothing to be ashamed of. You deserve it."

"And are you that man?"

"I could be."

She sought his eyes, glittering in the moonlight, and searched for the truth. She saw certainty and desire, hard and bright. But she also saw need, a raw need that answered her own and pleaded with her not to reject him. It was the plea that pushed her over the edge, not the strength or depth of her own needs but the overwhelming desire to give this man the fulfillment for which his eyes so eloquently begged.

In that moment, she felt imbued with a great power — a heady and frightening power — because she knew the decision was hers. Jared was making a request that was hers to grant or deny. Her answer would profoundly affect the course of the rest of their lives, either together or apart. For a moment, she relished the novelty of the power he had bestowed upon her. It gave her the courage she needed to speak aloud the answer that would bring either her salvation or her downfall.

"Yes." The answer to all the questions between them.

A crushing weight lifted, and her face broke into a triumphant smile.

****

Jared was stunned. He couldn't believe his eyes and ears. When Lisa's smile didn't fade, he grinned fiercely in return and pulled her into his arms.

Weeks and months of suppressed and frustrated desire erupted in his kiss. This was no tentative exploration, but a fiery culmination, and yet only a beginning. His breath fused with hers as their tongues tangled and mated. Emboldened by her silent consent, he allowed his hands their first access to the generous bounty of her breasts. As the firm, swelling curves filled his hands for the first time, a restless satisfaction surged through him. She felt every bit as good as he'd imagined during the long nights alone in the hired hand's room, but he was impatient with the layers of clothing that still separated them, flesh from flesh.

As he pressed kisses along the soft column of her

neck and nuzzled the tender skin beneath her ear, he pulled her hand away from its place around his neck and placed it boldly on the swelling at his groin. She started to jerk back, but he gripped her wrist and refused to allow her to pull away.

"No," he rasped. "Don't be afraid. Touch me, sweetheart. Feel what you do to me. This is because of you."

When her fingers tentatively explored the rock-solid contours of his body through the smooth wool fabric, he groaned. He couldn't stand much more, but he couldn't bear any less. He was breathing hard. Control became more and more difficult as he felt himself coming close to the edge.

"Lisa, honey, as much as I want this to go on forever, we've got to stop." He captured her hand and paused to catch his breath. "I swear I'm not going to make our first time like this, in the bushes, in the dark, with people all around."

She blinked at him, dazed.

He went on. "I want us to have the comfort and security of our own bed in our own home, where I can see every beautiful inch of you and we can take all the time we want. This is too important, and I've waited too long not to do it right."

Our own bed? Our own home? What had he said? He couldn't think straight—it must be all the blood rushing away from his brain. No matter. It sounded right, felt right.

Somehow, she must have understood. She nodded.

Still holding her hand, he rose and led her across the garden to the back terrace where the party was in full swing. His pulse pounded and his spirit soared.

She had said yes, to exactly what he wasn't sure. But she had at least acknowledged a desire as strong as his. He felt a powerful urge to make some gesture to announce to the world she was his, but he curbed the impulse. Neither of them was ready for that.

He made his way around the dancers and through the small clusters of guests engaged in lively conversation looking for Martha. When they reached her, she was pink from exertion and the heat.

She beamed at her daughter. "There you are, dear. It seems like hours since I've seen you. Are you enjoying yourself?"

Jared glanced at Lisa and saw the rosy flush rising in her cheeks all the way to the tips of her ears. He stepped forward and took her elbow. "Your party is a great success, Martha. Tomorrow you'll be the toast of the county."

"Why thank you, Jared. How gallant you are."

He smiled. "Right now, though, I think it's time for me to take your daughter and grandson home. It's getting pretty late."

"Unless, of course, you need me for anything else," Lisa added hastily.

Martha leaned forward to kiss her cheek. "Oh, no. You do look tired, dear. You go on home, and thank you for your help."

"But I didn't do anything."

"Nonsense. Now, do you need some help with that dress before you leave?"

Jared's impatience got the better of him, and he answered for her. "I promise to be very careful on the way home. The dress will be fine. We'll manage somehow once we get there."

He could have bitten his tongue when he saw the

embarrassment on Lisa's face. What had made him say such a thing to her mother, to imply he would help her undress?

However, Martha smiled and replied, "Fine. Have a safe trip home. We probably won't see you in church tomorrow, because I doubt Ben and I will be up before noon after we finally get rid of this crowd."

Lisa mumbled something in response and bolted up the stairs to the room where Andrew slept. Jared followed and closed the door behind them. She stood beside the bed, staring down at her son slumbering amid the pillows.

"I'm not sure I can do this," she whispered.

He crossed the room to stand behind her and enfolded her in his arms. "Don't give up on me now, sweetheart. Everything's going to work out. I need you...and you need me."

She turned in his arms. "Do you really think so?"

"I know so. I'll make it so. Trust me."

"I want to. You can't imagine how much."

Her heart was in her eyes with all her feelings laid bare, and it nearly overwhelmed him. He tightened his arms and captured her mouth with a ferocity that made her gasp. He relaxed his grip but not the intensity of his kiss. The responsibility of the gift she offered humbled him. He wanted to give her something in return, but he couldn't articulate his emotions in his mind. They were such a jumble of protectiveness, possessiveness, tenderness, and passion. He wanted her to feel all of them, so he tried to express them the only way he knew.

When he finally raised his head and looked into her face, her expression was dazed, but full of yearning. "Let's go home."

Chapter Twelve

The ride home seemed longer than ever to Lisa, although they made good time thanks to the bright, silvery light cast by the full moon. A tangle of thoughts and feelings tumbled through her head, leaving her tense and confused. She loved Jared — she was sure of that. But were they doing the right thing? She feared that when the storm of passion had passed she might be left with nothing but regrets.

The heat of the day had dissipated, and away from the crush of people, the cool night air chilled her damp skin. Instead of feeling refreshed, she hugged her arms across her chest and shivered.

He reached his right arm around her, pulled her across the bench, and snuggled her against his side. "Cold, sweetheart?"

"A little." She burrowed against him under his arm, seeking comfort and courage more than warmth.

He hugged her. "It's going to be all right. I promise. I'll take care of you. You've got to trust me."

She drew back and searched his face. "I know, and I do. But I'm scared."

He draped the reins across his lap, and Old Pete continued to plod the familiar road unguided. Jared turned to her and took her face in his hands, stroking her cheekbones with his thumbs. "Fear is the last thing I want you to feel. I'll never hurt you. This can be a new beginning for both of us, but you have to want it, too. I'd never force you."

She gave him a wobbly smile. "I know, but it's so important. It could change everything."

His expression remained serious, and his gaze seared her with passionate determination. "You're right. It is important. It might be the most important night of our lives."

Like a wedding night, she mused, but without the wedding. That sobering thought brought back memories of her wedding night with Dan. She remembered the things he had done and her reactions to them. She shuddered and pulled away.

Jared slid his hands down to her shoulders. "Lisa, please tell me why you're so frightened. Are you worried about what people would say if they knew? Or are you actually afraid of what we're about to do?"

She didn't look at him. "Yes," she whispered, "all of it."

He removed one hand from her shoulder, slid it beneath her chin, and lifted her head until she met his gaze. "As for other people, no one will know. This is just between the two of us. I don't know how things were between you and Dan, and I don't want to know. But I promise I'll make it good for you. I'll make you forget you've ever been with another man. It will be like the first time, only better."

His frank discussion of such an intimate subject embarrassed her, even though his words sent a thrill radiating from her core to every cell in her body. But she had to try to make him understand.

"It's not only that." Her voice all but disappeared. "I'm afraid I'll disappoint you."

"Oh, sweetheart," he groaned, gathering her to him in an all-encompassing embrace. "You won't disappoint me. You could never disappoint me."

She tried to gain confidence from the conviction in his voice.

He released her with a sprinkling of soft, restrained kisses across her brows, her cheekbones, and ending on the tip of her nose. He might have meant the kisses to be reassuring, but she found his light caresses even more arousing than the forceful ones. Her lips, which he had bypassed, hungered for the taste they'd been denied, and a tingling glow began to build in the most feminine parts of her body. It soon became an ache that caused her to shift position on the wagon seat and filled her with an absurd desire to snatch his hands and pull them to her needy breasts.

When she opened her eyes, he was smiling.

"We're home." His simple announcement brimmed with promise and anticipation. "I'll take care of the wagon and Old Pete and tend to the rest of the livestock. You take Andrew inside."

He climbed down and raised his arms. She allowed him to take her weight and once again marveled at the strength that lifted her so easily and slid her down against his big body to the ground. Jared held her briefly against him, his arms tightening around her, allowing her to feel the hard planes of his chest and thighs, as well as the full force of his arousal.

"You go on up," he whispered, even though there was no one to hear them except Andrew, who could sleep through an earthquake. "I'll join you in a few minutes." He handed her the basket with the sleeping baby and sent her on her way toward the house with a lingering caress on her bottom that started her tingling all over again.

She carried the baby into the darkened kitchen and set him on the table while she located a lamp. When she found one, the shaking of her hands made it difficult to light. She took a slow, deep breath, trying to calm her agitated nerves. She reminded herself she loved Jared, and he seemed to have feelings for her beyond mere lust. He'd promised everything would be all right and asked her to trust him.

She drew another ragged breath. She would do it. She would grab this chance for happiness, however fleeting, and make the most of it. Determined, she lifted Andrew from the basket, taking care not to wake him, picked up the lamp in her other hand, and carried them both upstairs to her bedroom.

By the time Jared came in from the barn, she had settled her sleeping son in his cradle and was standing motionless in the center of the room. She didn't know what to do next. Nothing in her experience had prepared her for this moment.

He had made it clear he intended their joining to go beyond the perfunctory basics, and she had only the vaguest idea what might be involved. When she allowed her mind to consider the possibilities, her pulse increased and an internal warmth flowed to her limbs as anxiety and curiosity battled for the upper hand. She was still lost in her imaginings when the bedroom door opened.

The sound and movement caught her attention, and she turned her head. There in the black chasm of the open doorway stood Jared, his damp, naked chest gilded by the light of the lamp he held. Tiny droplets of water glistened in the curling black hair that covered the thick muscle and tapered into the waistband of his trousers.

Some part of her mind realized he must have washed up outside before coming in, but she was incapable of conscious thought. She could only stare. She had seen him without a shirt many times, but not under these circumstances, not when she knew those arms would soon hold her against the heat and solidity of that chest. Soon she would be able to feel him, to smell him, and even, if she wished, to taste him. A rippling shudder of excitement passed through her at the thought.

He crossed the room, but she remained rooted in place. Her eyes never left him until he stopped inches in front of her. Then her lids fluttered down, unable to withstand the heat of his gaze. Strong arms closed around her, and her breathing quickened.

Her chin tipped up automatically, and her lips parted to receive his kiss. She felt as if she were floating, without a will of her own, content to give herself over completely into his hands. And those hands roamed up and down the length of her spine from shoulders to hips, soothing and arousing her flesh at the same time, while his lips worked persuasively on hers.

Eventually his lips relinquished her mouth and moved across her cheek to her ear. The combination of warm breath and sensuous nibbles had her gasping for breath and clutching his shoulders for support. Never in her life had she imagined such a devastating sensation. When she thought she could bear no more, he pressed one last kiss on the top of her hair and drew back.

"I never got to finish the dance."

She opened her eyes and tried to focus on his face. "What?" Her dazed brain struggled to follow his train of thought.

"At the party. We never finished our dance."

"You want to dance? Here? Now? But we don't have any music."

"We'll make our own. Come on."

He swept her into waltz position and began a slower and more intimate version of the dance than any she'd seen at the party. Instead of maintaining the customary distance, he tightened his hold until she pressed against him from shoulder to knee. Then he began to move around the room in smooth, sinuous steps, keeping perfect time to some internal orchestra. Soon, she could swear she heard the same music as she followed his movements. The muscles of his back stretched and bunched under her hand.

His hand slid from her lower back to her hips and held her firm against him. Abruptly, he brought them to a halt.

"It's a good thing I didn't really get a chance to dance with you at the party," he said with a shaky smile. "I might have embarrassed us both."

She flushed at his reference.

"I think it's time we got Andrew settled for the night," he continued.

She glanced at the baby asleep in his cradle at their feet. "But he is settled. He's sound asleep."

"Lisa, look at me," Jared commanded softly.

She obeyed and was mesmerized by the depth of the need she saw etched across his hard features.

"Just for tonight, I'd like to put him in the room across the hall. He'll never know the difference, and I want you all to myself. Tonight, I want you to forget everything but you and me, forget you're somebody's widow, or daughter, or mother for a few hours, and just be a woman—my woman. Can you do that?"

She swallowed. He was asking a lot. She had never put her own desires ahead of her obligations to others. "I'll try."

He kissed her. "That's all I ask." Then he leaned down and picked up the cradle. "You bring the lamp."

She led the way to the other bedroom. As she watched Jared set the cradle on the braided rag rug, her heart clenched. She felt as if she were abandoning her son. Andrew looked so tiny in the big, dark room. Then Jared's hand slid up and down her arm.

"He's going to be fine. You'll be right across the hall with the doors open. You'll hear any sound he makes."

"I know, but..."

She knew he was right. Andrew would be fine. But she hadn't slept apart from him since the day he was born, and it seemed so strange leaving him all alone in the dark.

"Do you want to bring him back in?"

She was touched by the concern in his voice. He could be overbearing at times, but at other times he showed a profound regard for her feelings. "No, you're right. I want this night to be for the two of us, too." She smiled with more confidence than she felt.

"Good." He bent and swept her up in his arms and carried her through the door. As they crossed the hall, he whispered in her ear, "Do you remember the first time I did this?"

"Carried me?"

"Yes."

She did, all too well. He had insisted on carrying her down the stairs on Christmas day, the day after Andrew's birth. Thinking back, she realized she had first become aware of him as a man that day, when he'd held her against his chest as he did now.

"I remember."

"I've never forgotten the way you felt in my arms."

"Neither have I."

When they reached the side of the bed, he set her on her feet, but kept her inside the circle of his arms. They stood watching each other and waiting. With each second, Lisa's anticipation rose.

Finally, a rueful smile crossed Jared's mouth and he spoke. "I've waited for this moment so long, I'm almost afraid to touch you."

His admission of uncertainty banished hers. "Don't be."

"Oh, God..." he groaned as he crushed her in his arms and plundered her soft, open mouth. His hands worked in a flurry of activity to divest them both of their clothing. Thick fingers struggled with tiny, feminine hooks and tapes until he nearly tore them in his hurry to see and touch every inch of her. Soon the beautiful fuchsia dress lay crumpled on the floor, forgotten.

When at last they stood naked before each other, he stepped back. She watched his heated gaze glide from the top of her disheveled knot of hair to the toes of her bare feet and waited. What would he think of her? Would he be disappointed?

Wordlessly, he reached up and removed the remaining pins from her hair, dropping them on the bedside table. Then he slid both hands into the thick mass and worked his fingers through its length until it lay in waves upon her shoulders.

"You're beautiful...the most beautiful woman I've ever seen."

The words were as soft as a flower petal floating on a breeze, but they set her heart free. She had never considered herself pretty, but under his adoring eyes, she felt beautiful. When he began to worship her with his hands as well, she closed her eyes and reveled in the sensations washing over her.

With her eyes closed, she felt his rough knuckles slide down the sensitive outer sides of her breasts. Up and down, ever so lightly. Then he turned his hands and brushed the full, heavy undersides. She bit her lip to keep from crying out when he brought his thumbs up to ply her nipples while he continued to caress the delicate skin under her breasts. Finally, for the first time, he allowed his hands complete access to the unfettered fullness and weight of her bare breasts. He squeezed, and she moaned, but not in pain. She leaned forward, pressing her breasts more fully into his palms, silently begging for more.

He groaned and squeezed a little harder. "You can't imagine how long I've waited for this, how much I wanted, needed, to feel you like this. You're perfect." He bent to capture her lips in a searing kiss.

When he dragged his lips away, she sagged against him. "Oh, Jared..." She didn't know what to say, how to tell him of the devastating joy he gave her.

He held her with one arm and flung back the

covers on the bed with the other. Then he lifted her and laid her on the mattress.

Her bare back and hips touched the smooth muslin sheets. Scanning his face as he leaned over her, she decided he was the most handsome man she could ever imagine. The golden light from the lamp cast shadows that accentuated the planes of his face and the contours of the muscles in his arms, shoulders, and chest. The hair on his chest and arms served to camouflage and soften the hard surfaces beneath. The effect intrigued her as she stared at him, and she reached out to touch the skin it shielded from her gaze.

He lay down beside her. It was too hot for sheets or quilts, but he rolled toward her and threw one leg over hers so she could feel him rubbing against the side of her hip but couldn't see him.

"Relax. I promise I won't hurt you, sweetheart." He placed nibbling kisses down the side of her neck.

She couldn't form a coherent thought with her skin tingling and prickling from his caresses. When he moved lower, she almost screamed in frustration.

His eyes glowed in the soft lamplight. "I've always envied Andrew. You taste better than your mother's Sunday peach pie."

She turned her head away.

He stroked her cheek, guiding her to face him again. "Don't be embarrassed. I love him like my own."

She stared into the dark depths of his eyes, searching for the truth.

He stared back as if willing her to see into his heart. When he continued, his voice dropped to a rough whisper. "I've imagined he's my son, you're mine, and we'll make another baby together. I'll watch it grow inside you and be there to bring it into the world, just like I was with Andrew."

His words were so close to the secret longings of her own heart tears started in her eyes. "Oh, Jared, I love you so much!" she cried without thinking. She flung her arms around his neck and pulled his mouth down to hers.

He kissed her with a new intensity, as if his very life depended on it. It was as if her admission of love had ignited the explosion of his desire and he had no wish to contain the flames. When he joined their bodies, Lisa's tender tissues seemed determined to reject his invasion. She couldn't suppress an involuntary flinch at the sharp shaft of pain.

Jared halted. "I'm hurting you."

"No, not exactly." What was the matter with her? She wanted so badly to please him. In her anxiety, she tensed even more.

"Relax," he murmured.

She gave him a feeble smile, which was the best she could do. This was not going well. And she had been so hopeful that being in love would make lovemaking perfect.

He leaned down and pressed soft kisses across her cheekbones and mouth. "Don't worry, just relax."

He continued to kiss her, murmuring soothing words between kisses. "Is that better?"

She didn't answer. Her lips parted, and her breathing came fast and even. A small sound escaped her, and he picked up the pace. Soon all thoughts of restraint fled as she joined the sensual battle for fulfillment.

"Come on, sweetheart. You're almost there." He sounded near pain.

What did he mean, almost there? Almost where? Suddenly, strange nerve endings she had never felt before shimmered all through her. "Oh, oh, oh...!" The universe turned upside down and inside out.

Jared gave a hoarse shout then collapsed, his breathing hot and ragged in her ear. When he had recovered somewhat, he eased himself from her and rolled to his side, taking her with him. He held her in the crook of his arm with her head nestled against his shoulder. She stared at the pounding pulse in his neck as it slowed, in time with her own.

After a few minutes, he nuzzled his nose in her hair and gave her a small squeeze. "How do you feel?"

She stirred. "Tired. Wonderful." She paused. "I had no idea."

He smiled. "I told you it would be a whole new experience."

"You were right."

"When you've had some rest and a chance to recuperate, I know several more delightful variations I can show you."

She gave him a lazy smile. "I don't know where I'd find the energy."

He slid his free hand up her thigh, over the curve of her hip, and down into the valley of her waist. "Don't worry. It doesn't have to be tonight. There's always tomorrow...and the day after..."

She wriggled away from him and sat up. "Tonight was very special, but you can't mean for this to continue."

His eyes narrowed, then eased. "Come here. Try to get some sleep, and we'll talk about it in the morning."

She struggled a little. "You can't sleep in here with me."

"Why not?"

"Well...it isn't decent."

"It's no less decent than what we just did, and that was good and right. If you're honest with yourself, you'll admit it." He pushed her head back down on his shoulder. "Now we're both tired, so relax and go to sleep. We'll sort this out in the morning, together."

She tried to think up arguments, but her mind was too fuzzy. Her body was sated and relaxed from the intensity of his lovemaking, and she was too comfortable in his arms to concentrate. He was right. They would have to sort it out tomorrow.

Chapter Thirteen

Sunlight streamed through the windows when Andrew's angry squall awakened Lisa from a deep sleep. She dragged herself upright and struggled to open her eyes. Her head felt fuzzy, and everything seemed out of place. The baby's cries sounded so far away. She was on the wrong side of the bed and seemed to be missing her nightdress. As she grabbed the sheet to cover herself, she blinked several times and noticed the large form of a man sprawled beside her.

Memories of the night came flooding back—the overwhelming pleasure as well as the gravity of what she had done.

Andrew's cries pierced her consciousness again, jerking her into the present. As she struggled to climb over Jared and get out of bed, he rolled over and yawned.

"Good morning." His husky early morning voice served as a potent reminder of the intimacy they had shared.

He reached out and captured her wrist. "How about a good morning kiss?" His bristly face still wore its satisfied smile from the night before.

"The baby's crying." She pulled herself free and scurried to the wardrobe to grab her wrapper. This morning she needed to cover herself against his probing eyes. She needed the protection while she worked to make sense of her feelings.

Jared frowned and climbed out of bed, reaching for his pants. "I hear him, but it's not the first time and it won't be the last. He'll be all right. He's just hungry." He followed her across the hall.

She bent and picked up the angry baby from his cradle. "Shh, precious, don't cry now. Mama's here."

Andrew quieted. Then he turned his head toward Jared and flashed him a big grin.

Jared reached a finger toward the boy, who promptly grabbed it. "See, I told you. He's fine."

"He was frightened in here all alone. He should have been with me."

"All right. We'll move him back tonight." His voice was still agreeable as he followed her back to her bedroom.

Lisa laid Andrew on the padded top of a small chest and began to change his soggy clothing. "You sound as if you expect to be in here again tonight."

Jared walked up behind her, placed a big, warm hand on the base of her spine, and began to rub in small circles. "Don't you want me here?" The seductive tone of his voice invited her to abandon everything and lose herself in the pleasures of loving him all over again.

"I think it would be best if you returned to your

own room." Her voice was sharp and tight from the effort to fight back her body's response to his touch.

His hand stilled. "Last night you said you loved me. Did you mean it?"

She lifted Andrew and carried him to the rocker without answering. As she opened her wrapper to bare her breast, she refused to raise her eyes to Jared, who had moved to stand in front of her.

"I asked you if you meant it." The tender understanding in his voice had given way to the gritty sound of rising temper.

She remained silent.

"Damn it, Lisa!"

She couldn't hold out against the pain mingled with his anger. She glanced up at him. "Yes. I meant it."

His frustration simmered in the air between them. "I know last night was good for you, and if you love me, how can you think of us not being together?"

"Because last night was wrong—wonderful but wrong. It was wrong for both of us. I will always cherish the memories, but it can't happen again."

"Your love must be pretty weak if you can turn it off just like that."

She gave a bitter laugh. "Oh, I can't turn it off. I love you, and it's probably my curse that I always will."

"Then what are you talking about?"

"I will not become involved in the kind of relationship you're suggesting. I can't, and won't, not without a commitment neither of us is prepared to make."

He narrowed his eyes. "What if I said I was ready?"

"I wouldn't believe you. If you're going to try to convince me you're suddenly in love with me because of what happened last night, you can save your breath. I don't have much experience with love, but I know there should be more to it than that."

He studied her for a moment. "All right. So, you won't believe me. But what about you? You say you love me, but you don't want any kind of future with me?"

She considered his question. Try as she might, she could no longer convince herself she was just being sensible, that she wanted nothing more than a quiet life with her son. She wanted Jared. She wanted to see him, talk to him, touch him every day. What was holding her back? Why couldn't she say she wanted to be with him forever?

As her mind formed the words, cold prickles ran up her spine to her scalp, and her stomach clenched. Forever. What could forever mean to a man like Jared, especially a man in his line of work? Until he moved to the next town? Until someone else was quicker on the draw? Her stomach rebelled. She couldn't do it.

"I don't want to talk about it. I will understand if you feel you can no longer stay here under the circumstances."

He turned away and began pacing the room. Then he stopped and turned. "No! Damn it! I won't do it. I refuse to give up. You're in for a surprise if you think you can relegate last night to *a wonderful memory*." His gaze burned her with its heat. "Every time you look at me you're going to remember my lips on yours and my mouth on your breasts. You're going to remember the feeling of me inside you. And you're going to want more. I'm going to stay right here and remind you."

Her body responded as if he had actually touched her, even as her eyes widened in alarm. "But you promised you'd never force me to do anything I don't want to do."

"I won't. I won't have to. You'll come to me. And I'm going to be here when you do." He turned and left the room.

All day, Lisa skirted Jared warily. His anger didn't dissipate. He reminded her of a cannon with a lit fuse of unknown length, as if he could explode without warning at any moment. The fact he didn't only made the anticipation worse.

Supper was strained, the silence broken only by Andrew's occasional babbles. Even the baby seemed tense, as though confused by the behavior of his favorite adults. He kept looking from one to the other with his head cocked and his little brows furrowed.

After she washed the dishes, Lisa carried the baby to the parlor where Jared was reading by the window. The summer sun was still high enough to make lamps unnecessary. "We'll go up now." She refused to look directly at him. "I'm feeling quite tired."

"That's what comes of missing so much sleep last night. Too bad you didn't think it was worth it."

It was his first reference since early that morning to what had happened the night before. She hoped it wasn't the start of the confrontation she'd been dreading all day. Without a word, she hurried from the room.

She was changing Andrew for the night when the bedroom door opened and Jared walked in. She looked up and frowned. "What are you doing here?"

"I came to say goodnight."

Her lips thinned. "All right. Goodnight. Now

please leave."

He relaxed and leaned against the footboard of the bed. "No. I want to say goodnight properly."

Her anger started to rise, along with a tiny thread of fear. Her body grew taut in defense. "I told you there will be no repeat of last night, and I'll fight you with my last breath if you try to force me."

He straightened, no longer relaxed. "Damn it, Lisa. I can't believe you'd suggest such a thing. You said you loved me. Give me credit for a little self-control. I would never force you, never. But that doesn't mean I'm going to let you ignore me, either. Now put that baby to bed so we can settle some things."

She finished dressing Andrew and sat down in the rocker to give him his last feeding while Jared watched. The excitement and late hours of the party the night before had taken their toll on Andrew, too. He fell asleep as soon as his stomach was full. She held him in the crook of her right arm while she tried to re-fasten her dress with her left hand.

"Here, let me have him." Jared reached for the sleeping infant.

She allowed him to take the boy from her arms and watched the big man carry the little bundle to his cradle.

Jared stopped in front of the cradle. He bent his head and pressed his lips to Andrew's downy black hair in a feather-light kiss. "Goodnight, son." His words were as soft as the night air as he placed the baby in bed.

Although his voice was barely a whisper, Lisa heard him clearly. Bittersweet emotion welled up inside her. Jared had never spoken of love to her, but his love for her son was obvious. Was that the reason he wanted to stay with them? He was so good for Andrew she was almost tempted to agree on that basis alone. But deep inside she rebelled against the idea of living with a man who didn't love her for herself, even one she loved as much as she loved Jared.

Then he was in front of her, reaching toward her with one outstretched hand. "Stand up." It was more of a request than an order, and his hand beckoned rather than commanded. She allowed him to draw her to her feet.

He stared into her eyes. "Relax. I'm only going to kiss you." His mouth came down to within a breath of hers. "You've said you don't want me in your bed, and I can live with that as long as you can, but I can't live without this. Please don't make me." He lowered his head a fraction until their mouths came together.

Her lips were parted and ready to receive his. If she had to deny herself the full expression of her love, she could at least have this. The fire that had consumed her the night before flared again as his tongue slid in and around hers, touching in turn the sensitive roof of her mouth and the sharp edges of her teeth. Without thinking, she wound her arms around his back and splayed her hands against the hard bulges of muscle beneath his shirt.

He gripped the back of her head with one hand, holding her in place, while the other glided down the length of her spine to cup the fullness of her hips. With his fingers so close to the source of her heat, her response grew until she throbbed with excitement. She knew she would never be able to hold out against this passionate onslaught. She had been a fool to even think it.

Then he drew back. He was breathing heavily and

his nostrils flared. The pupils of his eyes were fathomless pits.

"I always keep my word. Never forget that. Goodnight, Lisa." He released her and strode toward the door.

She stood shaking, staring at his back, and wondering how she would ever survive this torture she couldn't seem to live without.

****

Her tension level continued to rise all week. Even Jared's three-day absence on a stage run did nothing to relieve it. On the nights he was home, he followed the pattern he'd established Sunday. He accompanied her upstairs to put Andrew to bed and then kissed her senseless before departing for his own room.

She was losing her mind. If his superhuman control didn't shatter soon, hers surely would. Every night he worked his sensual magic to bring her to the brink. Then he stepped back and waited in silence for her decision. When she didn't speak he left, leaving her alone to toss and turn all night and question every moral precept she had ever embraced.

A small ember of anger and resentment for what seemed calculated and callous treatment began to glow in her belly. After a week of sleepless nights, it flared into fury. Saturday night, when he reached for her, she rebelled.

She slapped his hands away. "No, I will not let you do this to me again. I will not let you use my feelings for you to manipulate me this way."

A small muscle in his jaw flexed as he clenched his teeth. "You never objected before. In fact, you've been damned eager."

The shame of knowing what he said was true did

nothing to diminish her anger. "You're tearing me apart, and you're doing it on purpose."

"I am not. I'm trying to show you how stupid and stubborn you're being, denying us both something we want so badly."

Their raised voices disturbed Andrew, who whimpered in his sleep.

Lisa lowered her voice. "Well, I don't want it. I don't want to feel this way. It makes me miserable. If you have any feelings for me at all, you will leave me alone."

Jared's voice lost some of its edge. "I can't leave you alone, and I wouldn't even if I could. What we have together is so much better than what we have apart. I won't give up until you accept it."

She reached for his hands. "You've got to stop doing this to me. If I give in to you only because I can't stand any more of this torture, it will kill something inside me." She closed her eyes against the pain, and when she opened them a tear rolled down each cheek.

He swore a crude oath, but his arms were infinitely gentle as he gathered her into their shelter. "Shh, sweetheart, don't cry. I never meant to hurt you. That's the last thing I want. And I don't want you to *give in* to me, either. I want you to come to me freely because you love me and you're ready to accept what I can give you."

He held her close while the old school clock on the mantel ticked the seconds off.

"I guess I chose the wrong method of persuasion, but I just want you so much." His arms tightened around her, and then loosened as he leaned back far enough to see her face. He tried a small smile. "If it's any consolation, this past week hasn't been any easier for me than it has been for you. If I promise not to kiss you the way I want to again until you let me know you're ready, could I have one last kiss tonight?"

She searched his face. Lines of fatigue and tension framed his eyes, and shadows darkened the skin beneath them. He was telling the truth. The stress of the week had taken its toll on him, too. His eyes were asking for forgiveness, and for a sign that he had not irreparably damaged the love she claimed to feel for him.

She brushed aside an ugly little urge to take revenge by denying him. Her love was too strong to allow revenge any place in her heart. She nodded. When he didn't claim the privilege she had granted, she understood. He was waiting for her. She reached up and pulled his head down until their lips met.

Tenderly, their lips joined and released, then joined again, to follow the same pattern over and over. He had given her the power, but she was neither the aggressor nor the seducer. In this union she was both the supplicant and the celebrant.

Finally, he cupped her face between his hands, and placing one last exquisite kiss on her forehead, drew back. "Thank you." His voice wavered. "You have my promise I won't touch you again until you ask me."

Inside, she rebelled at the knowledge of her impending loss, but she stepped back and nodded. "Thank you. Goodnight."

"Goodnight." He brushed a long, rough finger down the satiny curve of her cheek. Then he was gone.

She stared at the closed door for a long time, wondering why she felt like someone close to her had just died.

In the morning, she was up early, preparing to go to church. Contrary to what she had expected, she was looking forward to it. She no longer felt guilty for the night of lovemaking she'd shared with Jared, but she recognized her weakness where he was concerned and needed to be reminded she was doing the right thing. Besides, the annual church picnic was being held after the service, and it would be a welcome distraction from the intensity of the past week.

She was shocked when she walked into the kitchen carrying Andrew and found Jared sitting at the table dressed in a suit. Except for the night of the Holladay's party, she had never seen him in anything except his customary work clothes. She frowned. "Where are you going?"

"To church with you." He said it as if it were the most natural thing in the world.

"But why? You've never come to services with us before."

"I think it's time I started. You don't have any objections, do you?" His smile dared her to protest.

"Of course not. I'm just surprised."

"When you recover, you can fix me some breakfast. I'm starved. Here, give me the baby."

Lisa handed Andrew into Jared's waiting hands and went to work slicing bacon and cornmeal mush for the frying pan. While she worked, she pondered his astonishing announcement. It seemed unlikely he had been visited by a sudden religious conversion, so he must have some other motive. Perhaps this was a strange new tactic in his campaign to wear down her resistance.

It took an extra hour to prepare and pack the chicken, rolls, and slaw for their lunch, and the dried apple pie to share, but finally everything was ready. Jared carried the basket to the wagon, then helped Lisa and Andrew climb aboard.

It was a beautiful, sunny morning and already quite hot when they set out for town. His cheerful whistling grated on her ears like a dirge. It was so unnatural—he never whistled. She became increasingly convinced something was afoot.

When they reached the small, white clapboard church, he unhitched Old Pete and tethered him in the patchy shade of the lone locust tree in the front churchyard. Then he carried the basket around to the table that had been set up along the north side of the building. Finally, he returned to the wagon for Lisa and Andrew. He insisted on carrying the baby, who chirped with delight, and kept a firm grip on Lisa's elbow as Jared escorted her across the dusty, trampled grass and up the steps of the church.

He smiled and nodded to everyone as he marched her up the main aisle until they reached the second pew, where Martha and Ben were seated. Lisa answered her mother's look of surprise with a lame smile as she slid into place next to her and reached over to take Andrew from Jared. She hadn't missed the speculative glances darting their way from many members of the congregation, particularly the women. Jared was making a spectacle of them both.

Perhaps that was his intent. He had draped his arm across the back of the pew behind her shoulders and was resting one booted ankle across the opposite knee. He looked like a prosperous farmer proudly showing off his wife and child. What a fraud.

She stewed for a while, but when the preacher began his sermon, he captured her full attention. She hoped it was mere coincidence he had chosen to preach about the evils of casting the first stone. Despite the message of forgiveness and charity toward the fallen woman, Lisa felt as if she were standing in front of the congregation with a large red *A* emblazoned across her chest, like the unhappy heroine of Mr. Hawthorne's novel.

By the time the service was over, all she wanted to do was escape. She had no stomach for the food she had packed that morning. When the benediction was over and everyone rustled around preparing to head outside for the picnic, she leaned over and tugged on Jared's sleeve. "Let's go home."

He turned and smiled, knowingly and without humor. "Now why would we do that? Our dinner is out back, and your mother told me she brought her famous peach pie. Besides, I'm looking forward to spending the afternoon socializing with the neighbors."

Her eyes narrowed. "What do you think you're doing?"

"I'm bringing you and Andrew to church. What's wrong with that?"

"You're enjoying this, aren't you?"

"You bet I am."

"But you know what everyone's saying about us."

He stopped in the middle of the aisle, blocking the flow of people toward the rear door. "No, what are they saying? You tell me."

"Jared, you're making a scene." Genuine distress ripped through her hoarse whisper.

He took pity on her and began to move again, but he held her elbow and leaned down until his lips touched her ear. "Calm down. Pretty soon their interest will pass. They just need time to get used to the idea of seeing us together."

"I'm not used to the idea."

His expression sobered. "Well, get used to it. I made some promises to you, and I intend to keep them. But I never promised not to be seen in public with you."

She struggled to control her fluttering nerves as she smiled at the preacher's wife, who was greeting people by the door.

When they stepped into the brilliant sunlight and stifling heat of the churchyard, Jared drew her aside. "I'll be beside you all the way to make things as easy as I can, but I won't let you try to ignore what's between us or keep it under a barrel forever. We've come too far to go back now, and one of these days you're going to recognize that. Now let's go join your mother and Ben."

Lisa's mind balked at his declaration that there was no turning back, that they had already passed the point of no return. He might have passed some milestone in his own mind, but she was nowhere near one herself.

Families and friends settled in groups in the shade of the oak and walnut trees that surrounded the clearing around the church. Baskets were unpacked, and conversation hummed as neighbors enjoyed the opportunity to socialize. The long table groaned with the spread of luscious cakes, dried fruit and molasses pies, bread puddings, and other specialties of the ladies of the church. Every year there was an informal, but very serious, competition to see whose creation would be the most popular. Martha's peach pie was always one of the first to go.

After everyone had eaten all they could hold, the men drifted off to pitch horseshoes and talk crops and politics and left the ladies to visit in the shade while the older children played and the babies napped. Lisa had left Andrew asleep with her mother and was at the table packing the empty pie tins when she heard her name.

"Why, Lisa McAllister, there you are."

Lisa shuddered. She was almost afraid to turn around. What was Eliza Worthington doing here? Her father was the Methodist minister. Why couldn't she content herself with tormenting his flock? She steeled herself and smiled. "Good afternoon, Eliza. How are you?"

"I'm just fine, thank you. But I've been so worried about you." Eliza's voice dripped with false solicitude.

"I assure you, there's no cause for worry."

Eliza fluttered her lashes and widened her eyes. "Why last Saturday night, you left the Holladay's party so early. Mr. Tanner practically dragged you out of the house. I was afraid you might be ill."

"I was tired, and I needed to get the baby home."

Eliza ignored Lisa's reply and gushed on. "And here I was afraid you might be getting lonely out there on the farm." She cast her gaze across the lawn to where Jared was pitching horseshoes with the other men. "But now that I think about it, I don't suppose that's a problem for you." Her voice had taken on a silky, feline purr.

Lisa gritted her teeth. But just as she was about to speak, another voice interrupted.

"Eliza Worthington, it's a wonder you don't trip over your own nose, it's so long from poking into other people's business."

Lisa turned in surprise to face an indignant Jessamine Randall. Her face relaxed into a smile. Jessy was like a fierce little terrier when called upon to defend a friend from attack.

Eliza, however, didn't smile. Her plain, pointed face twisted into a mask of spite. "You're a fine one to talk, Jessy Randall," she spat. "You with your school for filthy little urchins."

Jessy's green eyes narrowed in fury, and she raised a white-gloved hand. "Get out of here this minute before I slap your face and tell your daddy all about what a fine *Christian* daughter he has."

Eliza backed down like a snarling alley cur who was all bark and no bite and scuttled off to find her father.

Then Jessy turned to Lisa. She grabbed her arm and dragged her over to a shady spot away from the others.

"Sit down," she ordered. Lisa sank to the grass. "Now, you mustn't pay any attention to Eliza. You know what a cowardly bully she is."

"But, Jessy, her meaning was very clear. Suppose everyone in town is thinking the same thing?"

"Well, they're not. Very few people are as small-minded as Eliza. Besides, everyone wants you to be happy, and you and Jared make a handsome couple. He seems to be fitting into the community very well."

Lisa glanced across the field. Jared had removed his black coat and string tie and rolled up the sleeves of his white shirt like the other men. His striking dark looks and formidable height and breadth caused him to stand apart in her eyes, but no one else seemed to notice. He was laughing and talking and appeared to be perfectly relaxed in the group. "He does, doesn't he?"

"Lisa, what is going on between the two of you? I don't mean to pry, and you know I'd never tell a soul, but I'm worried about you. You look miserable."

Lisa dragged her gaze away from Jared and focused on Jessy. Genuine concern radiated from her friend's serious countenance. She took a deep breath. She had told Jessy about Clay—did she dare tell her about Jared? It would be such a relief to share at least a small part of her burden of silence. Finally, she broke down and admitted, "I *am* miserable."

"Is it Jared?"

"Yes, partly...mainly. I love him."

Jessy smiled. "I thought so. So why aren't you happy?"

"I love him, but I don't want to. It's hard to put into words. He stirs me up. Does that make any sense?"

Jessy nodded.

Lisa continued, following her train of thought. "He's such a contradiction. He's a strong man with a violent job, but sometimes he can be unbearably gentle. He aggravates me beyond words, but he's wonderful with Andrew. He's overprotective and keeps most of his feelings hidden, but sometimes I just want to melt into his strength." She shook her head. "You must think I'm crazy. I think I'm crazy."

"I don't think you're crazy. I think you're a woman in love."

"He makes me feel safe, but I want to feel strong. I don't ever want to lose someone I love again. I don't think I could stand it."

"What makes you think you would lose him?"

"One way or another, I'd lose him. He's going to

leave town whenever the company decides they need him somewhere else, if some outlaw doesn't shoot him first. I can't even bear to think about it." She closed her eyes and rubbed her temples. Suddenly, a new thought whispered in her brain and she glanced at Jessy. "You know, I'm not proud to admit it, but I think I might be afraid to love him."

"Afraid? Why? Because of Dan?"

"And Papa, and Seth. It hurts so bad. You can't imagine if you've never lost somebody like that."

"I'm so sorry. And you're right—I don't really know what it feels like. But I do have some idea what it feels like to be in love. Don't you think it might be worth the risk? Does Jared love you?"

"I don't know. He hasn't said so."

Jessy frowned. "Well, he must have some feelings for you. He appears to be devoted, and I'm sure you wouldn't have gotten yourself into this situation all on your own. You're far too sensible to fall in love with a man who doesn't return your feelings."

Lisa shook her head with a rueful smile. "Believe me, sense has nothing to do with this."

"So, what are you going to do about it?"

"I don't know."

"Well, you'd better decide before you have two babies on your hands." Lisa's eyes widened in shock, but Jessy continued, "Jared doesn't look like the kind of man to be put off very long."

Lisa blushed. "He's not. But what would you know about a thing like that?"

Jessy lifted her chin. "I'm not as innocent as you think."

"Jessy, what do you...you aren't still seeing Morgan Bingham, are you?"

"Yes," Jessy answered, proud and defiant.

"You haven't...?"

"No." Jessy looked disgusted and disappointed. "But only because he won't. He's too honorable to make love to me before marriage, and since he's convinced we can never be married, he won't do it. I've tried to tell him it's not important, that I don't want to get married, but he won't listen."

"It sounds like he cares for you more than you know."

"I only know I love him. I just wish he weren't so stubborn." Jessy's expression lifted and she shrugged. "Oh, well. Maybe it will work out in time. I'm trying to wear down his resistance. Besides we have other things to worry about now."

Lisa was trying hard not to judge her friend, but she found Jessy's ideas about love so startling and alien she could hardly comprehend them. "What else do you have to worry about?" she asked, half afraid to hear the answer.

Jessy's expression sobered. "Do you remember Eliza's nasty remark about filthy urchins?"

"Of course."

"Well, she isn't the only one in town who feels that way. I've been receiving threatening letters from some group calling itself the Masked Riders, and someone has been painting the letters "MR" on the walls of the school building. So far, I've washed them off and tried to ignore the whole thing, but it's getting harder. I'm starting to worry about the safety of the children."

Lisa frowned. "This sounds dangerous."

Jessy nodded. "That's what Morgan says. He's trying to find out more about the group without attracting attention. I don't want him in any danger on my account."

"Have you told your father about this? He is a judge, and I'm sure he could arrange some kind of protection for you."

"You know how my father is. If he knew anyone had threatened his precious baby, he'd lock me in my room from now until doomsday."

"You're probably right." Judge Randall had always indulged Jessy's whims, but he had also sent her back East for safety at the first sign of trouble in the county when the war started. "Have you considered closing the school, at least temporarily?"

Jessy bristled. "Certainly not. I refuse to be intimidated by a bunch of renegades who don't have the courage to speak their ugly views in public."

"Will you at least let me talk to Jared about it? After all, protection is his job."

"Only if he promises not to say anything to the sheriff. He'd only tell my father, and besides, for all I know, he may be a part of it."

Lisa didn't like the idea that some of her neighbors—people she had known since childhood—were capable of threatening, or maybe even harming, innocent children or a lovely, spirited young woman like Jessy. "I know Jared will be able to do something," she said with conviction. "And I promise he won't tell the sheriff."

Jessy hesitated then nodded. "All right. Go ahead and tell him, but remember, he has to be discreet."

"Don't worry. Jared can be very closed-mouthed if he has a mind to." Lisa glanced back at the men playing horseshoes. Jared had broken away from the group and was heading her way. "Here he comes. Smile sweetly, and I'll tell him later.

Chapter Fourteen

As Jared approached, Lisa couldn't help noticing the way his white shirt clung damply to his chest and arms and his hair glistened with perspiration. She couldn't remember ever having found a sweaty man appealing before, but the sight of him set her pulse humming. When he stood beside her, she could swear she felt the heat radiating from his body. And she could smell him—a clean, hot, male smell. It was heady and unnerving.

"Good afternoon, ladies." He bowed.

"Good afternoon, Mr. Tanner," Jessy replied. "It's a warm day, isn't it?"

Lisa watched her friend's gaze slide over Jared's body, taking in every detail, and felt a surge of unreasonable jealousy. "It certainly is," she agreed, before he had a chance to respond. "Jared, I think we ought to take Andrew home now, out of this heat."

"I came to ask if you were ready to leave."

She handed him the picnic basket filled with dirty dishes. "If you'll take these to the wagon, I'll go see if I can pry Andrew loose from Mama."

"Of course." Jared took the basket. "It was a pleasure to see you again, Miss Randall."

As he sauntered off, Jessy's gaze followed every step.

Lisa pressed her lips together in a tight line. "You can stop drooling. Not five minutes ago, you told me you were in love with someone else."

Jessy turned and laughed. "I am, but that doesn't mean I've been struck blind. I wonder if you appreciate what you've got."

"I haven't *got* anything."

Jessy changed the subject. "If you think Jared might be able to help with my problem, go ahead and talk to him. I'll drive over Tuesday morning to find out what he has to say."

"Don't you have class?"

"No. Only in the afternoons. Most of the children have too many chores to be able to come to school in the morning."

"I'll see you Tuesday then, and be careful. I worry about you." Lisa gave Jessy a quick hug and went to retrieve her son.

After Jared helped her into the wagon, she waited until they were out of earshot of the churchyard before speaking. "Jared, I have to talk to you. I'm worried."

He maintained his easy posture, but his gaze darted over to her. "What about?" His voice remained casual.

"Well, practically everything, if you want to know the truth. But there's one thing in particular I want to discuss with you."

"What's that?"

"It's about Jessy."

"I think your friend enjoys shocking people. What's she up to now?"

Lisa frowned. "This is serious."

"I'm listening."

"Have you ever heard of a group called the Masked Riders?"

He paused to consider. "I think I may have heard it mentioned, but I can't recall any details. It's some kind of new secret society, isn't it?"

"I don't know anything about it, but Jessy has been receiving threatening letters from them, and her school has been vandalized. She's worried about her students' safety, and I'm worried about her."

He pursed his lips. "I knew her school wasn't too popular with some folks in town, but I didn't know things had gone that far."

Lisa leaned over and placed her hand on the warm flesh of his arm below the rolled-up sleeve. "Can you help her, please?"

"I'll ask around and see what I can find out."

Some of her worries eased. "But you have to be very discreet. I promised Jessy you would. She hasn't told anyone else about this except Morgan Bingham."

"Is she still seeing that lowlife?" Jared scowled.

She wasn't sure why she felt called upon to defend Morgan, but she did. "It isn't necessary to call the man names. Jessy has been teaching him to read. She claims he treats her with great respect and consideration." She didn't mention that her friend also thought she was in love with the outlaw.

His frown remained in place. "Then she isn't as smart as she looks. You can always judge a man by the company he keeps."

Lisa chewed her lip. "I'm not sure he's keeping the same company he used to. If he's been spending as much time with Jessy as she indicated, I don't see how he could still be riding with Clay and the James boys."

"Maybe not, but she still ought to be very careful around him."

"People can change."

"Sometimes, but not often." Jared tilted his head and studied her. "Are you hoping Clay will change?"

Her lips tightened. "For his own sake, yes."

"But not for yours?"

She turned away. "I hope I never see him again."

"Good."

She heard the hard satisfaction in his voice. She could almost believe he was jealous, but that would be ridiculous. More likely, it was just his usual over-protectiveness. But back to the matter at hand. "Now about Jessy's problem—"

"I said I'd ask around, very discreetly, and see what I can come up with. I'll also talk to Bingham. If he's as devoted to Jessy as she claims, he's probably concerned, too. Maybe he's heard something."

"But wouldn't he have told her?"

"Not necessarily."

"Why not? Surely he'd realize how important this is to her?"

"Sometimes a man shields his woman from things he thinks will frighten or upset her." Jared's answer was matter-of-fact.

Lisa drew back. "That's outrageous. Jessy is an adult and deserves to know the truth."

He held up his hand against her indignation. "Hold on. I didn't say he was keeping anything from her. He may not know anything at all."

But she refused to be mollified. "I want your promise that if you learn anything you will tell me the whole truth, without holding anything back. Is that a promise?"

He eyed her speculatively. "I'll tell you what I find out if you'll promise not to go running to Jessy with it until we decide what needs to be done, if anything. She's foolhardy enough to rush into a situation without considering the consequences, and she might get herself hurt."

Lisa didn't want to be disloyal to Jessy, but he had a point. Jessy could be hotheaded if she got stirred up. In the end, her concern for Jessy's safety won out. "I promise."

"Good. Now, was that all you wanted to talk about?"

The sudden heat in his glance belied his casual words and suggested he was thinking of something more personal than Jessy Randall's problems. Lisa guessed he was referring to his promise the night before, and she knew she didn't want to talk about that. "Yes."

He shrugged. "All right. You know where to find me when you're ready. Just don't wait too long."

Neither of them spoke again the rest of the way home, leaving Lisa to ponder what he meant by his comment. Was he suggesting if she put him off long enough, his ardor would cool? Or was he threatening to go back on his word and try to force her to accept a physical relationship? She didn't want to contemplate either possibility.

The next evening, after saying goodnight to Jared in the parlor and settling Andrew in his cradle, she sat in front of the open window in her room brushing her hair in long, even strokes and watching the purple twilight steal over the tobacco fields across the road. It was such a peaceful time, that gentle bridge between day and night, when the daytime sounds had stilled, and the night sounds were just beginning. She could almost convince herself her mother was across the hall preparing for bed and she had only imagined the problems that plagued her.

Gradually, her ears picked up the ringing sounds of a horse's hooves striking rocks. She rose and walked closer to the window. It was almost dark, but she could discern the outline of a horse and rider walking toward the main road. There was no mistaking the form astride the horse. From the size and the posture, she knew it was Jared.

Man and horse picked their way as if trying to make as little noise as possible. For a moment, she thought about shouting out the window and demanding an explanation. But before she could bring herself to shatter the silence, the horse and rider moved out of calling distance.

She leaned back from the window and tried to bring to mind all the possible explanations for Jared's nighttime departure. She was certain he wasn't leaving on a job. He would never go off for a day or more without telling her. Since he plainly didn't want her to know what he was doing, he must be planning to return before morning.

So where could he be going? To meet someone, perhaps?

For a split second, the idea that he might be heading for a rendezvous with another woman flashed through her mind. After all, she had told him to find someone else.

No, her heart insisted. He had sworn he wanted her and was prepared to wait until he got what he wanted. But she had no idea how long a man like Jared would wait for a woman.

If it wasn't another woman, what could he be doing? An image of Jessy popped into her head. Lisa had asked Jared to do something about Jessy's problem. He might be trying to find out something about the group threatening her. That could be dangerous. If the men involved were intent on keeping their membership and activities secret, they might resort to violence to maintain their anonymity.

She bit her lip wondering what she had gotten him into and wished with all her heart she had never mentioned the situation. She couldn't bear it if he were hurt on her account. Besides, then what would happen to Jessy? Jessy was too brave and proud to ask anyone for help, and she might truly be in danger. Lisa tried to remind herself of all the reasons she had given for wanting to involve Jared—of his abilities and experience—but her concern for his safety rose and drowned out every other argument.

She stewed for a few minutes but knew she would never be able to sleep until he returned, so she picked up her lamp and went down to the parlor to wait.

The minutes ticked by with agonizing slowness while she tried to concentrate on her book. The dark outside became a blackness that penetrated into the corners of the room, making her feel small and very much alone. Several times, when she could stand it no longer, she got up and walked to the window to stare out into the obscurity, but she couldn't see past the front porch.

The hours dragged, marked by the loud chiming of the clock. Each time, she glanced up with a start, and her anxiety increased as she noted the hour. Jared had been gone so long—she prayed nothing had happened to him.

A little after eleven, she thought she heard the sound of a horse. She rose and went to the window, but the dark obliterated everything. When the sound grew louder, her heart began to pound. She clenched her hands until the knuckles went white and whispered her wish that the rider was Jared.

The horse was coming fast, and its rider made no effort to muffle the sounds of the hooves. She pressed her nose against the glass of the parlor window and cupped her hands around her eyes in an effort to pick a shape out of the darkness.

Suddenly, the horse and rider raced into view. She had a momentary impression of a whirl of black more solid than the surrounding space. Then the dark mass split in two and the rider leapt down onto the front porch.

Even though she should have been expecting it, the loud banging on the front door caught her by surprise. She was still standing at the window, staring out; everything had happened so fast. She rushed into the hall and started to turn the heavy lock. Then it occurred to her—why would Jared come to the front door? And why would he knock when he had a key?

"Lisa, let me in!"

Lisa flung open the heavy door, and Jessamine Randall burst into the hall. Her auburn curls were loose and flying wildly around her head.

"Jessy, what are you doing here at this hour? Has something happened?"

Jessy's eyes scanned both parlors and the hall to the kitchen. "Is Jared here?"

"No. What's the matter?"

"Where is he?"

"I don't know. Now calm down and tell me what this is all about."

"Morgan's gone."

"What are you talking about? You're not making any sense." Lisa reached for Jessy's arm. "Come into the kitchen, and I'll make us some coffee. Then you can tell me what's going on."

Jessy allowed herself to be led into the kitchen and waited at the table while Lisa stirred the fire and set the coffee pot on the long-legged trivet.

"Now," Lisa said, "start at the beginning."

"Morgan's gone. He was supposed to meet me tonight, and he never showed up."

"Meet you? Where? Do your parents know about this?"

Jessy thinned her lips in exasperation. "Of course not. But that's not important. I'm worried something might have happened to him, he might be hurt."

"Is Morgan still riding with the James gang?"

Jessy shook her head. "No. He told me he's finished with them for good, and I believe him. He says he hasn't seen them since the day they came back here to pick up Clay."

"Jessy, sometimes it's hard for a man to change that much." Lisa was surprised to find herself echoing Jared's words.

"He has changed. I know it. Besides, I think I know where he went tonight."

"Then why are you worried?"

"I think he and Jared may have found out where

the Masked Rider group is meeting and gone to investigate. Jared came by the school this afternoon to talk to Morgan. They went out back, but I'm sure they were talking about all this nonsense."

"It is not nonsense," Lisa insisted. "You and your students might be in serious danger."

"I think all of you are making too much of this. I'm careful, and besides, who would try to harm us in broad daylight?"

"It's not broad daylight now," Lisa pointed out. "Under the circumstances, do you think it was smart riding here by yourself in the middle of the night?"

"Well, if they're all at the meeting, no one could hurt me, could they? Besides, I didn't tell anyone I was coming, not even my parents."

Lisa frowned. Her friend was entirely too glib. "They could have men watching your house. You never know what some people will do to put a stop to something they don't like."

Jessy brushed the admonition aside. "I arrived safely, so there's no need to discuss it further. Besides, I didn't come here to be lectured."

"Why did you come?"

Jessy stood and began pacing. "I came here because I was worried. If Jared had been here, I was going to ask him if he knew where Morgan was. Since he's not here, I can only assume they're together."

"That had occurred to me, too."

Jessy whirled around to face her. "Well, aren't you worried?"

Lisa hesitated then nodded. "Yes. Sneaking around to spy on secret meetings in the middle of the night seems foolhardy even for a lawman and an ex-outlaw."

"If anything happens to either of them on my account, I'll...I'll...oh, I don't know what I'll do!" Jessy's temporary calm had given way to her naturally dramatic temperament again.

Lisa crossed the kitchen and extended a placating hand. "We won't do Morgan or Jared any good by getting hysterical."

Jessy looked at her, tears glistening in the corners of her eyes in the dim firelight. "Hysterical?" She laughed. "You never get hysterical. You're the most self-composed person I know."

Images of herself with Jared flashed into Lisa's mind. Oh no, she was not always cool and calm. Whether it was tears or passion, he provoked a fire in her that resisted all efforts to contain it.

She shook her head. "I'm not always calm." Then she gave Jessy a small smile. "I think you bring it out in me."

Some of the tension left Jessy's shoulders, and she returned the smile. "That's probably a good thing. I don't think I could stand to be around you if you were just like me."

Lisa put her arm around her friend and gave her a hug, which Jessy returned. "Why don't you stay here and wait with me for a while? We can worry together."

"Thank you. I need to be home before dawn, but I know I won't sleep a wink until I'm sure Morgan's safe."

"You really love him, don't you?"

"Yes," Jessy replied without hesitation. "The way you love Jared."

"Yes," Lisa answered, more to herself than to Jessy.

The next two hours passed with agonizing

slowness. After a while even Jessy ran out of things to say, and Lisa struggled to keep her eyes off the clock. She tried drawing the drapes to block out the cold staring eyes of the night-black windows, but it made the room stuffy instead of comforting. At one point, she hunted through a cabinet and brought out a deck of cards. Although she didn't know how to play any card games, Jessy offered to teach her five-card stud poker. Unfortunately, neither of them could concentrate long enough to play a single hand.

By one o'clock, Lisa's nerves were brittle with anxiety and fatigue. She had chewed a sore place on the inside of her lower lip, and the front of her dress had long, damp streaks where she kept wiping her hands down the length of her thighs.

Suddenly, Jessy bounded to her feet, her hands balled in frustration. "I can't stand this a moment longer. Do you have any whiskey in the house?"

Lisa's hands stilled in her lap. "Whiskey? Since when do you drink whiskey?"

"I don't, yet, but this seems like the perfect opportunity to start. I've heard it steadies the nerves."

"I haven't kept a bottle in the house since Clay left, but all it did for him was turn him into a braying jackass. I think I can do without that tonight, thank you."

"Well, I have to do something. I'm going crazy!"

Just then, Lisa tipped her head to the side and held up her hand, signaling Jessy to be quiet. They both listened. There was definitely a sound coming from outside, a quiet, rhythmic sound.

"Do you think—?" Jessy began.

"Shh."

They listened again. The sound, though still soft,

was growing more distinct. Soon they were able to make out the steady tread of a horse's hooves.

"Do you think it's Jared?" Jessy whispered.

"It had better be." Lisa's nerves drew even tighter. She had been waiting and worrying so long she wasn't sure how she'd react when she finally saw him. Would she scream at him or throw herself into his arms?

Then she noticed the sound had stopped. Every sound seemed to have stopped except the inexorable ticking of the clock.

Crash!

The front and back doors splintered open simultaneously, and Lisa and Jessy froze. When they heard the heavy sounds of intruders in both places at once they grabbed each other and screamed.

Seconds later, Jared and Morgan Bingham burst in, guns drawn. They scanned the room for intruders then holstered their weapons and advanced on the stunned women standing in front of the fireplace.

Morgan was the first to speak. "Jessy, what are you doing here? You scared us half to death."

Jessy came to life. "We scared you?!"

"Yes," Lisa added as she stepped toward Jared, who was glowering fiercely. "What do you mean by breaking down the doors and charging in here like a couple of mad bulls?"

Jared's expression remained unchanged. "We saw the lights through the curtains and the horse out front. I didn't expect you to be entertaining a visitor at this hour. We thought you might be in trouble."

"I'm not the one who's in trouble tonight," Lisa countered. "Where have you been?" Her relief at seeing him unharmed was overshadowed by fury at the fright he'd given her.

Jared ignored her question. "What are you doing up?"

Lisa crossed her arms and glared back. "Waiting for you."

Morgan had moved to stand in front of Jessy. His normally impassive features now looked as forbidding as Jared's. "Jessy, what are you doing here?"

She lifted her chin. "When you didn't show up tonight, I came looking for you."

"You shouldn't be out alone in the middle of the night. Come on. I'm taking you home. We can ride double on your horse."

Jessy crossed her arms in front of her chest. "I'm not going anywhere until I get some answers. Where is your horse?"

"Shot out from under him," Jared said.

"What?"

Jessy bristled with outrage, but Lisa's head spun and her stomach clenched. *Shot.* It could just as easily have been Jared.

He stared at her hard and motioned to Morgan. "Get Jessy out of here, Bingham. You can explain on the way."

"Right." Morgan took Jessy by the arm and half-dragged her into the hall.

As soon as they were gone, Jared reached for Lisa. She went without a word. For a long time, neither of them spoke. She stood with her arms wrapped around his middle and her face buried in the fabric of his shirt, deeply inhaling the reassuring scent of him. He was alive. He was unhurt. He was here. He was hers. Nothing else mattered.

He stroked her long, unbound, hair, pausing from time to time to press light kisses on her crown or temple and murmur soothing words which comforted more by their sound than their meaning.

Finally, she raised her head. "Someone shot at you again."

He ventured a crooked grin. "But this time they missed."

She didn't return his smile. "What about next time, and the next? When will this stop?"

"You asked me to help Jessy."

"Yes. But when I asked, I didn't realize it would be so dangerous." She loosened her arms and stepped back. "Tell me what happened."

"Come sit down." He led her to the sofa and sat beside her. "I nosed around town a little bit and talked to Bingham like I said I would. We learned that the group calling itself the Masked Riders was meeting tonight in an abandoned barn about five miles from here. We rode over to see what we could find out."

"Surely you didn't just ride into the middle of a group like that. It's a wonder you weren't both killed."

He made a face of disgust. "Give us credit for having a little sense. We left our horses tied in the woods and sneaked up to listen."

"Could you hear anything?"

"A little. Enough to know there's a lot of resentment around here for what some people regard as government handouts to the former slaves. Many people are suffering since the war, and they're ready to lash out at anyone they can."

"Do you think they would attack Jessy or the children?"

He shook his head. "I doubt there will be any overt attacks, but you never can tell. If Jessy's smart, she won't go anywhere alone or at night. Probably they'd only try to scare her, but a couple of men were pretty vocal in their anger at what they view as betrayal by one of their own."

Lisa leaned back against his arm and closed her eyes. "We had so much turmoil and hatred around here during the war. Why won't people see that peace is better for everyone?"

"Human nature, I guess."

She was silent for a moment, then she straightened and looked at him. "You still haven't told me how Morgan's horse was shot."

"Someone came out of the barn, so we made a run for the horses. He chased us and fired several shots. One of them hit Bingham's horse, so I brought him back with me."

Suddenly, a frightening idea popped into Lisa's mind, and she grabbed his hand. "Do you think that man could have recognized you?"

"I don't think so. It was pretty dark, and we were running fast."

"Yes, but your size alone might give you away. There aren't many men around here as big as you."

"Relax. If he did, which I doubt, there's nothing we can do about it now. I'll be careful. I've been taking care of myself for years. I don't want you to worry."

"But I do worry. I've been worried ever since you left tonight. Why didn't you tell me where you were going?"

"For just this reason. I didn't want you to worry."

She dropped his hand and stood. "We'll give Jessy your warning, and then I don't want you involved in this mess anymore."

He rose, too. "I think Bingham will be keeping a pretty close eye on her. He's a better man than I thought. She'll be all right."

"I hope so." Lisa raised her eyes to his. "I'm tired now. It's been quite a night. I think it's time for bed."

Jared reached out, and his hand grazed her cheek. "You do look tired. Go get some sleep. I'll see you in the morning."

She raised her hand to cover his. Then she turned her lips into his palm and pressed a kiss against the sensitive flesh. When she looked back into his eyes, they blazed with need. "I want you to come with me."

His hand shook where it touched her face. "Are you sure?"

She nodded. "I spent hours tonight wondering where you were and thinking about what my life would be like if you never came back. I realized that life is filled with uncertainties. The only thing I know for sure is I love you, and I want to be with you, in every way, for as long as I can."

"Oh, sweetheart!" He pulled her into his arms, crushing her against his chest.

Lisa could barely breathe, but she didn't care. To be in his arms again was the most wonderful feeling in the world, as if they could meld into a single being.

He loosened his hold. When he drew back enough for her to see his face, she could swear she saw love shining in his dark eyes. Her breath caught. How she loved this man.

He said nothing, but bent down, swept her into his arms, and carried her up the steps, two at a time.

Chapter Fifteen

When they reached the bedroom, and before Jared could set her down, Lisa wrapped her arms around his neck and tugged until their lips joined. He lowered his head and shifted her position to give her better access, curious to see how far she would go. She attacked his mouth like a starving woman, nipping and nibbling and thrusting her tongue between his teeth. Soft moans of need and desire emanated from deep in her throat.

The force of her passion took him by surprise. In his experience, no matter how ardent a woman's response might be to lovemaking, it was always that—a response. He had never been with a woman who wanted him badly enough to take the upper hand. Yet, Lisa was practically assaulting him. And she was driven by love. The knowledge acted on him like a powerful aphrodisiac.

He groaned as his arms tightened around her, and his mouth plunged and plundered, only to be plundered in return. But it wasn't enough, and frustration began to pound inside him. He held Lisa in his arms, but he couldn't touch her, not in the ways and places he wanted to. Without being able to use his hands, he was a prisoner of her desire, unable to give or take what he wanted.

She squirmed in his arms, seeking more and more contact until he could stand it no longer. He adjusted his hold, sending her sliding to the floor, but without breaking the bond of their lips. Freed of their burden, his hands began a frantic exploration to find the woman beneath the enveloping layers of clothing.

"You wear too many clothes," he growled as he pulled up handfuls of her skirt. His breathing was ragged. "Turn around. We've got to get this off you before I rip it."

"Only if I get to do yours next." Her full lips tilted in a sultry smile.

He tried to return the smile, but he couldn't. His need was too great. "All right. But you'd better make it fast. I'm about to explode."

She turned her back to him and lifted the silky tangle of her hair. He had to concentrate to keep his hands from shaking but made short work of the fastenings of her dress and undergarments. When she turned back, she was gloriously naked and unashamed.

"Now it's your turn."

She made no effort to match his speed. Instead, she allowed her fingers to linger over his chest and shoulders, sliding into the hair on his chest and stroking his biceps as she pushed the shirt down his arms. Jared drew in his breath but forced himself to stand still and endure the sweet torture. His hands balled into fists when she began to work the buttons on his pants. Finally, he could stand no more and brushed her hands away.

"I'll do that."

In seconds, he had stripped off the rest of his clothes and discarded them in a careless heap on the floor. When he reached for Lisa again, she stopped him.

"No. I want to look at you first," she murmured. "Last time I was too nervous and embarrassed to really look at you, but now I want to see every inch."

She stepped back, and her eyes wandered over him slowly, lovingly, from his shoulders to his chest and below. Jared clenched his jaw in an effort to control himself. He had never been in this position before. If any of his previous lovers had admired his body, they had never done so in such a brazen, blatant, loving, and exciting way. Lisa looked as though she wanted to eat him alive. Was it possible she felt a desire as strong as his own? If he had felt ready to burst while they were still dressed, it was nothing compared to the way he felt now.

"That's enough, woman," he ordered, reaching for her. "Come here."

She smiled and stepped into his arms.

He had her flat on her back on the bed before she had time to object. Nor did she protest when he pinned her hands to the pillow on either side of her head.

"Jared, please!" She tossed her head in frustration. She wrapped her legs around his back and wriggled to increase the contact.

"Yes?" His voice was tight and husky.

"I need you," she pleaded.

Abruptly, he rolled off her.

Lisa raised on her elbows and looked at him in dismay.

"Show me," he demanded.

"What?"

"Show me how much you need me."

She drew her brows together. "How?"

"Make love to me. I'm ready. I'm more than ready."

When she hesitated, he reached over, and, putting his big hands on either side of her waist, lifted her to straddle his abdomen.

Light dawned in her eyes. "Can we do it like this?"

"If we don't, I think I'm going to die." He pushed up against her for emphasis. She was so ready for him.

Soon she was following his rhythm. Faster and faster they came together, until her fingers dug into his shoulders. When the startling magic overcame her, she cried out.

He watched the mask of ecstasy slide over the face of the woman above him and felt an enormous satisfaction. It paled, however, beside the satisfaction that gripped him he allowed himself to join her in the maelstrom of release.

When it was over, Lisa collapsed onto his heaving chest, both of them unable to move a muscle. He felt as though he had been totally, blissfully drained of every spark of energy. He must have dozed when she moved atop him, and a tiny groan escaped her lips.

"My legs...I think they're cramped."

He kissed her. "Poor sweetheart. I guess you're not used to so much exercise in this position."

She made a face. "I should hope not."

He kissed her again. "Here." He reached down to grasp her ankle. "Let me help you." He slid her right leg down until it was straight then did the same for the left.

She sighed in relief. She was still draped across him with their bodies intimately joined.

He rolled over with her until she was on her back. Then he eased back to lie on his side and propped his head up with one hand. The other hand began a lazy journey down her body from shoulder to knee, taking the time to explore and appreciate all her beauty now that the initial driving heat of his desire was past. Before, he had never had the opportunity to look and touch his fill, and he meant to take full advantage of it.

"You're so beautiful." He leaned down to drop a light kiss on one soft, pink nipple. "I can hardly believe you're mine." His eyes challenged her to deny the proprietary statement.

She smiled and reached up to twine her fingers through the hair on his chest. "I could say the same."

He didn't return her smile. "I'm serious. I'll never get tired of seeing you like this. You're a dream come true, all warm and relaxed, damp and flushed, with your hair spread across the pillow. It makes me want to give you the world."

She reached up to stroke his rough cheek. "Let's just give each other what we can, while we can. That's enough."

Her words tripped something in his brain. It wouldn't be enough. It could never be enough. He had to have more. He captured her hand and held it against his face. "No, it isn't. I want everything with you, a home and a family. And I won't be satisfied until I get it." And suddenly he meant every word, with his whole heart.

A look clouded her chocolate eyes. He couldn't be

sure what it was, maybe uncertainty, maybe something more.

"Please. I don't want to talk about it tonight," she said. "I'm tired, and I want to feel your arms around me while I sleep."

He hesitated for a second before he slid down beside her and wrapped his arms around her. He wouldn't press her tonight, but soon. Now that his desires were crystal clear, he had to know hers.

Lisa curled up against his body as if she had been made to fit there and promptly fell asleep, but Jared lay awake, pondering the woman he held close to his heart. In a few short months his whole world had changed. How had he missed the signs? His only excuse was lack of experience. He'd known so little of love in his life he'd allowed it to ambush him, and now it held him a willing prisoner.

****

Lisa awoke and reached across the bed for Jared. Her lips curved into a smile as memories of the night past drifted back into her mind. What a powerful, yet tender, lover he was, and how much she loved him. But his side of the bed was empty. The room seemed bright, too. She squinted at the clock. It was already eight o'clock. They had slept well past normal rising time. Then she opened her eyes fully and glanced across the room to see him, stark naked, lifting a wiggling, fussing Andrew from his cradle.

"Hush, son, let's try not to wake Mama, shall we?" The baby quieted and regarded him quizzically. "Hoo-eee, you sure are wet!"

He held the soggy infant away from his body and looked for a safe place to deposit him. "I'm afraid you're stuck with me this morning." He gave the dangling baby a grimace. "Let's hope we both survive this."

He carried Andrew to the dresser and began to remove his soaked clothing. Holding the wriggling baby with one hand, he rooted around in the drawers until he found the clean diapers and gowns. With the other hand, he grabbed Andrew's ankles and lifted them, raising his plump little bottom, and attempted to slide a clean diaper underneath. Then the baby jerked one leg free, and the battle began.

At first Lisa merely smiled, but she couldn't contain her laughter for long.

Jared whipped his head around. His dark hair was tousled, his jaw was shadowed with beard, and he had a pin in his mouth. He looked wonderful.

"You're very good with him, you know," she said.

He removed the pin. "I love him." His tone was matter-of-fact. "Just like I love his mama."

The shock hit her like a brick wall. "Y-you never said you loved me."

He turned his attention back to his task. "I just figured it out myself, but a blind man would have seen it all along. I may not have said the words, but I told you in every other way. I told you I wanted you, I wanted to be a father to your son and to make a family with you. What did you think?"

"I—I don't know."

He loves me. He loves me!

"There!" He announced with a flourish. He swung back around brandishing Andrew, who chortled with glee and ignored the crookedly pinned diaper that threatened to slide off any second. "Why don't you feed him, then we can decide what we want to do today." He handed Andrew to Lisa and climbed into bed beside her.

As she settled the baby at her breast, she thought about the picture they made. All three of them in bed together and the baby the only one with anything on. Scandalous, no doubt, but oh, so right.

She smiled at Jared. "What did you have in mind?"

He stretched out without a shred of self-consciousness and crossed his arms behind his head. "Well, I was thinking about taking a holiday. I have four days off before I have to go back out, so we could take today and do anything we want."

"No work?"

"Nope. We could relax and enjoy the day like a real family."

She thought about that for a moment. It was so tempting. There could be no harm in pretending, just for a day, while she tried to come to grips with his stunning announcement. She relaxed and smiled. "I think that would be lovely."

While he finished his chores in the barn, she tidied the house and packed their lunch in a basket. It was a shimmering hot, midsummer day, perfect for a picnic in the orchard. She relaxed on a blanket beneath the shady limbs heavy with unripe fruit and nibbled a piece of cold fried chicken while she watched Jared tickle Andrew's bare toes with a long blade of grass. The baby's chortles of glee filled her heart with a warmth that outshone the heat of the sun.

Afterwards, Jared filled a huge washtub with cool water from the well. A delicious flutter of anticipation started in her stomach when he peeled off his shirt—she would never tire of the sight. He teased and cajoled until she stripped to her chemise and petticoat and joined him splashing and playing until they were both soaked to the skin. Andrew crowed to join the fun, so Jared removed his diaper and let him frolic in the cool water until his yawns spelled naptime.

Lisa carried the sleepy baby into the house and laid him in his cradle. When she turned, Jared was standing beside the bed. A sheen of moisture gleamed on his chest, and a lock of still-damp hair hung across his forehead. He held out his hand, and his smile offered an invitation she accepted with joy.

When they came together, she reveled in the feel of his hands against her body, still slick with water. His fingers grazed and caressed. Hers stroked and squeezed. Their mouths licked and sucked, tasted and cried out. Until, at last, they fell apart, spent and exhausted.

He was the first to speak. "So, what are we going to do about this?"

She had known it was coming, but she'd hoped for a few more days before she had to face his questions and demands. "Enjoy it?" she ventured.

"I intend to. But that's not what I meant."

"I know. But do we have to do anything more right now? I'm not ready."

He rolled over to face her. "I want us to be together. We love each other. We've got to deal with that."

"I want us to be together, too."

And she did, but how could she explain what held her back? She wanted to love him, but she was afraid. She wanted his love, but she also needed to feel secure. She couldn't remember ever really feeling secure. She'd hidden behind a mask of strength and independence since her father died. It might have fooled everyone else, but that mask no longer hid her from herself.

She plucked at a wrinkle in the sheet, unable to meet his questioning gaze. "I'm a coward."

He reached out to stroke her face. "Is this the same woman who faced down a posse with a wounded man in her root cellar? What could you be afraid of now?"

"I don't know, everything. Afraid of loving you too much. Afraid something will happen to you. Afraid you won't love me enough."

His finger slipped beneath her chin and lifted it until she was forced to meet his gaze. "I don't know what more I can do to prove it to you. Life doesn't come with guarantees. Sometimes you have to take chances. Only you can decide if the prize is worth the risk."

He was right. She would have to make a decision, and soon. As wonderful as the day had been, it was just pretend, a day out of time. Real life would come rushing back.

"I have to think." Her eyes pleaded with him. "I need more time to be sure I'm doing the right thing. Just a little more time, please."

He stared at her long and hard before he replied. "A little more time is all there is."

"I know." They had crossed a line, and there was no going back to the way things had been. Either they made a permanent commitment or he would have to leave, and that thought caused an ache deep in her chest that wouldn't go away.

****

Lisa didn't mention the subject again during the next three days. With great effort, Jared avoided hounding her about her decision. He was conscious of it every second, whether he was doing chores in the barn or sitting across the table from her at supper. He had never been a patient man, and the temptation to throw Lisa and the baby into the wagon and drive to town to see the preacher gnawed at him.

He felt like a man waiting for a judge to pass sentence. It was agonizing, but necessary. He wanted her to choose him, but she had to do it willingly, with her whole heart. He wanted her to be certain this was what she wanted above all else. So, he waited.

Although he didn't allow himself to try to influence her decision with words, he couldn't help trying to influence her with actions. He spent those three days showing her, in every way he could think of, how good life could be if she would reach out for it. And he spent the nights taking her body to ever-new heights of passion, pouring his love into her and hoping it would be enough.

****

The last night before Jared had to go back to work, Lisa sat across from him at the dinner table, pushing her chicken and dumplings around with her fork and watching him. She loved him, of that she was certain. She knew he loved Andrew. And he said he loved her. That should be all she needed. But did she love him enough to risk losing him? And what did he want from life? They had never discussed the future. The whole concept of a future together was too new.

"Jared?"

"Mmm?"

"I know you spent your childhood in California. Would you want to move back there?"

He didn't hesitate. "No."

"Why not?"

258

"I don't have a single good memory of the place. I've spent the last twenty years trying to forget it."

"Why? What happened there?" When he didn't answer, she reached across the table to touch his arm. "I want to know. I want to know everything about you."

He hesitated, then squeezed her hand before releasing it. "My father was a no-account miner always waiting for that big strike. He'd take off for weeks or months at a time, leaving my mother to take care of herself and me any way she could. When I was about six, he didn't come back. I was relieved because when he was home he spent most of his time drunk, slapping us both around."

He stopped and leaned his head back, closing his eyes. "After a couple of years, my mother decided to go looking for him. We traipsed around the California hill country, going from one mining camp to another looking for that worthless scum. We slept in a tent, and my mother took in laundry to make enough money for food and a few basic supplies. We never found him. Instead, when I was twelve, some drunken miners were celebrating, shooting up the town. My mother caught a stray bullet in the chest, and there wasn't a damned thing I could do to save her."

He opened his eyes. "After that I swore I'd never be helpless again. And I'd never watch another innocent person die. No, I don't want to go back there. I never want to see it again."

Lisa rose from the table and stood behind him. She leaned forward and slid her arms around his neck, pillowing his head between her breasts as if to absorb some of his pain. "I'm sorry."

"Don't be. I'm not. I'm mad as hell about it, and I

probably always will be." He turned and looked up at her. Anger still burned in his eyes. "A man, a real man, takes care of his responsibilities, and that includes his woman and child. No matter how hard it is. He doesn't cut and run after the promise of easy money."

She trembled. His passionate words helped explain his feelings about Andrew and his desire to protect everyone he thought needed protection. They formed the basis of the masculine code of honor at the core of his being.

"I know how important this place is to you," he continued. "It's important to me, too. It's the first real home I've ever had. We're not going to leave."

Her heart swelled. How could she not love this man? Not only was he the strongest, bravest, and most honorable person she had ever known, but he valued everything she cherished.

Chapter Sixteen

The next morning, before the sun rose, Jared pressed a soft kiss on Lisa's forehead and slipped out of bed. He had to leave early for Atchison and didn't want to disturb her. It had been a long night, and he wanted her to sleep while she had the chance. After hours of lovemaking, they'd finally succumbed to exhaustion only an hour or two earlier.

He'd tried again to discuss marriage, but she wouldn't hear it. When words failed, he'd tried passion. She had responded with every fiber of her being, and he was sure he'd found the answer he sought. How could a woman love a man so thoroughly and still hold anything back?

He gathered his clothes and paused by the cradle to look down at the sleeping baby one more time before going downstairs. Perhaps soon Andrew would be his son. *His son.* He liked the sound of the words. If Lisa agreed to marry him, he wanted to talk to Judge

Randall about adopting the boy and giving Andrew his name. Then it would be as if they'd always been a family, and in many ways, they had.

As he washed and dressed in the dark kitchen, he was struck again by how much this place had come to be home. There might be some tough times ahead, but this would always be home. Their son and their love had both been born in this house, and he was determined to make sure both had a chance to grow here.

As much as he hated to leave Lisa, he always enjoyed the early morning ride to the stage office in Atchison. The countryside was so quiet, it gave a man a chance to think. As the sun nudged above the horizon and began to burn off the haze of humidity, his mind whirled with the possibilities that lay ahead. He pondered where he should take Lisa for a honeymoon. Kansas City would be nice. It was close enough that he might be able to persuade her to leave Andrew with Martha for a few days, and it was reported to have every modern convenience from fancy hotels to indoor plumbing.

When he reached the stage company office, the stage he was to accompany was already waiting out front being loaded. This morning's run to Denver was not a passenger trip. Instead, two men were dragging big sacks of mail across the dusty street and heaving them into the coach.

A grizzled old man with a tobacco-stained beard and bowed legs stumped out of the office, staggering under the weight of a large wooden box banded with iron.

"Tanner! You going with me today? If you are, come over here and get this dad-blamed thing. It weighs more than my wife and her sister put together!"

Jared grinned, picturing Eulalia Benson, who was easily twice the size of her diminutive husband. He walked over and relieved the man of his load.

"Are you driving today, Curly?" The old man's nickname was a joke around the company, for beneath his battered brown hat, his head was as smooth as a billiard ball.

"Yep. Better tie that strong box down on top where you can keep an eye on it. That there's the payroll for the whole western region. The boys in Denver are like to be a mite unfriendly if we lose it."

Jared nodded and hefted the box onto the high seat. Then he climbed up and lifted it onto the roof of the coach before securing it. When he was finished, he climbed back down, but only long enough to fetch his gear from his horse and ask one of the men to take it around to the stable in back. He didn't want to take his eyes off the box for a minute.

A payroll. That would bring out every outlaw within shooting distance. The news traveled fast whenever the stage was carrying a large sum of money. Maybe this would be his chance to take care of some of the bandits who had been plaguing the line for the past few months. After all, that's what Mr. Holladay paid him for.

He waited a few minutes on the high seat of the stagecoach with his rifle resting across his knees. He also wore a pair of revolvers, one strapped to each thigh. If the outlaws chose to attack, he would be ready for them. Finally, Curly came out of the office, climbed up to take the reins, and they set off.

For the first hour or two, Jared kept his guard

high, peering into every clump of trees for signs of men or horses. It was here that robbers were most likely to strike, where they still had cover. The rolling, grass-covered contours of the flint hills farther west offered few places to lie in wait undetected.

By the time they passed the little settlement of De Soto, he began to relax. Maybe he'd been wrong. Maybe the outlaws were occupied elsewhere and this run would go smoothly. He felt a stab of disappointment. It would be satisfying to finally win a battle in the long, ongoing war. He leaned back on the board that served as a seat and returned his rifle to his knees.

Curly was pushing the team at an accelerated pace since there were no passengers to complain about being bounced and jostled. At this rate, they'd make Lawrence by early afternoon, and Jared had no objections. It was a long, hot, dusty, and usually boring ride across the plains of Kansas and western Colorado before they sighted the Rockies and knew they were in the final stretch. He was in favor of anything that would shave a few hours, or even a whole day, off the trip. Besides, they'd both get a bonus if they arrived early with the cargo intact.

The rhythmic thud of the horses' hooves and the creaking of the coach made conversation difficult, so they rode in silence. There would be plenty of time for jawing when they stopped for dinner and a change of horses in Lawrence.

Suddenly, a pistol shot cracked the air a split second before a bullet whizzed past his ear. He whipped around and raised his rifle in one fluid motion. Six mounted men rode out of a ravine down toward the Kaw River, their guns blazing. They had pulled bandanas over the lower halves of their faces, but Jared had no time to waste wondering about their identities. He crouched on the seat, using the strongbox on the roof of the coach for cover as he tried to pick the riders off in spite of the wild bouncing of the stage.

Curly snapped the reins and yelled to the frightened horses to get all the speed he could out of them. However, the six horses harnessed together were no match for the single mounts of the outlaws, and soon two of them had ridden up alongside the coach. Jared threw his rifle aside because he didn't have time to reload and fired his pistol at the man bearing down on him. He felt a surge of satisfaction when he heard a grunt and saw the man collapse forward across his horse with a spreading stain of blood on the back of his left shoulder.

That sound was followed by a much louder groan to Jared's right, and he turned to see Curly slumped forward with a small, round hole in his temple. A blinding rage seized him, and his shout of fury rose above the report of the gun in his hand. The second outlaw jerked and fell from his horse.

The shots frightened the driverless horses further, and they plunged ahead at breakneck speed, hauling the stage helplessly behind. Jared leaned forward and grabbed the reins that had fallen from Curly's dead fingers. He pulled hard, trying to control the frantic horses. His whole body strained with the effort until he finally brought the team and stagecoach to a halt.

When they stopped, he realized the attackers were no longer following him. He turned and saw them riding off in the opposite direction as fast as they could, leading two riderless horses. The body of the man who'd shot Curly still lay in the dust. Jared assumed the man was dead and his comrades had taken the other wounded man with them. Glancing back at Curly's body, he felt no remorse for the man in the dirt. As his mother used to say, you reap what you sow.

His heart was heavy as he lifted the driver's slight body from the seat and stretched it out inside the coach. There was nothing to do except drive him back to Atchison and deliver him into the hands of his grieving widow. The futility of his death made Jared sick with anger.

When he finished, he climbed back on the high seat and turned the team around. He squinted beneath the brim of his hat in the hot noonday sun, and his anger grew as every step brought him closer to the body of the dead man lying beside the trail. He pulled up next to the body, jerked on the reins, and set the brake before climbing down. He was half tempted to leave the man for the buzzards and coyotes, but reason won out. He'd haul the carcass back and let the sheriff deal with it. He walked over and squatted beside the man in the dusty, flattened grass.

There was something gnawingly familiar about the size and shape of his body and the matted, sandy hair on the back of his head. Jared's gut clenched as he reached over and shoved the man's shoulder, rolling him onto his back.

Clay Ferguson.

It was him all right. And the glazed, staring eyes and gaping mouth left no doubt about his death. *Damn.*

Jared had told Lisa he wouldn't kill Clay, and now he'd gone and done just that. Would she be able to understand the circumstances and the necessity?

Damn! He cursed Clay for everything—for shooting Curly, for forcing him to kill him, for every second of his miserable, wasted life.

Then he lifted the body and carried it to the stagecoach for the long drive back.

****

Lisa had spent the morning doing laundry, watering the garden, and missing Jared. Every time she thought of him a warm glow rose inside. She loved him so much, and he was so positive everything was going to work out for them. She almost dared to let herself believe it. His strength and determination made anything seem possible.

That afternoon while Andrew napped, she sat on the back veranda in the shade, spinning pictures in her mind. She allowed herself the luxury of imagining what life might be like if she agreed to marry Jared. Indulging in such thoughts was a secret, guilty pleasure, not unlike the candy she'd bought earlier that spring at Mr. Cody's store. She didn't want to share them with anybody, not even Jared. Maybe by the time he returned from his trip she would have made a decision she could live with.

After supper, she washed the dishes in a bucket of hot, sudsy water in the dry sink and tried to keep one eye on Andrew, who was sitting on the floor banging the bottom of a tin pot with a wooden spoon. He was able to sit up pretty well by himself now but occasionally tipped over and hadn't yet discovered how to get back up. A thump followed by an angry squall told her it had happened again, so she bent and sat the baby back up on his well-padded little behind.

The heavy sound of boot steps on the back porch startled her, and she whipped around to look through the window. Jared wouldn't be back for several days.

Dear Lord, please don't let it be Clay.

Before she could make a move toward the door, it opened and Jared stepped into the room. She started to smile until her brain registered the lines of tension around his eyes, the grayish color of his skin, and the bloodstains on his shirt. Her smile faded and she rushed to him.

"Are you hurt?" She grabbed his arms with both hands.

He didn't move. "No."

"Come sit down. What happened?" She was frantic. There was so much blood, and he seemed to be in shock.

He came into the room but ignored her request to sit. "Six armed men held up the stage just this side of Lawrence." He paused. When he continued, his voice was tight with pain. "Two men were killed. One of them was Curly Benson, the driver."

"Oh, no!"

"He was a good man. I've just come from breaking the news to his wife. She's taking it pretty well. She's a strong woman."

Lisa turned away and brushed her hair back from her temples with damp hands. More bloodshed, and this time men had died.

"I'm afraid there's more."

She turned back to face him.

"There's no easy way to tell you this, but you might as well hear it from me. The other man was Clay."

Oh Lord, no. Her mind had accepted the possibility of his death after he'd been dumped bleeding on her doorstep, but she'd hoped against hope he would learn his lesson before it was too late. Apparently, he'd run out of time.

She leaned back against the kitchen table and grasped the edge with both hands. "Clay's dead?"

"Yes."

"How?"

Jared's black eyes sparked as anger re-kindled their fire. "He was one of the gang. He rode up beside the stage and shot Curly, straight through the temple. The man was dead before he knew what hit him."

She winced at the brutal image, but there was another question she had to ask. She dreaded the answer, but she had to know. "Was there anyone else riding with you?"

His lips thinned, but his gaze never wavered. "No."

She closed her eyes. "Tell me it wasn't you. Tell me you didn't kill him."

He took a step toward her. "Lisa, stop it. I did what I had to do. He brought it on himself, and you know it."

"I never wanted him dead. I swear it." She shook her head back and forth.

He reached for her with both arms. "What do you mean, you never wanted him dead? It had nothing to do with you. I'm not glad I killed him, but I'm not sorry either. Clay shot an innocent man in cold blood with no more remorse than if he'd been a rabbit or a squirrel. He got what he deserved."

"Who are you to say what he deserved?" Her eyes were open and her question harsh. "You didn't even know him."

"I knew him well enough to know what kind of man he was. Have you forgotten everything? I

269

haven't."

"No, I haven't forgotten, but he didn't deserve to die for anything he said or did to me. Who are any of us to say who deserves to die?" She jerked out of his grasp. "I'm just so sick of it all, all this violence and killing."

"Lisa." His voice was almost pleading. "You have to accept that Clay's death was inevitable. If it hadn't been me, it would have been someone else. Choosing that way of life was almost like committing suicide."

"But he didn't commit suicide. You killed him."

"You make it sound like I wanted it, like I planned it."

She made a small sound of disgust. "Of course, I know you didn't plan it, but don't you see? You've chosen this life, and besides putting your own life constantly at risk, it's made you a killer."

"That's how you see me, as a killer?" His voice rose. "Yesterday you were ready to consider me for your husband and the father of your children. Don't try to deny it."

It was true, but clearly it had been an illusion. Now she feared the blood on his hands would taint their life together and fuel her nightmares. "Yesterday you hadn't killed Clay."

"And now you're having second thoughts?"

"I never said I'd marry you. You just assumed."

"You gave me every reason to make that assumption. You told me you loved me, and you showed me in ways that still make me hard just thinking about it."

"Don't be crude."

"Sometimes I get crude when I'm mad."

"You have nothing to be mad about. I'm simply

not going to marry you. You can move on to your next assignment free and unencumbered."

"I don't want to be unencumbered." He was shouting, as if her mind could be changed by sheer volume. "That's what this is all about."

"I'm sorry."

"Lisa, you're being completely unreasonable."

She sighed. "Maybe, but I don't feel reasonable right now. There's no reason in any of this."

"I don't see how Clay's death has anything to do with us, and I want to know why you've changed your mind about getting married. My feelings for you are the same as when I left this morning. Clay's death hasn't changed anything."

"I'm afraid it has."

"I didn't even know who he was when I shot him, and under the same circumstances, I'd do it again."

The argument was going in circles, and she didn't want to hear any more rationalizations. "Where is his body?"

"The sheriff in Atchison has it for the moment. Why?"

"There's no one else to claim him, to give him a funeral."

"You're going bury him?" Jared was incredulous. "He's not your responsibility."

"Not legally, perhaps, but I feel a moral responsibility." She paused, then continued in a softer voice. "Maybe because his killer was living under my roof."

He began pacing around the room before he stopped and spoke. "That's so absurd, I'm going to pretend you didn't say it. Are you going to tell me you're willing to throw away everything we have and could have together because of that criminal?"

She didn't answer. She couldn't meet his eyes. A numbing weight pressed down on her. In her heart, something wonderful had died, and it had nothing to do with Clay.

"Lisa, look at me," Jared commanded. "You could be carrying my child even now. Have you thought of that? You have to marry me."

She still refused to look at him. "I'll tell people I don't know who the father is. I'll tell them I was attacked by a stranger."

"Damn it!" He banged his fist on the table so hard she jumped. "I won't have any child of mine branded a bastard, even if I have to shout the truth from the top of the town hall!"

Silence quivered in the air, and then Andrew started to scream. She had forgotten him, sitting on the floor with his pot and spoon. She rushed to pick the baby up and cuddled him. Then she turned to face Jared. "I won't marry you, and you can't make me. I want you out of this house, now."

He eyed her as if considering his options. "I'll go, for now. But don't think you're getting rid of me this easily. You're mine—you know it and I know it. I'm willing to wait until you can see things more clearly, and I can wait as long as I have to."

He turned and left the room without a backward glance.

****

As Jared saddled his horse and threw his saddlebags over the back, he wondered if he was doing the right thing. Even with Clay dead, he hated the idea of leaving Lisa and Andrew alone and unprotected. How would she be able to manage the farm by herself?

He'd taken on so much of the work around the place, she'd be shocked when she realized how much there was to do. He pondered those questions and more as he rode down the road toward town.

By the time he reached Weston, he'd decided what to do. He rode through the center of town and crossed the bridge that led up the hill to Ben and Martha's small house. Tying his horse to the post in front, he stepped onto the porch and knocked.

Ben opened the door. "Jared! I didn't expect to see you tonight. Martha, we've got company."

Martha bustled out from the kitchen, wiping her hands on her apron. "Jared, how nice to see you. Have you brought Lisa and Andrew for a little visit after supper?"

"I'm afraid not." His countenance was grim. "In fact, I'm looking for a place to bunk down. Have you got a spare bed?"

"Oh, dear." Martha took him by the arm, drawing him into the parlor. "You'd better come in and tell us about it."

He sat and proceeded to tell them everything, from his hopes for marriage to Clay's death and Lisa's reaction to it. When he finished, Martha shook her head.

"I was always afraid Clay would come to a bad end, but I'm surprised Lisa's taking it so hard. I suppose it's natural for her to grieve for the man—after all, she's known him all her life. But she also ought to feel at least a little relieved."

"Maybe she will, when she calms down and has a chance to think about it," Jared replied. "But right now, she seems to have the harebrained idea she's responsible somehow because I'm the one who shot him."

Martha pursed her lips. "That's ridiculous. Living like that, he was bound to run afoul of the law sooner or later. This time it just happened to be you."

"I couldn't make her see that."

Martha stood. "I wonder if I ought to go and stay with her for a while. It would probably only make matters worse if I tried to insist she move into town right now."

"Don't worry about the work. I'll ride out every day to keep up with the chores.

She smiled. "That's very kind of you. Lisa's a lucky woman to have a man like you."

"I don't think she sees it that way right now."

"No, but I'm sure she'll soon recognize it."

****

The day of Clay's funeral was damp and dismal, a rarity for August, and Lisa's mood matched the weather. She had arranged a small, private service and a burial plot in a discreet corner of the cemetery. The black skirts of her mourning dress hung limp in the heavy mist as she stood beside the open grave wondering if what she felt was true grief. She felt sorrow, certainly. What could be said about a man, scarcely more than a boy, who had thrown his life away and died a thief and a murderer? The minister said a few words about finding peace at last, but they gave Lisa no comfort. Clay's death represented the waste of a life, pure and simple.

Only a small band of mourners gathered at the cemetery. Her mother and Ben were there, of course. And Jessy had come with Morgan Bingham. But Lisa knew they had come only to offer support to her. No one had come to truly mourn the deceased. It was a sad commentary on a sad life.

Jared had insisted on attending, too, even though in Lisa's mind he had no place at the funeral of the man he had killed. He stood behind her with his hands clasped in front of him. In spite of his role in the whole tragedy, he was a wall of strength, and the temptation to lean on that wall was strong. But she couldn't. She needed to make her own place in the world now, a small haven of peace and security, as far as possible from the shooting and killing.

When the short service was over, and with the sounds of earth hitting the simple wooden casket still ringing in her ears, Lisa turned to leave. Jared took her elbow and fell in step beside her. She hadn't seen him since the day he'd brought the news about Clay, but he didn't speak, and she found she had no words for him, either.

As they walked back toward the cemetery gate, a small buggy pulled in. She looked up through her black veil and was surprised to see Eliza Worthington and her father. Neither of them had ever had any connection with Clay.

Reverend Worthington climbed down from the buggy and turned to help his daughter. Together, they walked over to Lisa and Jared, and the reverend reached out to take her hands.

"Lisa, my dear, I wanted to tell you what a fine Christian act this was, providing a final farewell for such a sad, lost soul. Such a pity." He clucked his tongue and shook his head.

He was such a sweet, earnest man. It was hard to imagine how he had ever produced such a spiteful child as Eliza.

"Thank you, Reverend," Lisa murmured. "You're

very kind."

"I'd like to speak to your mother for a moment, if you'll excuse me..."

"Of course, Reverend."

He walked away, leaving Eliza with Lisa and Jared.

As soon as her father was out of earshot, Eliza spoke. "Yes, how awful about Clay. To think an outlaw and murderer was living right here under our noses! It must have been a terrible shock for you." She paused, and her beady little eyes watched Lisa for a response.

"Yes, quite a shock," Lisa replied.

"And how kind of you to take care of his funeral. But you two were always so close."

Lisa gritted her teeth before answering. "I wanted Clay to have a decent burial."

Eliza nodded. "Of course. What a remarkable coincidence that the man who shot him was living right in your very own house."

Jared glowered. "Miss Worthington, what are you suggesting?"

"Why nothing at all Mr. Tanner. Lisa's always been so popular with gentlemen. I guess it's just a case of *may the best man win*." She paused. "And clearly he did."

"Do you think I killed Ferguson out of jealousy?"

Eliza gave him her mean little smile. "Well, you have to admit it's quite convenient. Now there's no one to come between you, out there on the farm all by yourselves."

Lisa's stomach turned over. Was Eliza still spreading her ugly gossip around town? She could only hope she wasn't pregnant. Nobody would ever believe Jared wasn't the father.

"Miss Worthington, has anyone ever told you that you have a filthy tongue?"

Eliza drew back as if he'd slapped her. "Mr. Tanner!"

Just then, her father returned, accompanied by Ben and Martha. "Have you had time to express your sympathy to Lisa, my dear? If so, I think we should be going home. I'm sure this has been a difficult day for everyone." He nodded to Lisa and helped Eliza into the buggy.

When they had gone, Lisa's knees buckled. Jared's arms shot out to support her, and this time she didn't refuse him.

Martha hurried to her side. "Are you all right?"

"I just want to go home."

"Of course, dear." She patted Lisa's hand, then turned to Jared. "You'll take care of her, won't you?"

He nodded and lifted Lisa onto the seat of the wagon for the ride back to the farm.

****

True to his word, Jared rode out every morning to perform the chores he'd long since come to think of as his responsibility but never saw Lisa. If she appreciated his efforts, she never gave a sign. She refused to come out of the house while he was there, and he couldn't bring himself to barge in uninvited.

Not that it wasn't a tempting notion. It would almost be worth the inevitable confrontation to see her again and assure himself she was all right. He also found himself missing Andrew more than he'd expected. At this rate, the little boy would be talking and walking before Jared saw him again.

Even Martha couldn't put his mind at ease when he expressed his frustration.

"I don't know what more to do for her," she said one evening when she returned from a visit to the farm. "She looks awful. She's thin and pale—I don't think she's eating right—and she has dark hollows under her eyes. I'm sure she's not getting much sleep. When I try to talk to her, she just walks off."

"Do you think I should take her and the baby away from here?" Jared asked.

Martha shook her head and sank into a chair. "I'm afraid you'd have to tie her up to do it. When I mentioned your name, all she said was she didn't want to see you, that you *remind her*. She wouldn't even say what it is you remind her of."

Jared stared out the window. "She doesn't have to. I know what I remind her of. I remind her she once had the courage to reach for her own happiness, the courage to fall in love." He looked back at Martha and crossed the room to sit across from her. "Seeing me also reminds her of Clay and the way he died."

He slammed his fist on the kitchen table, making the dishes clatter and jump. "Why can't she understand she had nothing to do with it? I did what I had to do, and I'm not sorry."

Martha reached out and rested a hand on his arm. "I think there may be more to her problems than Clay's death. She was such a lively, cheerful little thing before her father died. After that, the nightmares started, and she became much more solemn and self-contained. I never knew what to do for her."

"Well, a sight like that was bound to affect her."

"A sight like what?"

"She told me she saw the accident. She saw her father shot."

"Oh, no!" Martha's brows knit in horror. "How

awful! She never told me. After it happened, there was so much confusion. I didn't see her, and when I went looking for her later, I found her in the barn. I assumed she'd been playing in there all afternoon. I can't believe she's been living with such a horrible memory bottled up inside all these years."

"She still dreams about it."

She looked pensive. "Is that what her nightmares are about? She never would tell me. She must trust you very much."

"Maybe once. Not anymore." He stood. "I don't know how much more of this I can take."

"I know it's hard, but please try to be patient. She needs you now more than ever." Her soft brown eyes were pleading as they sought Jared's. "Please don't desert her."

"I won't desert her, but I've never been much good at waiting. I guess it'll have to do until I come up with something better."

Chapter Seventeen

As the heat of August gave way to the shorter days and cooler nights of September, Lisa slipped into a safe, if lonely, routine. As long as she stayed on the farm with only Andrew for company, she could convince herself she was moving on with her life. At least until the sun went down, Andrew went to sleep, and she was alone in the dark, silent house.

The summer weather had produced a bumper crop of apples, and the trees in the orchard groaned with their burden. In another month and a half, it would be time for harvest, and she had to start planning. She hoped she could afford to hire a couple of men to help as she and her mother had done in years past, since she doubted she could handle the job alone. Standing on a ladder all day picking apples was backbreaking work, and even if her mother took care of Andrew, hauling the heavy bushels of fruit to the root cellar would be a formidable task. And then there was the canning to be done. She hoped to take a wagonload of jars of applesauce to Mr. Cody to sell at the mercantile this year.

Jared would help if she asked him. Even though she refused to see him, he still rode out every morning to do the heavy chores. And every morning, her anxiety built as she wondered whether he would show up again that day or whether her resistance had finally driven him away. From her hiding place behind the lace curtains in her mother's old bedroom, a near-painful rush of relief flooded her every time she saw his tall figure astride his horse riding up the road.

Not that she would allow herself to be close to him again. That could never be. She had been able to put Clay's death into perspective, but she vowed she would never join her life to a man who made his living with a gun. Regardless of the reasons he had killed Clay, killing was part of Jared's job, and she refused to have any part of that tragedy again.

Unfortunately, her vow did nothing to quash the deep yearnings of her heart. Every time she saw him, she remembered—remembered his patience and gentleness with Andrew, his hard work around the farm, and, most disturbing of all, his husky voice murmuring words of love while his hands and lips worked their magic on her body. She told herself she'd had a lucky escape when it became obvious she was not carrying his child. *Lucky.* If she was so lucky, why did she feel a sense of loss for something that had never been more than a wisp of hope?

"Good afternoon, Lisa."

She dropped the wooden clothespin from her teeth, and the wet sheet in her hands slapped against her apron leaving a long, damp streak. She whipped

281

around as Jessy Randall crossed the yard. She'd been so lost in her own thoughts she hadn't heard her friend drive up. "Good heavens, you startled me."

"Good." Jessy gave a vigorous nod. "You need to be startled. You've been out here all by yourself so long, you've probably forgotten there are other people in the world."

Lisa laughed in spite of herself. It was the first time she'd laughed in a long time and it surprised her. It also felt good, very, very good.

"I haven't been that bad."

"Oh yes, you have. You've been hiding out here like a hermit." Jessy's coppery curls bounced with each word.

"My mother visits every few days."

"But do you visit her? Or go shopping, or to church? No." Jessy paused, whether for effect or to catch her breath Lisa couldn't be sure. "And what about Jared? He loves you, and your mother says you won't even talk to him."

"I can't, don't you see? I love him, too, but I can't spend my life with him."

Jessy dismissed her objection with a wave of her hand. "That's plain irrational."

"Maybe so," Lisa said, bending to pull another damp sheet from the big willow basket, "but since when have feelings been rational? He's a killer, justified or unjustified, and I refuse to get involved with someone like that."

"He's a man, a man who loves you. I think you should at least talk to him."

Lisa turned away and snatched up Andrew, whose fistful of grass was half-way to his mouth. "There's no point."

"You're being very stubborn."

"Maybe, but it's my life. Now, if you've finished scolding me, would you like to come into the house for a glass of buttermilk? You can fill me in on everything you think I've missed."

Jessy opened her mouth and then paused, apparently thinking better of what she'd planned to say. "All right. Well, now let me see. Sarah Wessel had a baby boy last week..." She picked up the laundry basket and carried it into the kitchen, keeping up a steady stream of chatter all the way.

Inside, Jessy claimed Andrew as Lisa poured two glasses of cool buttermilk from the pitcher she'd brought in from the well house earlier.

"So how is your school going?" Lisa asked, taking a sip.

Jessy kept her attention on Andrew, who sat on her lap, showing off his two new teeth in a big grin. "Wonderfully well. I've started on a full day schedule this month, and the students are learning so fast."

"Are you still teaching Morgan?"

When Jessy raised her head, her cheeks were pink. "He picked up reading pretty quickly, but we still get together to...uh...study."

Lisa decided she was in no position to lecture her friend on the perils of ill-conceived romance. Jessy would have to find her own way through that minefield. "You're happy then?"

Jessy glowed. "Yes, very." Then a frown clouded her brow. "Except for this one annoyance." She reached for her reticule with her free hand and pulled out a folded piece of paper. "Look at this. Of all the melodramatic, ridiculous..."

Lisa took the paper, unfolded it, and read. The

words hit her like a fist. It was a crudely written, but very explicit threat. According to the writer, the upstanding citizens of Weston were fed up with Jessy's do-gooding, and if she knew what was good for her, she would stay away from her school on the fourteenth. It was signed *The Masked Riders*.

"The fourteenth—that's tomorrow. Have you told anyone about this? What are you going to do?"

Jessy sat taller. "Well, I'm certainly not going to abandon my school to a bunch of hooligans!"

"Have you told your father or the sheriff?"

"No. I'm sure they would both try to prevent me from doing what I know is right."

"I'm sure they would try to protect you." Lisa shook her head. "What about Morgan? What did he say about this?"

"I didn't show it to him."

"Why not?"

"He's as bad as my father. He doesn't seem to believe I can take care of myself."

"But Jessy, these men could be very dangerous."

"Whoever they are, they're probably men I've known all my life, and I refuse to believe they'll do anything to harm me if I'm standing on the front steps of the school."

"I wouldn't be so sure. Jared told me a couple of months ago public sentiment is running high. So many people are having a hard time making ends meet they resent anything being given to anyone else."

"Well, I don't intend to let that kind of short-sighted selfishness go unchallenged."

Lisa sighed. There was no arguing with Jessy when she was up on her soapbox. She'd been so cosseted and pampered all her life, she would never understand the extremes to which people could be driven by desperation. "At least promise me you'll be very careful, you won't do anything foolish to provoke these people."

"I won't deliberately provoke them, but I won't allow them to intimidate me, either."

Lisa took a deep breath, then released it slowly, giving herself time to think. "If you're determined to stand your ground, perhaps I should drive into town tomorrow and stand with you. Two women might be more of a deterrent than one."

"Don't be foolish, you're a mother. You have Andrew to consider."

"Then you admit this might be dangerous."

"I tell you, I am not in any real danger. Now, I must get back to town." Jessy rose and handed Andrew back to Lisa. "I want your promise you'll come and visit me soon. This self-imposed exile has gone on long enough."

Lisa followed her friend out to her buggy. "I promise. I don't know how soon I can come. There's a lot of work to be done around here, but I'll come."

Jessy smiled and reached down from the buggy to squeeze Lisa's hand. "Good. I'll see you soon." She snapped the reins, and the well-trained horse slipped into a trot. Jessy turned to wave. "And don't worry about me," she called over her shoulder.

As if that were possible. Lisa chewed her lower lip. She had to do something to protect Jessy if she was too reckless and naive to recognize the danger for herself.

By the time she finished cleaning the kitchen after supper, Lisa had worked herself into a state. She had to try to prevent any harm from befalling Jessy, but how could she do that short of kidnapping her? She could tell the sheriff or Ben, but they were both long past their prime and might end up getting hurt. She would never forgive herself if Ben were injured or killed because she asked him to intervene against an unruly mob.

She could ask Jared. He could handle any situation. And he would do it, too, if she asked. But she hadn't spoken to him in over a month. Besides, her heart whispered another fear, what if he were hurt? No matter how big, how strong, or how competent a man was, it only took one bullet to bring him down. Bile rose in her throat at the thought. But what else could she do? Jessy's life might be at stake.

She loaded Andrew into the laundry basket and settled it on the floor of the wagon. He could sit up by himself now, but there was no way to keep him firmly on the seat beside her and drive with one hand, not even with a horse as docile as Old Pete, so he stayed in the basket. Within minutes, they were on the road.

Lisa figured there was still about an hour of daylight left, almost enough to drive into town, persuade Jared to help Jessy, and drive back to the farm if he didn't take too much persuading. If it got late, she and Andrew would have to spend the night with her mother and Ben. Then she realized they couldn't do that. It was a tiny house, and Jared was already staying there. Oh, well, she could drive back in the dark if necessary.

By the time they reached the Wainwright's house, dusk had deepened close to nightfall. It would be fully dark by the time they were ready to head home. She lifted Andrew out of the basket and carried him up the walk to the front door. She shifted him to one hip and knocked.

The door opened, and the light from the parlor silhouetted the large, dark form of a man. Before Lisa's senses could send a message to her brain, Andrew began to wriggle and chirp. He reached with both hands and leaned his weight away from her.

It was Jared. As her mind registered the fact, big hands reached for the boy and lifted him from her arms. She tried to grab the baby back.

"Give him to me and come on in."

She closed her eyes. That voice. How she had missed that voice. It had haunted her dreams for weeks. The sound stirred every sense she possessed.

She tried to compose herself with a sharp reminder of why she'd come and followed Jared and Andrew into the parlor where Ben sat reading and Martha knitted.

"Look who's here," Jared announced.

Martha dropped her knitting and was out of her chair in a flash. "Lisa, what a wonderful surprise."

"Hello, Mama."

"Come in, dear, and sit down. Would you like a piece of pie?"

Lisa wet her lips and glanced around the room. "No, thank you. Actually, I came to talk to Jared."

Jared stopped playing with Andrew in mid-tickle and stared at her.

Martha's brows rose, but she covered any surprise with characteristic smoothness. "Why don't you go out on the front porch? I'll hold Andrew." She walked over and plucked the baby from Jared's motionless hands.

Lisa stepped outside and Jared followed.

After the front door closed behind them, she stepped over to lean her elbows on the railing. She'd had the whole trip to plan what she wanted to say, but now that they were alone, she didn't know where to start.

After a brief silence, Jared spoke. "What do you want?"

She turned. The twilight masking his features made him appear even darker and more dangerous than usual. She wet her lips again. "I...uh...came to ask you a favor."

"What kind of favor could you want from me? I'm a murderer, remember?"

"The favor isn't for me. It's for Jessy."

"Then why doesn't she ask me herself?"

"She's being very stubborn. She's in danger, and she refuses to tell anyone about it."

"What kind of danger?"

Lisa began to pace across the porch, and her speech picked up speed with her agitated movements. "She got another letter from those Masked Rider people, but this time they actually threatened her. They warned her to stay away from her school tomorrow. Of course, Jessy is taking the whole thing as a challenge, but I think they're serious, and she could be in real danger."

"What do you want me to do?" His pose leaning against the post was casual, but tension emanated from him like a coiled snake poised to strike.

She continued pacing and threw her hands upward. "I don't know. Protect her. Keep those people away from her. You always seem to know what to do."

He leaned forward and stepped away from the post. "But you don't always like what needs to be done. If I interfere, someone could get hurt, maybe even killed."

"Don't you think I know that? But I don't know

what else to do?" The pitch of her voice rose, and she stopped in front of him.

"Are you prepared to deal with the consequences if I do what you ask?"

"Well, I'm certainly not prepared to deal with the consequences if you don't. Jessy is my oldest friend."

"Yes, and sometimes she's a damned fool."

She wasn't going to argue that point. "Are you going to help, or not?"

He took one more step forward and captured her arms in his hands. "How important is this to you? How much do you want my help?" His fingers glided sensuously up and down her arms.

She steeled herself against the waves of longing that washed over her. She had to hold out against him. She had to. "Is this your price?" Her voice as cold as she could make it. "You will help my friend only if I submit to your advances?"

He dropped his hands as if he'd been scalded. "No, damn it. It's not my price. I just wanted to see if you still had any shred of feeling left for me."

She closed her eyes. If he only knew.

"I shouldn't. I can't," she whispered.

He must have heard because he reached for her again and drew her against his chest, enfolding her in a protective embrace. They stood together for what seemed like an eternity. Because his arms demanded nothing, she allowed herself to take what he offered in silence and without resistance.

Finally, he set her away and gazed into her face. "I'll help Jessy. I don't want you to worry."

She searched his face in return. "Thank you."

Those two little words were so inadequate. She wanted to say more, to more eloquently express her relief and gratitude, but the barrier between them remained. They stared at each other in silence then he opened the door and followed her into the house.

In the parlor, Martha looked up from her knitting. Her gaze darted from Lisa to Jared and back. "Andrew fell asleep a few minutes ago, so I put him to bed in the laundry basket."

Lisa nodded. "That's fine. Hopefully, he'll sleep all the way home."

Her mother frowned. "You're not planning to drive back alone in the dark, are you?"

"What else can we do?"

"You can stay right here, of course."

"But you don't have room for two more," Lisa protested.

"They can sleep in my room," Jared interrupted from behind her.

She turned. "I couldn't put you out of your bed."

His black eyes glittered. "That's the least of my problems."

She flushed as her mother's brows rose.

"I'll just clear out some of my gear." Jared headed for the narrow staircase. A few minutes later, he returned with an armful of clothes and shaving utensils. "It's all yours."

"Thank you." Lisa bent down to retrieve the laundry basket holding her sleeping son, but Martha stopped her.

"Why don't you leave him down here with us, dear? He's sure to wake if you jostle him all the way up those stairs."

"All right." Lisa reached out and brushed her hand across Andrew's silky curls in a silent blessing before climbing the steep stairs alone.

The tiny attic bedroom was tucked under the eaves. The roof rafters were so low, even at the peak, she wondered how Jared managed to get dressed in the morning. He wouldn't be able to stand up straight anywhere in the room. She crossed the loose, rough floor boards and sat on the narrow bed.

He had lit the kerosene lamp before coming downstairs, but the glow extended only a few feet. Beyond that, the rafters and planking faded into blackness. The room contained only the bed, a small chest of drawers that didn't match, and a washstand with a cracked bowl and pitcher. Of course, Ben and Martha hadn't planned on having houseguests. According to their plan, Jared was supposed to be comfortably ensconced in the hired hand's room at the farm.

Sighing, Lisa removed her shoes and slipped off her dress, stockings, and petticoat. Wearing only her chemise and drawers, she threw back the top sheet and quilt, and lay down on the bed. The minute her head hit the pillow, a wonderful, familiar, arousing aroma rose to engulf her. It was Jared's smell—not the smell of any hairdressing or cologne, but the unique smell of his body. She would recognize that scent anywhere, and she would remember it until the day she died.

She turned her face into the pillow and inhaled deeply.

It was sweet torture, but she couldn't help herself. Even though she had to deny herself the true fulfillment of his love, she wasn't too proud to take this small bit of comfort. Sleep was a long time coming.

In the morning, she rose early and went in search of Andrew. She found the rest of the family in the kitchen preparing for breakfast. Martha was frying bacon, and Ben was playing with the baby.

"Good morning, everyone."

Martha turned, fork in hand. "Good morning, dear. I hope you slept well. If you'll slice this bread for me, breakfast will be ready in a minute."

Lisa walked to the cupboard and picked up the wicked-looking bread knife. "Where's Jared this morning?" She drew the knife through the firm, brown loaf.

"He rode out to the farm before first light. Said he wanted to get the chores done early because something had come up that he had to deal with today."

"Mmm." Lisa had a pretty good idea what that something was. He was going to try to find out what he could about the threat to Jessy.

After breakfast, she announced it was time to go home. Just as Martha was trying to talk her into spending the day in town, Jared walked in.

"You're back," Lisa said, unable to think of anything more profound.

"Yes."

"I was just getting ready to take Andrew home."

"That's a good idea. And keep him there. I don't want you coming back to town. Do you understand?"

"Why would she come back so soon?" Martha asked, clearly puzzled by his strange demand. "She was just here last night and this morning."

Jared glanced at her. "With Lisa, you never know." With that cryptic reply, he turned and walked out.

"That was certainly odd." Martha's gaze followed him from the room.

"It certainly was." Lisa didn't want to get into a discussion about Jared's comment, and it was next to impossible to fool her mother. "I really should be going now."

"All right, dear. We enjoyed your visit. Come back soon."

"We will."

She wanted to go home, not because Jared insisted on it, but to keep herself busy. There was always work to be done at the farm, and it would help distract her until nightfall. The Masked Riders would likely wait for the cover of darkness to try anything, so she decided to drive back around seven. That should allow her plenty of time to drop Andrew off with her mother and Ben and walk over to Jessy's school.

Even though she had asked for Jared's help, she had no intention of following his orders. She would go crazy waiting out at the farm, worrying and wondering what was going on in town. She might not be able to protect everyone she cared about, but she could be there if, God forbid, she had asked more of Jared than he was able to fulfill.

Chapter Eighteen

After supper, Lisa loaded Andrew into his basket and carried him outside. As she glanced toward town, she saw a thick, roiling plume of smoke rising above the trees. Breathing deeply, she caught the strong, acrid smell of wood smoke. *Jessy's school!* It was hard to imagine the Masked Riders were so brazen as to set fire to it before nightfall, when their identities would be hidden under the cover of darkness. If they had, what had happened to Jessy? And Jared?

Struggling with the heavy basket, she ran to the barn. She hitched Old Pete to the wagon as fast as she could, climbed aboard with Andrew, and shouted as she snapped the reins. Unfortunately, Old Pete only had one speed, and that was slow. All the way to town, she hollered and cursed at him with tears of fear and frustration pricking her eyes, but it did no good. He could only go as fast as he could go, and that wasn't fast enough.

As she pressed on toward the billowing smoke, she couldn't suppress visions of Jessy trapped in the burning building. The closer she got, the thicker the smoke became, and occasional bright tongues of orange flame flickered up through the gray cloud. She prayed her friend had had enough sense to stay away from the school, but it was unlikely. And Jared. She'd asked him to help Jessy, but he must not have been able to prevent the attack. Had he been injured? Or worse? He wasn't the kind of man to stand aside and let something like this happen.

Then she heard the irregular crack, crack...crack of gunfire. Oh, Lord, it was worse than she'd feared.

She snapped the reins and shouted at Old Pete, but as the smell of smoke grew stronger, the old horse grew balky. Tears spilled over and ran down Lisa's cheeks.

"Please, please," she begged. "Don't do this now. It's just a little further."

They were close enough to see a solid wall of flames shooting up from the schoolhouse roof through the smoke above the trees. A crowd had gathered in front of the mercantile two blocks away, and random shots rang out above the din. Lisa pulled in front and tossed her reins to Ben, who stood with her mother on the porch of the store.

"Lisa, what are you doing here?" Martha asked in alarm.

Lisa handed Andrew to her mother before climbing from the wagon. "I saw the smoke."

"It's just awful! I can't understand what could possess people to do a thing like this."

"Has anyone been hurt? Where's Jessy?" Lisa peered out over the crowd.

"She was apparently at the school when someone rode by and tossed something burning through one of the windows. Ben said Jared and some other man were with her. She's over there now attending to the young man with the worst burns." Martha pointed toward a grassy area beneath a spreading elm tree where Jessy bent over a prostrate form that looked like Morgan Bingham.

"But who is shooting? And where is Jared?" Lisa's throat was so tight from smoke and fear she could barely get the words out.

Ben answered. "I think he's over there around the side of the blacksmith's shop. I tried to help him, but those Riders have got him pinned down. Between the gunfire and the smoke, I couldn't get close enough to do any good."

Panic threatened to suffocate Lisa. "This is all my fault. I have to do something."

Martha frowned. "Your fault? Don't be silly. How could this be your fault?"

"When Jessy told me about the threats, I asked Jared to help her. If he's hurt, it's my fault. I have to find him."

Ben reached for her arm. "You stay right here Jared wouldn't want you anywhere near this."

Lisa shook her head and pulled away. "Don't you understand? I have to. I love him. He's in danger because of me." It didn't matter if no one else understood. She had to save him. Her brain could think of nothing else. She turned to her mother. "Take care of Andrew for me."

"But..."

Lisa bolted past her mother without waiting to hear another word. She stumbled through the crowd, shoving people aside and ran on, following the sounds of the shots until she reached the street across from the blacksmith's shop. Two men crouched behind barrels on the porch of the tobacco exchange, and there appeared to be a body in the alley beside the building.

The sharp *ping* of gunfire rang out in erratic bursts, but she couldn't see Jared. She had to know if he was safe or injured. Her life depended on it.

"Jared!"

"Lisa, get back!" His head popped out from the side of the blacksmith's shop.

He was alive. Sweet relief pounded in her chest.

Immediately, one of the men behind the barrels aimed his rifle and fired. Jared's head disappeared.

"Noooooo!" she screamed. The whole core of her being rebelled. She had watched one man she loved die. She would not watch another. She had been helpless the first time. She would never be helpless again.

With that last thought, all reason fled, and blind fury took its place. She raced across to the wounded man in the alley. He moaned when she pulled the gun from his hand but didn't have the strength to stop her. Her mind barely registered the cold metal against her palm and the weight of the pistol in her hand. She began firing blindly into the air.

"Stop! Stop! Stop!"

She had no human target, only an overwhelming need to stop the madness of hatred and violence before it robbed her of everything she cherished.

A shot cracked again from the direction of the barrels on the porch. Then another. Her gun still in the air, Lisa turned to stare at the two masked men. She was too numbed by the extremity of her emotions to feel fear. The men stared back. Then they turned and ran, their boots thundering across the elevated boards. She stood frozen in the street, unable to comprehend what was happening. Seconds later, she heard the pounding of hooves, and the men raced out of the alley and down the street, leaning low across their horses' necks and slashing them with the reins. She stared after them, still frozen, as they tore out of town and disappeared into the smoky twilight.

Slowly, she lowered her arm and stared at the gun in her hand as if seeing it for the first time. The reality of what she had done penetrated the shell of insensibility surrounding her mind.

"No, no, no..." Her voice trailed off into an aching whisper of pain and horror. She loosened her grip on the gun, and it fell from her fingers before she sank to the ground sobbing.

Jared raced to her side and caught her in his arms. She clung to him, clutching his arms and pressing her face to his chest.

"How could you do that to me?" he demanded in a rough voice. His arms tightened. "You scared me to death."

And she had. He couldn't believe his ears when Lisa had called his name. And when he'd seen her standing in the street, his heart had almost stopped.

He kissed the top of her head, over and over, and held her tighter, as if he could protect her by absorbing her into himself. "How could you take a risk like that? What were you thinking?"

She inhaled with a shuddering breath and drew back far enough to see his face. Her eyes were red-rimmed, and her thick black lashes spiky with tears. "I had to s-stop them. Don't you understand? I couldn't let them kill you."

Did she mean what he hoped? Or was she just determined not to have any more bloodshed? He had to know because, by God, he loved her with all his heart. Now that he had her in his arms again, he wasn't sure he could let her go, no matter what her feelings.

"Why?" It was such a simple question, but his whole life depended on the answer. He held his breath, hopeful but desperate to hear the words from her lips.

"Why?" She looked confused.

"Yes. Why couldn't you let them kill me?"

"What kind of question is that?"

"A very important one."

She regarded him with a serious expression. "Because I love you."

His heart soared. He had waited what seemed like a lifetime to hear those words again. "And you risked your life for me."

Her beautiful brown eyes looked even more confused. "What else could I do?"

He grinned. In that moment, he felt like he could outrun a locomotive or swim the Missouri River in a single breath. He hugged her. "Sweetheart, they weren't going to kill me. I wouldn't let them."

She squirmed in his arms. "They seemed pretty determined. And you weren't stopping them."

"You've got to have more faith in me. I wouldn't let them kill me because I wouldn't let them take me away from you and Andrew. I love you."

She didn't smile. "You still love me? In spite of everything?"

He hated the uncertainty in her voice, in her eyes.

"Because of everything. I love you for your beauty, inside and out, for your spirit and your principles.

Seeing you with that gun in your hand, knowing you were facing your worst nightmares for me..." He shuddered. "I swear I'll do everything in my power to make sure you never have to make that choice again."

"But there was no choice. I had to do it."

And it was that simple. Jared stared at the love, plain and unadorned, glowing in her eyes. It was simple for him, too. Fear couldn't steal what they had. He tightened his arms and brought his mouth down on hers in an urgent, questing kiss.

"Lisa, I love you. Marry me. Soon. Tomorrow. Please. I don't care what people say. I'll quit my job and move back to the farm. I've missed you and Andrew so much. I don't want to live another day separated from you by anyone or anything."

She still looked so solemn, he couldn't tell what she was thinking. A fist tightened around his heart.

"Please," he pleaded in a whisper.

"Yes."

Yes. Such a simple word. Joy surged through him. "Do you mean it?"

Then she smiled. "There is no choice. I have to."

****

The next afternoon, they were married in a simple ceremony in Judge Randall's chambers, attended by the people they loved—Martha, Ben, Andrew, and Jessy. Jessy was bubbling over with the news that she planned to marry Morgan Bingham as soon as his injuries from the fire healed sufficiently. Lisa noted Judge and Mrs. Randall pretended not to hear a word. She had misgivings as well but was too filled with joy to say anything to dampen her friend's excitement. At that moment, she wished everyone in the world could feel exactly as she did.

When the vows were said, she turned with Jared to see their family and friends dabbing at tears. Even the little court clerk was blowing his nose into a big white handkerchief. Only Andrew beamed up at them from his place in Martha's arms. He raised his chubby little hands and cried, "Mama, Dada!"

Tears started in Lisa's eyes, and she glanced at Jared. His Adam's apple bobbed. She took her son from her mother's arms and hugged him. When she spoke, she could hardly get the words out. "Yes, precious, it's Mama and Dada."

Jared turned and wrapped her and Andrew in an encompassing embrace that would bind them together for all time.

ABOUT THE AUTHOR

I haven't always been a writer, but I have always embraced creativity and relished new experiences. Seeking to expand my horizons beyond Kansas City, I chose a college in upstate New York. By the time I was twenty-one I had traveled the world from Tunisia to Japan. Little did I suspect I was collecting material for future characters and stories along the way.

I began writing when my daughter entered preschool (she's now a full-fledged adult) and became addicted to the challenge of translating the living, breathing images in my mind into words. I write romance because that's what I like to read. The world provides more than enough drama and tragedy. I want to give my readers the happily-ever-after we all crave.

I've been married to my personal hero for more than thirty-five years. After decades of living in the Midwest, we heeded the siren call of sun and sea and moved to the most breathtakingly beautiful place imaginable - the gorgeous central coast of California. I look forward to bringing you all the new stories this place inspires.

Alison

Made in the USA
Monee, IL
30 July 2023